A HISTORY OF THE
GREAT ZOMBIE WAR:

THE SIMPSON EXPERIENCE

PROLOGUE

You have seen much of what I've seen, heard much of what I've heard and felt much what I've felt. We are all survivors, and we lived through the same hell, but all of our experiences are different as well.

Many of the best accounts of the Great Zombie War, like Max Brooks' *World War Z,* develop a global overview. Others focus on a small group of survivors or, in some cases, an individual account (for an excellent example, see J. L. Bourne's *Day by Day Armageddon*). These are invaluable approaches, but in this book, we have tried to find a middle ground by describing the experience of an entire community – our community – Simpson College.

We were some of the lucky few to survive. In peacetime Simpson's community included around 1400 full-time students, about 400 part-timers, 100 faculty members and over 100 staff. By September of Z-year this dwindled to a few hundred – sullen, starving, and divided.

As a history professor, I became interested in documenting the zombie apocalypse fairly early on. Clearly, as the most important single event in human history, it needed to be recorded, analyzed, and understood. The faculty of Simpson College facilitated this by creating a special "Z-Term" in the summer following the Great Panic, during which a wide variety of courses were offered in an effort to provide training and to help people maintain some sense of normalcy in the midst of the apocalypse. My "Zombie History" course was an effort to record and document the events at Simpson immediately before and after the outbreak. Although the course ended abruptly after only three weeks, the efforts of the students in this course provided a foundation for later research, which this book represents.

This book began as a group project, and it ended as such. It has been an honor to coordinate the dedicated team of young historians who successfully brought this project to fruition. This was *our* Simpson experience.

Hopefully, other communities can use this as a model. It is our hope that this work represents the first in a series that will document the Great Zombie War throughout North America.

Nicolas W. Proctor, editor

Chapter 1: FEBRUARY

1.1 "World Politics" course chat room, transcript

In the early days of the outbreak rumors abounded, but few took them seriously. A multitude of false and absurd theories metastasized on the Internet. This panicked some people, but most reacted with a mixture of derision and apathy. Even when accurate information seeped into the discourse it was usually ignored in favor of more sensationalist perspectives. Many faculty members seized upon the rumors for class assignments. In this case, small groups from a World Politics course developed ideas about the "single greatest threat to global stability."

AlEx36: So, terrorism, right? What else could it be?

GraysOn: Energy policy? Offshore drilling?

ScO: National debt?

bhattman: Let's stay away from the obvious. What about that thing in Vietnam? It's super swine flu or something. That could be cool.

docZen: Can we say H1N1 instead? My family raises hogs.

AlEx36: Is it a mutation or something?

CAPITAL-Liszt: More like the commies made the disease.

SenorStache: haha yeah damn REDS

GraysOn: I have an uncle in Thailand. He said that people over there are going nuts. The airport is shut down.

bhattman: I have an uncle in Idontcare-istan. He kills for freedom.

EddieMagic: FOX reported that it's from hookers! It's like an STD or something.

bhattman: Things aren't looking good for your uncle then, GraysOn. Bangkok crotch-rot is a tough way to go. Sorry pal.

docZen: CDC says it's nothing to worry about if you follow their guidelines

GraysOn: @bhattman: FU cholo.

docZen: Wikipedia says they defining the disease in patients brought back to the US.

GraysOn: How many patients? Where?

EddieMagic: IDK – the CDC site looks crashed.

CAPITAL- Liszt: We should call it the mao virus.

SenorStache: It didn't crash. It was HACKED.

AlEx36: Apparently, there was another outbreak in Brazil yesterday.

ScO: Actually, Peru.

AlEx36: No. Brazil. Look at the NYT site.

EddieMagic: Maybe both?

ArmApocalypse: This is God's punishment for the unbelievers.

docZen: I heard something happened this morning in NYC -- on a plane?

ArmApocalypse: All sinners will be purged from the earth. The faithful will be at his side forever in heaven.

SenorStache: REPENT sinners! or get eaten by MAO!

AlEx36: Anyone see about Korea? They just declared martial law.

CAPITAL- Liszt: I think their "Dear Leader" is getting ready to toss a nuke at someone.

bhattman: Hope it's France

1.2 Katie Sanders, journal

This journal documents some early student perspectives on the encroaching disease. Idle speculation and a sense of absurdity and incredulity were typically more common than worry or preparation.

February 12th: Creative writing class reflective journal entry three. (As you can see, Professor Glover, I've lapsed for the last couple of weeks. I'm going to try to remedy that since I need another 28 entries before the end of the semester. ☺)

Today in Human Physiology, one of the kids in the back of the room, I don't know him—he must be an athletic training major—interrupted Dr. Marks and asked about those weird rumors of a disease in Asia and if she had any idea what was causing it. She said that a microbiologist she knew was calling it a type of rabies virus—the effects weren't really known yet, but shots to the abdomen with rabies immune globulin could deal with it. She also pointed out that the Chinese have the technology and resources to treat something like this and that there's absolutely nothing to be worried about.

But then someone said he saw a YouTube video of someone with the disease. She was staggering around like a drunk, and something about her looked off. (The video didn't last long because the Chinese cops grabbed her a minute or so after the video began.) Dr. Marks said that the rabies virus damages your brain function. Dr. Marks explained that motor function is exactly what we are talking about with the autonomous functions of the nervous system and went off on that. You could hear some audible groans. I think those five minutes of class were the first five minutes everyone was paying attention all year, but then she ruined it by dragging us back to the text. (Not myself, of course, I usually get so many pages of notes from each class that my hand is cramped for a while afterwards.)

I was curious about that video so I searched it on YouTube. For some reason, they had taken it down. The page said it was due to some 'infringement' thing, but that sounds suspiciously like the Chinese government pulling strings to keep everything under wraps. Just like their whole beef with Google and their censoring of people and those poor Tibetans. It would suck to not have any freedoms.

Anyways, I thought this would be a good time to do some stumbling on some of my favorite sites for random stuff. I found a cool recipe for "freaky candy" and a great page on the Church of the Flying Spaghetti Monster, and then, on Boing Boing, I came across a link to a video that looked like a really bad horror movie.

There was this chick stumbling around wearing hooker clothing (slit dress to the crotch and thigh-high leather boots). It was really grainy, like it had been shot on a cameraphone, but I think it had been manipulated because she started running around with this jerky motion. It looked like it was fast-forwarded or something.

Then she tried grabbing this guy who was poking her with a stick or something. He hit her, but she leapt up on him. Then the camera started jiggling around and the video ended. It was weird. Some amateur thing jumping on all the rumors or something. Yeah... those screams were *really* convincing. *Blair Witch 2?*

I posted the link as my status on FB anyway.

I like the disturbing-ness of it.

1.3 Wesley Smyth, sermon

The outline of a sermon read to the student body on a night of campus worship, this was intended both to (as a note along one margin remarks) "rebuke and bring back into the fold those who had lost themselves."

Preaching Text: Matthew 7: 1-5

Do not judge, so that you may not be judged. For with the judgment you make you will be judged, and the measure you give will be the measure you will receive. Why do you see the speck in your neighbor's eye, but not notice the log in your own eye? Or how can you say to your neighbor, 'Let me take the speck out of your eye', while the log is in your own eye? You hypocrite, first take the log out of your own eye. And then you will see clearly to take the speck out of your neighbor's eye.

What's this I hear? (cup ear)

"I don't know this first hand, but have you heard about Sally losing it in Thailand?" "Do you know if Dave has an STD?" "Let me tell you about how 'easy' Kathy is." "I didn't know James was such a man-whore, did you?"

I'm hearing rumors, innuendo, insinuations and allusions to viruses and sex and your fellow students!

It's like we are all back in junior high - only with a twist! We are more vicious. Do you remember junior high school, where everything is fair game, with everyone keeping one eye on the mirror and the other on what everyone else is doing? We are keeping our ears open only to what is being said about us and using our mouths too often to simply repeat the juiciest of what we have heard about everyone else.

Remember... there was little, if anything, self-reflective about junior high school. It was a time of smoke and mirrors... there was no moment when we weren't acutely aware of ourselves, painfully self-conscious. From what I am hearing and the way in which we are behaving, it is as though we have returned with a vengeance to that inexperienced and awkward time.

Remember what it was like?

Was it helpful...? Nurturing? Life-giving? Gentle? Kind? Accepting?

How sad for us! How typical of us and how easy it is for us to slide into patterns so young and so destructive. I remain fascinated by our ability to be so small and to be so caught up in such small worlds. I acknowledge that I am a full participant in this small world.

I am not above listening to a dripping, juicy bit of gossip. I read the headlines on the front covers of the rags in the racks at the grocery store; at the doctor's office, I flip through the pages of *Us* and *People* with quiet curiosity. The temptation to be focused on others and to be small and snitty is part of who we are, I suspect, and that predisposes us to embrace the destructive ways and means learned so well and painfully in junior high, shared too quickly these days.

Recognizing this, Jesus accentuates it – just so we don't miss it. Today's preaching text is part of Jesus' great Sermon on the Mount, a collection of the sayings and teachings of Jesus that Matthew pulled together and placed early in the public ministry of Jesus. He's in his home territory, not too far from Nazareth where he grew up: about equidistant from Tiberius and Capernaum on the shores of Lake Galilee. It is a land and a people he knows well. As we sit on the hillside, listening to him, we can feel the breeze off the lake.

"Judge not, so that you may not be judged." Attend to the log in your own life before you pull out the tweezers on someone else's splinters. What is this we are hearing? Jesus expanding the law to include desire, everything we think, what we do and what we leave undone? Listen to him go on: love your enemies and pray for them, give to everyone who asks of you. If you lust after someone as far as God is concerned you have slept with them. If you are angry with someone it is the same as having killed them. Don't worry about anything. Live as the lilies of the field, do not resist the evildoer - offer the other cheek.

He's on a roll, but I am not sure I'm too happy with where he is rolling. If this is true, then we are all convicted. Certainly we are all too intimately acquainted with what he is declaring. I know deep within, when I admit it, this is who I am.

In our century, 2000 years removed from this sermon, we too easily focus on the doing. We are what we do; we are defined by our behavior, our employment. So we take this sermon as imperative rather than indicative. We translate Jesus into actions before we sit with the truth he has just described. As a result, we end up with a new set of laws. This is how you are *supposed* to behave . . . look, Jesus said it: it's right here in Matthew's gospel.

What is Jesus seeking to do? Well, that unfolds throughout the rest of Matthew's gospel. Jesus proclaims God's realm to be present and around us, that the time is already at hand for this realm to open in our midst. Jesus is describing the truth in God's realm by pointing to the distance between us, a distance that is seen in the depths of our hearts and the ways in which we fall so short of God's desires.

Jesus, then, proceeds to live... and die... in such proximity to God's realm that the whole world is restored, that creation itself is reconciled. A sweet by-product of this reunion opens up new possibilities in which we might examine our choices and our behaviors. We do this *not* in order to get it right – God has already accomplished that. Rather, we are invited to renewed life in which we begin to see those around us with new eyes, listen with new ears, live with newness in Jesus.

It is precisely this capacity with which we are sent into the world. Grace and peace, friends, *is* from our gracious and accepting God. Let's live with it! Amen.

1.4 Zoe Kinsley, email

The "helicopter parent" phenomenon intensified as a result of the news of early outbreaks. In some cases, this included helicopter *grand*parents.

From: raging.granny@gmail.com
Sent: February 16, 1415
To: zoe.kinsley@simpson.edu
Subject: Just Checking In

Zoe, Honey, have you heard?

There's some new virus out there. I know: what now? They say it might travel through the air, so if you hear of anything, stay in your room awhile; the professors will understand.

Maybe you should just come and visit me. You would be safe here and we could bake cookies.

The virus sounds something like it starts with flu symptoms, so don't underestimate a cough or anything. If you start coughing, go see the nurse or a doctor right away. Don't take any chances. Anyway, you just watch out and keep an eye on the news.

I sorted everything out with the dining hall people, and you won't have to deal with them anymore. Why they were still keeping peanuts in the kitchen with all these allergies is beyond me, but we straightened things out, so they won't be keeping them there anymore. You'd best carry your epi-pen just in case.

So, you can't blame me for my curiosity; I haven't seen you in a while and I'm a lonely old granny: have you found yourself a boy yet? Did you do anything for Valentine's Day? We old ladies have a running joke that all you have to do is show a little skin to reel them in. Some say ankles, but I think you should toss caution to the wind and show some calves. Ha! Oh, I'm just joking, but you just be safe and be who you are. I am proud of you.

Take care, and I will see you soon over Spring Break. Just call when you head home.

Love,
Raging Granny

From: zoe.kinsley@simpson.edu
Sent: February 17, 0132
To: raging.granny@gmail.com
Subject: RE: Just Checking In

Hey Granny,
    You always ask so many questions! Don't worry about me. I will keep an eye out for this stuff. I don't want to be sick when I don't have to be.
    Oh, and no, I am not dating anyone. Or anything like that. I eat supper in my room and get some good homework done.
    You and your friends are hilarious, but are you sure your old tricks will work anymore (haha)? The rolls were great, and of course I have plenty of food. Ever since we...you...arranged for my board plan to end, I have been having a good time eating in my room -- it's all totally peanut free, of course—don't worry.

Love,
Zoe

1.5 Paul Dule, media log

As events began to unfold and anxiety intensified, many began to keep journals. Some of these were sporadic and quickly played out. Others were dense and almost impenetrable. Like many, Dule's journal began as a class assignment. Consequently, it skips around a great deal, but it provides a good commentary on the dawning awareness of the crisis for a typical Simpson student, though the facts can be quite sketchy when it comes to world politics, leaning toward the sensationalist.

February 18.
Topic: the suspension of travel for HIV+ people by China.

I thought this was going to be lame (sorry), but let me tell you, it is actually pretty weird and interesting.

Just last week China announced that it was *restoring* a travel ban on people with STDs. One of my professors – one of the liberal knuckleheads (not you Professor S.!) – mentioned this in class. He seemed outraged about it, but then again, he seems outraged about almost everything, so I started to tune it out.

Then I thought to myself: This may have entertainment value. With the gay angle, I figured it would get pretty good play online, so after class I watched my favorite news feed: TrueTruthiness.com. Naturally, they were already hammering the "gay agenda," and their talking heads were trying to figure out how this action could make them hate *both* China *and* the gays even more. It was a tough contest, but as they yelled at each other, I think the Chinese came out on top, hate wise.

Clicking around other less screaming news sources, I discovered that the Chinese actually lifted a ban on HIV+ travelers about a year ago. They apparently decided that keeping HIV+ people out did not really help them control the disease any better – it just forced it underground. More importantly: it was hurting tourism. You've gotta love communists with a profit motive.

So, the standing question is: why did they restore a travel ban?

Only after I researched this did I notice that when they lifted the ban on HIV, they also lifted a ban on people with leprosy. Leprosy? Seriously? I think I'd keep a ban on that, but as far as I can tell, people with leprosy can still travel to China. Let's go, lepers!

Number of media sources examined: 3 (+Wikipedia – does that count?)

February 21.
Topic: Continued hijinks in the PRC

That didn't take long. Today China announced a ban on *all* international travel. TrueTruthiness went wild. They reported that the Chinese were calling up their military reserves. They reported that the North Koreans were gearing up for war. They "reported" all kinds of things, but they didn't offer much evidence other than fellows of various think tanks holding forth on their research and "sources."

The high point of their coverage was when they showed some video of an Iranian imam denouncing this as proof that God hated both gays *and* communists because they both encourage promiscuity, which they showed back-to-back with a honey-toned, white-haired televangelist explaining how homosexuals and communists were in an unholy pro-abortion alliance with the feminists. Classic.

Imagine the froth! Who to hate more: China, homosexuals, or Iranian clerics?

Excitement! I cruised through the TV news channels and stopped on some grainy cameraphone video of a border crossing from China into Russia or Kazakhstan or someplace. There was an English voice-over, which said the video had been shot by a Russian border guard.

The foreground was dominated by a huge, white arch with red Chinese lettering all over it. Behind it, there were cars backed up to the horizon (it was steppe country, so the horizon was a long way away) and thousands, *thousands,* of Chinese people were stacked up along the road and scattered along the double wire at a border post. There were only a few uniformed Russian guys with AKs and they looked nervous. The speaker pickup on the cameraphone was not good, but the Russians sounded nervous. The Chinese side was more heavily manned with a couple of armored personnel carriers and dozens of armed and uniformed guys. There were a couple guard towers and a few apartment-type buildings in the distance on the China side too. I'm not sure if the Russians had these too – the camera never swung around.

Then, at some point, the Chinese civilians decided they'd had it and they just started to surge towards the line. The Russians got excited, but the People's Liberation Army got down to serious business and started firing into the crowd with their AKs and with the heavy MGs on the APCs. No warning shots -- they just drilled into them. Pretty fucking gruesome. This part wasn't more than a few seconds. It got smoky and loud and then the Russian with the camera decided that his bunker was the place to be, so the video ended.

I was lucky (in a way, I guess) to catch this on TV. Apparently, like the 9/11 WTC jumper videos, this was the only time it was broadcast. But even though the networks shut it down it went viral on the web.

Renewing a boycott of STD-infected people and machine-gunning your own population is a weird thing to do if you are gearing up for war … unless you are an atheistic, homosexual, abortion crazed feminist! (jk).

So, I found this place on Google Earth. Its name is Manzhouli, which doesn't really sound Chinese or Russian, and I noticed that here the border runs pretty much along the "Genghis Wall." Did the Great Khan build it to keep people out or were people trying to keep him out? I'll try to find out more. Why is research fun when you aren't doing it for class?

Number of media sources consulted: 4 (+GoogleEarth)

1.6 Felix Reiche, cmail (translated)

This series of emails from a foreign exchange student and his brother living in Germany illustrates varying international levels of awareness about the outbreak. Like most exchange students Reiche possessed considerably more interest and knowledge about the world than most other Simpson students.

From:	Felix Reiche [felix.reiche@simpson.edu]
Sent:	Monday, February 8, 8:02 AM
To:	[reiche_ma05.yahoo.de]
Subject:	RE: RE:

We went to the bar Saturday. But then she went outside with her friend and took forever so I started dancing with these two girls from my biology class. She came back and was angry, so I took her home. We made out for a while so she got over it. She gets clingy like that—there is this girl I met at a party Friday who was hitting on me pretty hard, so I will probably take her out next weekend. The ladies cannot help themselves!!

So what is going on with you? How are mom and dad? I heard about some bad flu going around over there.

From:	[reiche_ma05.yahoo.de]
Sent:	Thursday, February 11, 7:33 PM
To:	Felix Reiche [felix.reiche@simpson.edu]
Subject:	RE: RE: RE:

Haha! Are you trying to get every Iowa girl to like you before you leave? Everyone is doing fine here. I am not sure about it being the flu, but there has been something going around. I know a couple people who have had to go to the hospital. Uncle Jan said there have been an unusually high number of assaults in the last week. He is not sure why, but he has theories. The best one: Some new food additive is driving people mad. Not sure what that has to do with people getting sick, but you cannot really get him to stop talking if he starts, right?!

From:	[reiche_ma05.yahoo.de]
Sent:	Tuesday, February 23, 12:10 AM
To:	Felix Reiche [felix.reiche@simpson.edu]
Subject:	RE: RE: RE: RE:

Hey, Felix. You there? Everything going okay?

From:	Felix Reiche [felix.reiche@simpson.edu]
Sent:	Thursday, February 25, 9:40 AM
To:	[reiche_ma05.yahoo.de]
Subject:	RE: RE: RE: RE: RE:

Sorry it has taken me so long to write back. It has been a little crazy here. Are you all okay?

I think whatever you all have been dealing with finally made its way over here. The news has been all over it; apparently a bunch of people in San Francisco overdosed on some drug and it sent them into a killing frenzy or something. PCP?
Now everyone has been talking about the flu and mental disorders; it is causing everyone to scare themselves and go a little wild. This girl at the bar the other night was really trying to get in my pants — and I mean IN my pants — right in the bar. I love this country!

1.8 Tête à Têtc, transcript

Even though almost no one listened to KSTM, the 10 watt student radio station at Simpson College, Political Science majors Ronald Schue and Harold Jackson used it to broadcast a weekly news talk show, Tête à Tête.

DATE: February 23
TIME(s) 18:00;18:26:33
DOCUMENT TYPE: Talk show
RECORD TYPE: Fulltext
LANGUAGE: English
SECTION HEADING: Political

TEXT:

SCHUE: Hello! I'm Ronald Schue!

JACKSON: And from the right, I'm Harold Jackson!

BOTH: And this is Tete a Tete!

SCHUE: We bring you the latest issues confronting our nation …
                 and the world.

JACKSON: Today's topic: China. Ron, disturbing news has been
                 circling around the blogosphere, stratosphere and various
                 other spheres.

SCHUE: That's right, Harold. This news has been all over on CNN,
                 FOX, NPR, you name it. But what is exactly going on?

JACKSON: First off background. Since our last show, China announced
                 a closure of its borders; no one gets in, no one gets out, and
                 this includes American citizens. The People's Republic says
                 it is due to a virus and they want to contain it, but when I
                 turn on my television I don't see images of people walking
                 around wearing masks; all I see is videos of riots.

SCHUE: The first video was posted on YouTube no more than a few
                 days ago, and it has been viral ever since. Chinese officials
                 denied the legitimacy of the video stating "Anyone could

have staged such a video." Well the logical response to that is: why would anyone do that?

JACKSON: Can you imagine his holiness the Dali Lama getting all the monks together for an ultra low-budget, mumblecore horror film in an effort to overthrow the government in Beijing?

SCHUE: Unlikely, but still certain to sweep the awards at Cannes, and I for one would pay good money to see it.

JACKSON: And that's why you are an idiot.

SCHUE: This from the man who considers "Kung Fu Hustle" the pinnacle of film as an expressive medium?

JACKSON: It is a beautiful picture about human dignity, mortality, and the power of community and secret kung fu moves. It is a perfect film in essentially every way.

SCHUE: How are those moves working against the federal budget deficit, mister bigshot?

JACKSON: I have many names.

SCHUE: Anyway. China. I think we might agree on this. China is experiencing political unrest and they don't want anyone to know until they've stomped it out.

JACKSON: You make sense at last. A revolution of rising expectations is finally destabilizing the system and the power elite seek to crush the political aspirations of newly urbanized proletarians ... just as they did in the masterful "Kung Fu Hustle."

SCHUE: I know that you tried to find out more about the videos that are leaking through the Chinese censors. What did you find out?

JACKSON: Well, I had a German test today. Also, I watched "Kung Fu Hustle" again last night ... so, nothing. Sorry.

SCHUE: And, with that, I believe our time is up. This is Ronald Schue.

JACKSON: And this is Harold Jackson.

BOTH: And this was Tete a Tete.

1.9 Jill Sammes, IM chat

By late February, fears about the contagion entered the news cycle. Even as rumors crystallized into terrifying reality and the contagion spread throughout the world, the vast majority of Simpson students remained almost totally unaware of the rising tide that would soon engulf them.

Me	3:45pm	How was class today?
Michael	3:45pm	Sucked as usual. What are you doing?
Me	3:45pm	hmwk. ... boo
Michael	3:46pm	Girl in my painting class / hot btw /was talking about this cult thing that's going on in Asia or something.
Me	3:46pm	Hot? Give me a name.
Michael	3:47pm	Sara something. Dietz doesn't call us by our full names. Duh.
Me	3:49pm	heikes?
Michael	3:49pm	idk
Me	3:50pm	look her up
Michael	3:51pm	how?
Me	3:51pm	really? Facebook you twit.
Michael	3:53pm	Yes. SARA HEIKES! That's it. HOT.
Me	3:53pm	You going to do anything about it?
Michael	3:54pm	Like what?
Me	3:55pm	Seriously? What is your issue today...did you lose your brain in class?
Michael	3:55pm	Just distracted. I might ask her to a discount movie Friday.
Me	3:56pm	Cheap date? $3? You truly are the last of the big spenders, my friend. CLASSY.
Michael	3:56pm	I don't want to impress her too early on or she'll expect it.
Me	3:56pm	You are so dumb.

Michael	3:57pm	So what's the deal with the Asian cannibal cult? She's into it, so I need to be into it.
Me	4:02pm	Probably some BS site.
Me	4:06pm	Thanks for nothing. I'm going back to hwmk.
Michael	4:11pm	dinner at 5:15?
Me	4:11pm	pfief or grill?
Michael	4:11pm	ttly the p-dog. It is nugget night.
Me	4:13pm	SAE party after?
Michael	4:14pm	mos def, but let's watch South Park first. It's a new episode about George Bush being a communist zombie or something.
Me	4:15pm	Right on.

Chapter 2: MARCH

2.1 Course Contingency Plan

When the outbreak began, the college implemented its course contingency plan, but these efforts were hampered by the requirements imposed on the college by state and federal authorities as well as the more immediate threat of the infected themselves. It is unfortunate that Simpson had not developed specific contingencies in advance like the University of Florida and a handful of other forward-thinking institutions.

March 12
Dear Students,

In response to the current crisis, the course contingency plan has been put into effect. In an effort to halt the spread of the contagion, the Iowa Department of Public Health has made an unusual request: All students, faculty, and staff must remain on campus for the duration of the emergency. This is part of a concerted effort to ensure our safety and that of our families. Despite the unusual nature of the emergency, I can assure the entire community that thanks to the cooperation of the Iowa National Guard, Simpson is well equipped to handle any disease outbreak on campus.

Courses will continue to meet and faculty and students should continue the educational process as best they can through the Scholar system with readings and online forums.

HIV-Z apparently causes massive damage and degradation of the central nervous system and brain, so please avoid the offensive use of the term "zombie" when referring to infected persons. Not only is this degrading and hurtful, but it also provides a great deal of misinformation. Those who have been infected deserve our sympathy rather than our scorn. In addition, please remember that the early symptoms of HIV-Z resemble those of many other illnesses. So, do not stigmatize the infected, but if you see anyone presenting symptoms immediately report it to your CA or department head.

As in the past, we encourage all students take precautions to avoid the transmission of this disease, such as frequently washing your hands, covering your mouth when you sneeze, and notifying the campus nurse and avoiding other students if you begin to feel ill. Please use the hand sanitation stations that are located throughout campus as often as possible. In addition to these measures, it appears likely the virus may be sexually transmitted. Students and staff are encouraged to remain abstinent to avoid transmission. Anyone wishing to remain sexually active should use impermeable protection. Condoms are available from all CAs and the health service office.

These are difficult times for all. The treatment of infectious diseases can be very frightening as the threat is an enemy that cannot be seen, but sometime next week the new HIV vaccine will be available for all un-inoculated students, faculty, staff, and guests. Furthermore, there will be a fundraiser event by the Student Government Association to send 10,000 units of the vaccine to Tanzania in an effort to stem the spread of the disease in the developing world.

If you have questions or comments related to health issues please contact the campus health service office at ext. 8735. If you have other questions or comments feel free to contact me directly.

Thank you for your cooperation in this time of crisis,

Jim Thorius,
Vice President for Student Development & Retention

2.2 911 Transcript

The following is the transcript of the 911 call from the Sigma Alpha Epsilon fraternity at 2:57 a.m., March 13. This document illustrates the mixture of paranoia and confusion in the early days of the outbreak.

DISPATCH: 911, what's your emergency?

CALLER: Hey, I need to get a ... an ambulance.

DISPATCH: Where are you?

CALLER: Uh, I'm at Simpson.

DISPATCH: Can you give me the address?

CALLER: I'm in the SAE house.

DISPATCH: Is that a fraternity house? Can you give me the street address?

CALLER: Uh ... [To someone else in the room: (inaudible)]

UNKNOWN: (inaudible)

CALLER: Uh, 701 E. Street, I think.

DISPATCH: What's happening, sir?

CALLER: Uh, I've got a guy who's passed out. He drank way too much.

DISPATCH: Is he breathing?

CALLER: I don't know. He's not waking up.

DISPATCH: How old do you think he is?

CALLER: Maybe 18, 19. [In background] Wake up, man.

DISPATCH: What is your name, sir?

CALLER: I'm Kraig. K – R – A – I – G.

DISPATCH: OK, Kraig, how do you know he was drinking?

CALLER: I got back to my room and he was passed out.

DISPATCH: OK, so he's passed out inside the fraternity house?

CALLER: Yeah, inside. [To someone in the room: "(Expletive deleted), man. What the (expletive deleted) did you guys do last night?"]

DISPATCH: OK, is he on the floor, or...?

CALLER:	He's on the floor.
DISPATCH:	Is he blue or cold?
CALLER:	He's not very cold. He doesn't look blue to me.
DISPATCH:	Do you see any injuries?
CALLER:	Well, he's face-down on the floor, so I'm not sure.
DISPATCH:	Is he breathing?
CALLER:	It doesn't look like he's breathing very much at all.
DISPATCH:	At all? Or not very much?
CALLER:	It doesn't look like it at all.
DISPATCH:	Is his chest rising?
CALLER:	Uh, no. I don't think so.
DISPATCH:	OK. Can you hold on one second for me?
CALLER:	Sure.
DISPATCH:	Don't hang up, OK?
CALLER:	OK, I won't. [To someone else in room: "Hey, is he breathing? Is he breathing?"]
DISPATCH:	Kraig, are you still there?
CALLER:	Yeah.
DISPATCH:	Look, Kraig. I think we have a special situation. So, what I need to ask you to do is to leave your room immediately.
CALLER:	Uh, what?
DISPATCH:	You need to leave your room. You need to lock the door. You go outside and wait for the patrol car.
UNKNOWN:	(Moaning)
CALLER:	Hey, wait. Wait. He's moving now.
DISPATCH:	No. You need to go. You need to go now.
CALLER:	Wait. He's … Oh, no. Oh, Jesus. Oh, Jesus. (Expletive deleted).
DISPATCH:	What's happening? What…
CALLER:	Oh, Jesus. Oh, Jesus God, no!
UNKNOWN:	(Moaning)
(Screaming. Sounds of a struggle.)	

An Indianola police officer arrived on site four minutes later. In the interim, the caller, Simpson sophomore Kraig Thomas, severely battered Simpson freshman Ryan Hervey with an aluminum

baseball bat. Hervey was transported by ambulance to the Mercy ER in Des Moines where he died of severe head trauma. Thomas was transported to the Warren County jail where he was awaiting charges when the Great Panic began.

2.3 Felix Reiche, email (translated)

International students struggled to understand what was happening both on campus and in their home countries.

From:	Felix Reiche [felix.reiche@simpson.edu]
Sent:	March 14, 10:22 AM
To:	[reiche_ma05.yahoo.de]
Subject:	RE: RE:

Marcus, you will not believe what happened yesterday; there was this party and someone got killed! I told you people were going crazy over here. My friend walked into the room just after it happened. He told me this guy was standing there with this bloody bat over the dead kid's body. The head was all smashed in and he was crying about how he found him and then the kid jumped up and was attacking him. He was just freaking out and crying and then the police came with an ambulance and took them both in and started questioning everyone.

Now all kinds of rumors are going around; it is insane here—never thought I would see this over here... this and all the news is really freaking me out.

I checked out Der Spiegel online and I read about some lunatics trying to bite people in Spandau. What is going on??? Have you heard anything new about this?

From:	Felix Reiche [felix.reiche@simpson.edu]
Sent:	Tuesday, March 16, 4:58 PM
To:	[reiche_ma05.yahoo.de]
Subject:	RE: RE:

Where are you Marcus? It never takes you this long to respond. Did you give up internet for lent because you started a little late? Is everything okay for you?

Everything is still going crazy here since that guy got murdered at SAE. No one has really gone out since then -- especially because of all these HIV rumors. This is all my human biology professor has been lecturing about for the last week. She's shifted the class so all we have been focusing on is sexually transmitted infections and stuff like that.

Is Hamburg as bad as it looks on TV?

2.4 Kate Snyder, journal

Opinions about the virus varied widely. Few at Simpson College took as extreme a view as Kate Snyder, but advocacy groups for the infected sprang up and spread almost as fast as the contagion – especially on college campuses.

March 17. There's this hunky runner named Clark Spencer who sits next to me in my calc class. Well, the last few days he keeps inching his desk closer and closer. I would've just thought it was in my head except Anne said she noticed too. And then today he asked if I'd be up for tutoring him sometime. He also said something about how big my head was, and that made me a little self-conscious, but then he got this gleam in his eye, so I guess it's OK. Do I have a big head? Maybe I should change my hairstyle.

Clark's a total genius, so it totally is just an excuse to spend time with me! Well, at least that's what Anne says. I mean, he did say he's been having trouble concentrating in class lately, and when everyone's talking about this virus thing, don't we all? A lot of kids have just stopped coming to class.

He's so cute when he raves about how defenseless Simpson is. I mean today he was complaining, "What's the good of paying $30,000 a year if they can't even kill something that's already dead?" And even though I'm totally against killing, and I don't think the infected are actually dead, I definitely see his point.

March 18. Yesterday was our meeting of the Environmental Awareness Club. At the meeting, I pointed out that our club's motto is "Reduce, Reuse, Recycle." I asked if a zombie outbreak was necessarily bad for the environment. It would, after all, reduce overpopulation and therefore our carbon footprint and use of petrochemicals. Nobody really liked that argument.

March 20. I feel bad for the "zombies." They're just using their survival instincts like any other animal. All they are trying to do is gather food. They are, in a way, more in touch with nature than we are. All everyone is trying to do is kill them with no sympathy for the state they're in. We need to try to understand what they're going through. Plus, even if they are trying to eat us, they have a right to live and exist.

March 21. I bet Monsanto did this. (Or BP).

March 22. When I try to talk about this stuff in class, Professor Spellerberg argues that the zombies are just like rabid animals. He says we must dispatch them quickly and efficiently so they can't contaminate the rest of the population. He is the type to act first and ask questions later. If he knew someone was a zombie, he'd "dispatch" him as calmly as if he were merely refilling his coffee cup. He'd probably use the blood that oozed from the body to write big red "F's" on my homework.

Clark seems to sympathize with my feelings though.

2.5 Incident Report

The first confirmed and documented stage IV case of HIV-Z on Simpson's campus appeared in a literature course.

Name: Professor Anastacia Fotiadis, Ph.D
Date: March 23
Place: Mary Berry Rm 120
Time: 2:15 p.m.

Incident: A male student (Fred Manchester, 21) in my Minority Literature class attacked a female student (Kristine Heinkel, 21).

We were watching *Eraserhead* (dark and brooding, this, the first full-length feature by director David Lynch, remains, perhaps, his finest work) when I heard whispering in the back of the classroom. Sadly, this is not uncommon. Too many of our students fail to engage in deep readings of the semiotics of late 20th century cinema. They seem to want "stories" with "characters." Someday I will figure out a way to crush their residual bourgeois sensibility.

Four male students and two female students were discussing one male student who had his head down on his desk and appeared to be sleeping. He was apparently ill; however he had chosen to attend class (no doubt due to my rigorously enforced attendance policy).

I instructed the students to be quiet, and moved to the back of the classroom to wake him, but before I could get there, he violently jerked awake. His face was contorted and his eyes were extremely bloodshot. He was looking around frantically and turned to the student closest to him, Kristine Heinkel.

He leapt out of his chair and attacked her, knocking both her and her desk onto the floor. He was grunting and screeching; Kristine was screaming.

The students in the proximity tried to subdue him, but he continued to attack the female. He bit her and scratched and grabbed at those restraining him. He never relented.

The students and I attempted to subdue him by hand. None of our attempts worked. He had no concern for those around him. He even appeared to be ripping and tearing at his own skin with his fingernails. I struck him repeatedly with my aluminum coffee mug to no effect.

By this point, he had scratched several of the students attempting to restrain him and had possibly bitten one or more of them. Then Nick Veneris (who had never previously struck me as someone to take the initiative) slammed his extremely heavy, clothbound organic chemistry book down on Fred's head. He did this repeatedly and he did it hard, probably breaking Fred's nose and dislocating his jaw. At this point, my colleague from the philosophy department, John Pauley, entered the room with a baseball bat. Without hesitation, he brought it down on the top of Fred's head. Fred went limp. Blood was everywhere. I believe the police arrived a few minutes later.

2.7 Anne Howard, email

Despite a clear reporting protocol established by college administration, most news about infections was carried through informal back-channels.

Professor Livingstone,

I am writing to you because I do not know what to do. I came to your office, but you were at a meeting or something. Maybe this email will help me organize my thoughts.

My friend Kate, who sits next to me in class, was my roommate freshman year, but then she joined Pi Phi and moved into the house. We have stayed really close friends, though. She always comes and hangs out at the apartment with me and my other roommates, and everyone has always really gotten along. Then about a week ago – right after Spring Break -- Kate started going out with her boyfriend, Clark, and things began to change.

From the start, I didn't like the guy. He is a cross country runner from ATO and he is completely full of himself. I still don't understand what Kate sees in the guy. He treats her poorly, and I am ninety-nine percent sure he cheats on her. I see him constantly flirting with other girls, especially at parties. He is even worse when he is drunk, which is more often than not.

Kate always brings him with her when she comes to our apartment, and it really pisses me off. I didn't want to turn her away, though, because she was my friend and I didn't want her to feel unwelcome. Just him.

Anyway, things were bad, but they weren't like they are now. I knew Kate and Clark were having sex, but they kept things pretty discreet. I'm not even sure where they were having it, because I knew they couldn't do it at Pi Phi, and I didn't think Kate would be comfortable at ATO.

Kate didn't really talk to me about it much (I didn't mind), but she did tell me that they didn't have sex as often as Clark wanted. He didn't push her, though, so I didn't think he was as huge of a butt-wipe as I originally thought.

That opinion didn't last long. One night I was at a party at ATO with a few of my friends. Kate wasn't there because she had to work really late that night. I spotted Clark, drunk as usual, talking with some slutty blonde girl. I watched them closely because I was instantly suspicious. Clark wasn't really doing the majority of the flirting because the girl appeared to do most of the work. Shortly after I first spotted them, they left together. I should have followed them…I should have told Kate, but I didn't want to see her hurt. Maybe none of this would have happened if I had just told her right away.

It didn't happen right after that night, but things started to change between Kate and Clark. She sometimes would call me in tears, telling me that she and Clark had just had a fight. I would ask why, and it was always the same answer, "He is mad because I didn't want to have sex tonight." I told her countless times to dump his sorry ass, but she never would, insisting that she loved him and he just wanted to "further solidify" their relationship. After awhile, I stopped getting her late night calls, so I figured they had worked things out.

I sat next to Kate in my American Women's History class and she stopped showing up, so a couple days after her last phone call, I asked her if things had gotten better. She didn't answer right away, but finally said that she had just relented and given into Clark's demands. They were having sex all the time, and not just at ATO. They did it in closets and bathrooms. They even did it in a study carrel in the library. This was weird enough, but I didn't get really worried until she said that he was getting rougher and more demanding while they were together. She sounded a little scared and a little sad. I told her, again, to just break up with him, but she refused insisting that he loved her and she loved him.

For the rest of that week, she simply would not speak to me. I was afraid that Clark was actually abusing her.

I tried to see her on the weekend, but her phone went straight to voicemail and she was never in her room. She didn't even post of FB, which for her was pretty unusual. I told my CA I was worried about her. She put me through a questionnaire. She didn't seem concerned about her emotional state, she just wanted to know if Kate was having muscle tics or something. What does that have to do with sexual abuse? The CA then told me that lots of people were cutting class, and not be worried. Well, duh, as if I hadn't noticed that my classes are half full and the parking lots have emptied. I was getting ready to go to the Dean, but the next Monday was a complete turnaround. She walked into class, sat down right next to me, and began chattering nonstop. She told me that things between her and Clark were great again. Her bubbly attitude freaked me out.

She seemed happy but tired. I was happy that she was talking to me again, though. She even began coming over to the apartment again, but she of course brought Clark with her. He was different -- even creepier -- and it made me nervous. I don't know what his problem was, but he was really short-tempered and he looked like crap. My roommate Carrie made the mistake of asking Clark to stop raiding the fridge. I mean, he ate a whole pack of raw hot dogs in a couple minutes.

He totally flipped out, smashed a lamp against the wall and shouted, "What's your problem, you fucking bitch?"

Carrie can be kind of a smartass; she just replied something like, "Your mom." Clark grabbed her and would have thrown her across the room had I not come up and slammed my fist into his face. It knocked him off balance and gave us enough time to run out of our apartment. We piled into Nate's apartment across the hall. He kept his door propped open for friends who were always coming and going in and out. I think the only time he shut it was when he was smoking pot – which was often – but luckily he wasn't toking up at the time.

It was a near thing. Clark almost immediately started banging on the door, and was hollering and cursing. Nate came out of his bedroom. Totally baked. He wanted to know what was going on. I told him that Clark was trying to kill us. Nate calmly walked back into his bedroom. He came out again a minute later with a video camera in one hand and a tree pruning thing in the other. It scraped along the ceiling, but he didn't seem to mind. The banging stopped after a while. I guess Kate calmed him down or something. I suppose I should have called the cops. I figured the CA would, but she didn't. (I later found out she'd high-tailed it for home). When I looked in the peephole the hallway was empty.

We were shaking with the adrenaline rush. To calm down, we played MarioKart on Nate's Wii for the next couple hours.

I didn't see Kate again until that weekend. It was Pi Phi's "Sisters with Sisters" weekend, where all of the sorority girls invited their younger sisters to stay with them. Kate knocked on our door Friday night. She looked like total crap. She was pale and her hair was all greasy. She had bruises on her cheek and arms. I would have given her a real interrogation, but she asked if we would be willing to watch her sister Nikki, because she didn't want to leave her at the house. Nikki was ten. I didn't say anything. I tried to catch Kate's eye, but she wouldn't look straight at me.

Kate said she'd be back in a few hours. I knew that she and Clark just wanted to get rid of Nikki for a little while so they could fuck. I was so pissed I almost said no, but I felt sorry for Nikki, so she and I watched cartoons together.

She and I both fell asleep on our couch, and Kate never came back. The old Kate would never have abandoned her little sister like that in order to be with a guy. I don't know what is going on with her, but I'm worried. She is so different, and it's only getting worse. I'm scared for Nikki and my friend.

2.8 Nikki Snyder, voice recorder transcript

Even in the early stages of the outbreak, some members of the wider community were caught up in the on campus chaos. For the most part, college authorities appeared unaware of their presence on campus.

I am at my sister Katie's college, and I'm alone. I don't know where Katie is. I stayed at her friend Annie's last night and we watched cartoons. This morning Annie woke me up. She said she was going to look outside for a few minutes but she was going come right back. She's not back yet. I've been here all day.

She told me to stay in the room and not to open the door for anyone. She also said don't make any noise at all. I'm up on her bed, clear next to the ceiling, whispering 'cause I'm scared. I want my Mommy or Katie.

Mom didn't want me to come and she was right.

I think I heard some screaming the morning after Annie left. Not here. Not in this building. Outside somewhere.

I wish my brothers were here. They were in Boy Scouts all the way till it was done, and they know a lot of things. They showed me too. I can do lots of first aid, but they are better. I'm scared. I want Katie to come back and take me home.

[recording ends]

I think I heard someone scream. I think it was in this building. I'm really afraid now. I'm hiding in a closet; maybe they can't find me here.

I've seen those "Home Alone" movies. This kid tries to keep bad guys out of his house by making booby traps. I should do that. Annie has lots of tacks on her bulletin board. Maybe if I quietly took them all down and put them by the door that would do something.

[recording ends]

I hear people somewhere outside. Maybe Annie is back. I shouldn't check though. She told me to stay in here. I'm going to think of some more booby traps now.

[recording ends]

It's night now. It wasn't Annie outside. I pushed up a chair and looked through the little peephole, and it was just some other girls talking and crying. I wanted to go hug them and ask where Annie and Katie are, but Annie said stay here, and she'd probably get back right when I go out and I'd be in trouble. She has to be back soon. Maybe she's just afraid to come back 'cause of what people are saying.

[recording ends]

It's quiet now. I think I'm going to try to sleep. If she isn't back in the morning, I'll do this again.

[recording ends]

2.9. Paul Dule, journal

In the chaos of the Great Panic, people surged on to highways in search of safety, friends and family. During this period, hundreds of additional students departed from campus, while a few others returned. Many accounts of this period are panicked. Others reveal a spirit of determination (or mere obstinacy) in the face of partially understood circumstances.

March 22.

A storm knocked down big branches from a couple of old trees back home, so I spent the weekend helping my father cut up the branches and cut down the dead trees that had not blown over yet. I didn't mind; I enjoyed it. It exhausted me and I finally got some sleep.

I drove back to campus in my 1970 Dodge Challenger. I turned on some Country and watched the landscape rolling by. It was still too early for things to be greening up, but the last of the snow was gone and you could tell spring was coming. Cows were browsing last year's stubble of corn stalks.

Traffic was pretty light.

There isn't much else to do on the boring two-hour drive – well, two and a half if you go the speed limit. But it's hard to go 65 when there is a 440 six pack under your hood. I shouldn't be speeding. The bright yellow stands out as it is, and I would rather not be pulled over with the whiskey and rum in my back seat. (For a man with a high school education, my dad understands the needs of a college man quite well.) I was reaching for my sunglasses when the music stopped.

I didn't really follow the news much before, but the whole China business and that big fight on the Mexican border, and the news that came out in the last few days about brutal mass murders in India and Thailand made me get real interested real fast. When these killings started happening in San Francisco, I wasn't that surprised, but it did bring it closer to home.

Last I checked, TrueTruthiness was saying there is some sort of new Islamo-fascist terrorist death cult behind the killings. One commentator said that this proves Islam worships death instead of God. Another wanted to know why the CIA didn't see it coming. Then one advocated nuking Mecca and Hanoi as well as Beijing and Hong Kong and about ten other places in China. Just to be on the safe side he said. Then he started talking about something called the "one-tenth of one percent doctrine." It is becoming increasingly clear that they are a bunch of morons.

The web is not much more helpful. According to what I found, there are bloody attacks happening every day just about everywhere, and that seems implausible to me. No conspiracy can be vast enough to motivate hundreds (thousands?) of people to commit bloody murder all over the world more or less at the same time. A lot of these reports must be made up. The parts about the terrorists *eating* people? I mean, come on.

So, it jerked me back to reality when the music stopped for the Emergency Broadcast System. I'd heard tests all my life, but I think that I'd only actually heard an actual emergency broadcast once, when there was a tornado. The announcer said that interstates and state highways were closed in and around Des Moines. He also announced the closure of bridges over the Missouri and Mississippi Rivers. There had been a lot of rain in the storm that knocked down those trees, but he didn't say anything about flooding, so I wasn't sure what was happening. I was thinking about possible routes around the city when I crested the hill and saw the roadblock.

They had big traffic signs with orange lights flashing STOP, concrete jersey barriers running off the road and into the ditches so you could not go around, a couple of heavy olive drab trucks and a tan humvee with a .50 cal. on top. There were probably a dozen guys in fatigues with M16s standing around. Needless to say, the first thing I thought (although I had no idea if I was pronouncing it correctly) was *Manzhouli!* It's here now.

I covered up the liquor in the backseat with a blanket as I pulled up behind a silver civic. A soldier stopped me. I rolled down the window and noticed that his eyes kept flicking from me to the blanket that I'd flipped over the booze. I was so busted. Then I thought: Hey wait – he wasn't a cop -- *posse comitatus*, man! He couldn't bust me! Right?

He said, "You won't be able to go this way."

"Why? What's going on?"

He looked back southward. "Des Moines is locked down."

I asked why a couple of times, but he started to get testy. Then another soldier walked up, tense, and said, "Turn around and go home now!"

I do not take kindly to rudeness, but I did not say one word. I turned, bumped across the median, stifled the urge to peel out and pelt them with gravel, and went back toward home.

I drove for a few miles thinking about following instructions and heading home, but I decided to head back to campus instead -- I guess, in a way, I just wanted to show up the soldiers at that roadblock. So, I pulled over, pulled out a map and looked it over. Iowa is pretty much on a grid, so unless there's a lake in your way, you can always find your way around anything. So, I found my way around.

2.10 Simpson College, medical bulletin

By late March, the mechanics of the disease were fairly well understood, but the number of the infected was still unknown. Fairly accurate information about the disease was widely disseminated, but by this time millions were infected worldwide.

From: (nurserita@simpson.edu)
To: Students; Faculty; Administration
Subject: HIV-Z Outbreak in Indianola

Everyone is encouraged to be aware of signs and symptoms, and report those that show them to CAs, department heads, and members of the student development staff.

The Center for Disease Control and World Health Organization, with the aid of Warren County Public Health Officials and the Iowa Department of Public Health, are investigating an outbreak of HIV-Z (a genetically mutated string of HIV) in Indianola. To date, six cases of HIV-Z have been found on Simpson College Campus and there have been two cases in the general population of Indianola.

Please fully cooperate with these officials and fully obey the curfew ordinance. Despite rumors to the contrary, this is a *statewide* curfew and Simpson College is <u>not</u> exempt.

Public health authorities are now fairly confident that HIV-Z is a mutation of HIV. It is spread through sexual contact or blood transfer. There are six stages of HIV-Z, each with its own symptoms.

Stage 1- 50-60 day latency period where the retro virus infects the body's healthy cells. During this period the infected may spread the infection through sexual contact, needle sharing, or organ donation.

To prevent the spread of this virus it is recommended that you remain abstinent and refrain from sexual intercourse until further notice.

Stage 2- Duration: 5-10 days. Physical symptoms begin to appear.
- Sweating
- Fever
- Small Muscle Tics

The virus attacks nerve cells, which results in damage to the brain and the central nervous system. This, in turn, results in loss of inhibition, ethical reasoning, and increased aggression. In some cases, these symptoms are accompanied by insomnia and paranoia.

To avoid contracting this virus refrain from sexual intercourse and travel in groups of three or more people to protect yourself.

Stage 3- Duration: 5-8 days. Physical symptoms continue to progress.
- Slight memory loss
- Muscle spasms
- Bleeding gums
- Pallor
- Confusion
- Impeded speech (In rare cases: glossolalia)

The infected still possess some urge for self preservation, and in rare cases they may still be able to communicate, but the aggression becomes psychotic in nature, and the infected begin to bite. If bitten by someone in stage 3, the infection spreads much more quickly through the initial stages. S1: 6-8 days; S2: 1 day; S3: 1 day.

It is imperative that you get away from anyone showing symptoms of this stage as quickly as possible. If escape is not an option, use any means necessary to incapacitate the infected person.

Stage 4- Duration: 50-100 (?) days. Physical symptoms continue to progress.

- Loss of fine motor control
- Inability to speak intelligibly
- Dehydration
- Hypertension

In this stage, higher reasoning abilities are gone. The infected go from assault to murder to cannibalism. If bitten by someone in stage 4 the infection progresses even more quickly through the initial stages. S1: 30-40 hours; S2: 10-12 hours; S3: 8-12 hours.

If you encounter anyone at this stage of the infection get away from them immediately. If there is absolutely no means of escape then you must incapacitate them. Many of those in stage 4 of HIV-Z are reportedly capable of surprising bursts of speed and strength. Consequently, flight is not an option, but you should not attempt to subdue them without assistance.

Stage5- Duration of four months. Infected are now slow and clumsy but feel no pain. Physical deterioration continues.
- No fine motor skills
- Skin and hair loss
- Loss of pain sensations
- Shambling gait

If bitten by someone in stage 5 the infection progresses even more quickly through the initial stages. S1: 20-30 hours; S2: 4-6 hours; S3: 3-6 hours.
If being attacked by an infected person at this stage, it is often best to attempt escape.

At present, there is NO vaccine or cure for this virus. If you encounter anyone showing signs or symptoms of the infected do not attempt to help them. Remove yourself from the infected, get to a safe area, and report any and all symptoms to your CA, department head, Campus Security, Campus Health, or the Indianola Police Department.

If you think you may have been infected or start to show symptoms related to any of the stages, please report to the nurse's office. You will be sent to a quarantined area for further examination and containment until it can be determined whether or not you pose a threat to those around you.

Go Storm!

2.11 Iowa National Guard ROE Card

This proscribed set of rules of engagement, was distributed to federalized Iowa National Guardsmen in late March in preparation for the construction and policing of quarantine areas across the state. Modeled on peacekeeping operations, the ROE are notable in that they do not address issues of contagion and do not yet reflect the nature of the new enemy. However, it is clearly designed for operations in hostile environments and ignores the *Posse Comitatus* Act. Simpson was declared a quarantine zone on the 30th of April.

Rules of Engagement
OPERATION VERDANT BADGER
(As Authorized by JCS [NORTHCOM Dir 55-47])

1. You have the right to use force to defend yourself against attacks or threats of attack.

2. In the event US forces are attacked or threatened by *unarmed* hostile elements, mobs, or rioters, the responsibility for the protection of US forces rests with the US commanding officer. The on-scene commander will employ the following measures to overcome the threat:

- Warning to demonstrators.
- Show of force, including the use of riot control formations.
- Warning shots fired over the heads of hostile elements.
- Other reasonable use of force necessary under the circumstances and proportional to the threat.

Hostile intent: When the on-scene commander determines, based on convincing evidence, that hostile intent is present, the right exists to use proportional force to deter or neutralize the threat.

3. Hostile fire may be returned effectively and promptly to stop a hostile act.

Hostile Act: Includes armed force directly to preclude or impede the missions and/or duties of US or allied forces.

4. You may not seize the property of others to accomplish your mission.

5. Detention of civilians is authorized only for security reasons or in self-defense.

Remember:

- Use of force only to protect lives
- Treat all persons with dignity and respect.
- Use minimum force to carry out the mission.
- Always be prepared to act in self-defense.

Finally, if necessary and proportional, use all available weapons to deter, neutralize, or destroy the threat as required.

Chapter 3: APRIL

3.1 National Guard Processing Form

After the National Guard constructed a perimeter around the college, they began interviewing everyone inside the wire in an attempt to determine the population, assess human resources, and study the outbreak. Some of these interviews rendered terse responses. Brian Allen, by contrast, seemed to want to talk about everything.

Date: 4 April
Case number: IA-SC-01034
Name: Brian F. Allen
Status: Simpson junior
Housing: Weinman (transferred to HA-1)
Age: 21
Sex: M
Height: 5'6"
Weight: 160lbs.
Eyes: Blue
Hair: Lt. Blonde
Skills: B1-2/1
Sexual contacts: Subject reported a sexual relationship with Simpson sophomore Michele Sprinkle (IA-SC-00954). Also, possible sexual contact with a probable II-Z (Likely IA-SC-0000023-ZZ).
Blood contacts: None reported, but subject reported scuffling with the same probable II-Z.

When did you first become aware of the zombie-virus?
Some would say I was a little too excited for the Zombie Apocalypse to appear. Like many other people, I watched the news and heard stories

about people being infected. While flipping channels on my way to Sports Center, I paused on a news story. I told my roommates something like, "Sounds like a bunch of zombies if you ask me."

They said I'd been watching too many movies, but I thought I'd have a great time blowing those dead bastards to hell. I'd sit up on the library with my .308, and just take my shots.

They wanted to know what I would do when I ran out of ammo. I was cocky. I just said that I'd go to Wal-Mart. Arrogance of youth, right? They were right here on campus, and I was confidently plotting their doom.

So, to answer your question, where I was when the zombie outbreak became official, I was sitting right here at Simpson College enjoying the good life, and man, did those zombies fuck that up.

Did you ever buy any ammunition?
No. I had a party to plan. I went to the liquor store instead. I went to Wal-Mart the next day and they were *sold out*. Sold out! How can you run out of bullets at Wal-Mart? This is America! We built this country on bullets!

Do you have any combat training or medical skills?
I'm an avid hunter. My favorite time of the year is hunting season, but I guess that has all changed now. It's kind of hard to go deer hunting when you have to worry about some zombie chasing you and trying to eat your brain. *I'm* the hunter; *I'm* not supposed to run away from anything. Everything should be running away from *me*. Humans just didn't go through millions of years of evolution to get to the top of the food chain so we could be the hunted.

So, you don't think of the infected as human?
You're joking right. Hell no, they ain't human no more. I'm ready for zombie season. Amendment two! I plan on exercising my constitutional

right to shoot those S.O.B.'s right in the head and follow that up with an "F. U." I mean, it is self-defense, right?

Have you interacted with any of the infected?
I sure did. It was at a party.

Where?
At my apartment. Remember my beer run? Anyway, my girlfriend was on one side of the room while I was chatting with my buddies about how much they sucked at flippy cup. The room was full of students who were drinking and having a good time. We know how to throw a party.

Around midnight, I decided that it was time to "break the seal" and go to the bathroom. I noticed some hot chick standing across the room staring at me. She was slender, long dark hair, and about 5'4 or so. Kind of pasty, but hot. Not goth hot, more librarian hot. Tina Fey hot. [Likely IA-SC-0000023-ZZ].

I knew my girlfriend would not like the way she was staring at me, so I made my way to the line waiting for the bathroom. After five minutes or so (everyone ahead of me in line was a fast-peeing guy), I entered and shut the door behind me without locking the door. Common courtesy dictates that a guy can pee in peace without any interruptions, or so I thought. I was in mid-stream when the door opened and that girl entered, closing the door behind her.

She scared the hell out of me and I darn near missed the bowl. Now that I saw her close up, she wasn't so hot. She looked like she'd been puking or something. Glassy eyed. Pale. I zipped up and told her, "Listen, I have a girlfriend and I don't think she'll be too happy knowing you are in here." I tried to push by her to the door knob.

She was quick. She slapped my outstretched hand away from the knob. Then she grabbed me and pushed me up against the wall and started to slide her hand down my pants.

I told her, "Get the hell off of me psycho bitch," and pushed her away. She stumbled and fell into the tub. I had enough of her and I flung the door open and walked back out to the party. I should have known not to leave her in there 'cause then she started to throw a damn fit. When I heard some glass breaking I was pretty pissed. My cologne is not cheap. I grabbed her and dragged her kicking and screaming out of the apartment with the help of a couple of my friends.

You said, "kicking and screaming."
Right.

Was she lucid? Was she screaming words, or was she just screaming?
Hm. Just screaming, I guess. Anyway, we slammed the door on her and she up and threw a rock through the window.

A rock?
Yes, a rock. A hunk of concrete or a brick or something. Damn near hit the plasma screen.

Did you call the police?
Yes. But by the time they got there, she'd taken off. The party never really fired up again after that buzz-kill. Looking back, I guess I should have shot her in the head.

Did she go into the bathroom with anyone else?
I don't know. Maybe.

Did you have any sexual contact after the party?
No. My girlfriend was too freaked out.

Recommendations and Actions:
Despite his potential weapons skills, subject is at high risk for infection. Despite his elaborate narrative it remains possible (likely?) that his description of the interaction with the infected [Likely IA-SC-0000023-ZZ] in the bathroom resulted in sexual contact. The description of infected matches the late, post-verbal stage 2 of disease. It is also

possible that in the process of ejecting her from the apartment, subject was scratched or bitten by the infected, although no recent injuries were apparent in his physical exam, subject has been transferred to Holding Area 1 (ARMC).

Subject was reluctant to divulge the names of the friends that attended the party, but when the dangerousness of the situation was stressed to him, subject produced a list of fifteen names [see attached]. Following protocol, since it is possible they all came into sexual contact with the infected, they have been moved up on the interview schedule and sequestered in Kresge Hall until further determinations about their status can be made.

Further recommendation: Conduct weapons search of subject's quarters.

Signed, SSGT Seth Borlag.

3.2 Eric Francis, journal

The following diary excerpt gives insight into the feelings and opinions of students on campus at the beginning of the Great Panic. It was executed in a fine calligraphic hand.

Last week, the National Guard showed up and erected a fence to quarantine the campus. They keep telling us that no one is allowed out for any reason, but they keep bringing in more students every day. They won't tell us why we're being quarantined, but we all know. It's this "infection" that hit China and spread out to other countries until it became bad enough that the World Health Organization and Center for Disease Control declared it a world epidemic. Now we're quarantined here.

It's not just us. It looks like they've done this to nearly every college campus in the U.S. because of spring break trips and students who have returned from studying abroad who may have contracted the infection. We're supposed to report any person showing signs of the symptoms. Being locked in we have no way to get weapons to protect ourselves, and I don't like that.

They thought they could contain us and we would just follow their orders. Most of the student body has, of course (lemmings), but I knew what to do. The first night after the fence went up I put on my camouflage hunting gear, grabbed a bag and snuck off into the darkness. I made it over the chain link without any problem and made my way to Wal-Mart. Once there I went to the sporting goods section.

Naturally, by this point, the guns were gone. So, I picked up some bottled water, a few canned goods, 5 lighters, a water purifying pitcher, and as many ramen noodles as I could carry to the checkout counter. It was a little trickier to get back inside the perimeter fence unnoticed because of the added weight, but I made it back to my room without incident. Once there I quickly hid the supplies by lifting a panel of my drop ceiling and sticking them behind an HVAC duct. I went out a couple more times for more supplies, but by Monday Wal-Mart was closed.

Then, when I woke up today I looked out my window to see a spiraling helix of razor wire topping the fence that, just last night, had been bare. I knew this meant things weren't going to get better. It could mean two things, the situation outside the fence were getting worse and we needed further protection, or the situation *inside* the fence was getting worse and we were locked in with these things that were trying to eat us. Either way I needed to see what was going on out there. I put on my camouflage again and made my way to the fence. Just before I threw a rug from the floor of my room over the razor wire to be able to cross over without being cut to pieces I saw the other wires. They'd electrified it. Then I saw some flashlights coming around the corner, so I had to get back inside *di di mau*. Clearly, they have stepped up security. I wonder if they knew I made a late-night trip to Wal-Mart. I couldn't have been the only one.

The Guard has removed all vehicles from campus. They only left the golf carts. They're making sure we can't crash the fences.

I've been lucky so far with my endeavors and keeping the fact that I have supplies (including two bottles of rum) a secret. I hope that I can continue to have this luck on my side because we were just told that the Guard had to put down two infected students this morning. Who knows how many more could have the disease and start attacking the rest of us. I'm going on a personal lock down today and I'm not leaving my room for anything but a necessary trip. If I do leave the safety of my room you can guarantee I will have my bat on hand. I don't care what the Guard says about not being allowed a weapon. I'm not letting myself be attacked by a "zombie" without making it regret the decision.

3.3 Grant Johnson, journal

On the evening of the 31st of March and the 1st of April, the Iowa National Guard erected a 10-foot chain link fence around the center of Simpson's campus. Students housed outside of this perimeter were moved in the morning of the 1st. Students, faculty and staff who had left the college in the preceding weeks were returned to the campus by local law enforcement. Although the fence was described as an effort to protect the inhabitants of the campus, many quickly came to consider it an effort to keep people *in* rather than something to keep the infection *out.*

Saw something terrifying today. Even worse than all the rumors floating around. People are fed up with the Guard. We just want to go home. I could drive out to you in four hours, tops, but something tells me that's not going to happen, now.

Earlier, maybe around 11:00 AM, some people started getting restless by the fence out near Buxton Park. I was just wandering around trying to get decent cell reception. Only every third or fourth call seems to be getting through. Anyway, I seemed to be having more luck out by the park, and while walking by I heard a lot of raised voices, definitely not friendly ones.

I got closer and saw some of the coaching staff and a couple of professors, big knots of people around them, shouting about laws and the Constitution and all kinds of stuff that I guess everyone's forgetting about now. A couple of the ethics profs were really getting into it— shaking their fists, making grand gestures. And apparently the students all loved it. I'd read about mobs before—in Intro. to Soc. or something— but I had never expected to see one in person. Seemed to me these people were getting close.

The Guard noticed too. I saw one on the other side of the wire watching them. A couple of minutes later seven or eight big trucks pulled up on the other side of the fence, outside the perimeter, and then soldiers poured out of them. They had those gas-mask looking things on. This didn't help the crowd's mood, of course. I think they just got more pissed.

The crowd was really growing by now. There were probably almost a hundred people attracted by the noise and commotion. All the nearby buildings were emptying out. I stayed close enough to see what was going on but no closer. I didn't like the idea of the Guard pointing guns at me. Much as I'd have liked to get out like everyone else, I was bullet averse.

The ringleaders started getting even crazier. They were leading the crowd to the wire. I have a feeling they forgot everything but their rage and fear for family and friends. I mean, they were terrified; they didn't know what was going on. They just wanted out, so they could feel like they were in control again. I guess running makes you feel safer than being trapped in a cage. Someone tried to calm them down, but it didn't work.

One of the guardsmen started bellowing orders through a megaphone. They were gathered right up to the fence now, shaking it and shouting at the guards. The Guardsman with the megaphone tried to explain, "Our orders are very specific! We cannot allow you past this barricade! Disperse now, or we will disperse you by force!"

He sounded confident that the Guard could deal with the mob, and I was inclined to agree with him, but I was too low down to see much. The crowd was just a seething mass of anger. They started shaking the fence, shouting *Out! Now! Out! Now!* People were jumping up and down and jostling at the fence. At this point, I jumped up onto a bench to try and see what the Guard was doing now.

Some of them were hauling crates full of something from their trucks. They laid them out in an ordered pattern and began opening them up. I saw a bunch of glinting metal cylinders passing between the Guardsmen. I figured it was some kind of gas or stun grenade or something. A soldier would grab hold of a couple cylinders and then move out to take position in a line stretching the entire length of the mob. There were two ranks of them, the front ones down and kneeling maybe fifteen feet from the divider. No one was pointing a gun yet—but the masks made them creepily inhuman.

I don't think they wanted a conflict any more than I did. God help them though, because the mob really seemed to be looking for one. They had another rhythmic chant going on now. "Let us out." They just shouted it again and again. *Let. Us. Out.* It was like hearing one angry voice, like the crowd was one single entity with only one thought. It was so loud, so desperate.

I never saw who threw the bottle.

I saw its path, though. It arched right up over the fence and glided smoothly down... right onto one of the Guard's helmets.

Now I'm no kind of military expert. I see a lot of movies, and I can guess how "realistic" they are. I know a thing or two more than most, though. I know that weapons aren't supposed to have the safety off unless someone has the intention to shoot.

The guy who got hit with the bottle, I bet he was only a little older than me, had probably been as panicky and afraid. Not every unit of the Guard from here had been sent into actual combat zones. Hell, I don't know. He might have even been a completely new guy who found himself joining at the wrong time and during the wrong situation.

One thing I'm pretty sure of, though, is that it was nothing but an honest mistake.

The bottle hit him and he stumbled a bit, surprised and off balance. And unfortunately for everyone there, he fired his M-16 right into the air.

It might as well have been a bomb for the effect it had.

The crowd went nuts, and I mean literally nuts, bonkers, crazy as hell. Some people jumped down to the ground to take cover. They really didn't care where they dived, just smashing into people looking for a place to hide. There were a lot of screams, pretty much a deafening chorus of them, in fact. Other people just scattered every which way. I even saw some idiots start fighting with one another, like they had just lost their minds and wanted to vent fear and anger on anyone nearby.

But they weren't even the worst. The worst were the ones who tried to go over the fence. Why someone would want to go OVER a divider toward the source of gunshots makes no sense to me. But then, mobs are not known for their spirit of cold calculation.

Ten or twenty jumped on the chain link fence, scrambling to reach the top. They moved so quickly and so desperately. The officers shouted something. The sergeants shouted it louder. Then every third or fourth person down the line drew out those canisters of tear gas, pulled some pins out and threw them over the fence.

As the gas released, it formed white clouds. The gas started seriously affecting the people the clouds came into contact with. The wind was blowing hard enough that I could still see fairly well, and at least it wasn't blowing toward me. A lot of the people, mostly those who weren't climbing the fence yet, started coughing and falling down. Some of them looked like they were retching, but they'd deployed it too late. Maybe the wind dispersed the gas before it reached the top of the fence. Maybe it was their adrenaline, or just sheer stupidity. Either way, a lot of them made it over.

They probably wish they hadn't, now.

I was surprised they didn't just shoot them. I mean, if it was a movie that would have happened, right? They would have blown them away.

I knew they trained our troops in some kind of close combat, but they really surprised me. Mostly they hit the crowd with the butts of their rifles. They didn't hold back either, at ALL. They formed a wall and just beat down anyone who wouldn't just lay there. A group of thirty or so unarmed idiots couldn't do much to a wall of strong, trained troops. It's harsh, yeah, but not deadly. It was probably nicer than a lot of those morons deserved.

They used zip cuffs to tie the wrists and ankles of the ones on the ground. The gas was drifting towards the center of campus. People were yelling everywhere. I saw three or four guys standing back a ways like me, muttering and whispering to each other. One of them pulled something from his pocket. It looked like a handgun, but it might just have been a camera or a transistor radio.

I'd had enough. I turned and sprinted for my apartment. I wasn't about to let these morons get me killed. I'm sitting here now, the lights low, worried that at any minute I'll hear more gunshots and screams. I heard from a friend on the floor that the Guard is going to start putting razor wire up.

3.4 Campus Perimeter

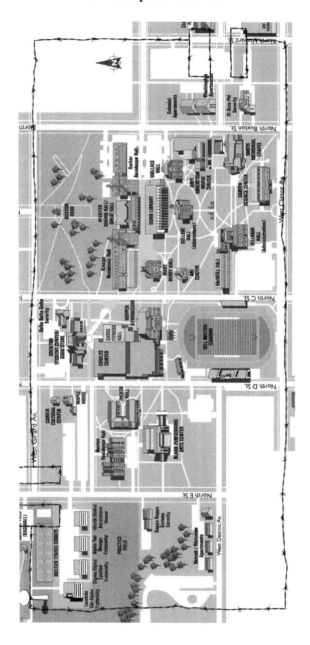

3.5 Photograph of Alexis Scott

Some students began arming in an effort to defend themselves from the infected within the perimeter.

3.6 Jack Landscombe, journal

This account, by a first-year music major, illustrates the ineffectiveness with which the National Guard policed the campus. Apparently, most of their efforts were concentrated on maintaining the perimeter, although at the outset they did conduct HIV tests and swept for weapons and illicit substances.

4-16. It's unnatural, but I can't bring myself to let her go -- let alone kill her. Sarah is going crazy in that chair I tied her to; she's rubbing her skin off in places and doesn't seem to notice at all. I am amazed that the knot I used to tie her is still holding. Who knew that Boy Scouts would prepare me for a zombie apocalypse? I gagged her too. I worry that people outside are going to hear her. I can't afford that, but I need to be sure I don't suffocate her by accident.

Last night I played some Debussy and she seemed to quiet down considerably, but the moment I quit she started back up again. What if I played something like Beethoven's Piano Sonata in C minor Movement 1... would she go nuts because it is fast and in minor? I might test this out tonight.

People around here are frequently trying to get out of the perimeter. Probably not a bad idea -- especially with Sarah being infected. It's been almost two months since I first made love with her, but I haven't felt any symptoms. This means I am immune, just like I thought before. The plus side to this is that I am unaffected and my woman is a zombie, so she can't turn me... but she still can kill me if she mauls me to death. Is it ironic that someone is immune, but in love with a zombie? I must be the most illogical person on the face of the Earth. To protect us, I made a pipe bomb just in case someone tries to enter my room without my permission.

4-17. She BIT me…. She got loose and <u>bit me</u>! I am running a fever now, but my wound doesn't look infected. I know I am immune, but damn it, this hurts. I managed to get her off of me and tie her down again, but my arm is all messed up from this bite. I don't know what to do. I have some first aid stuff so maybe that will help ease the pain. Maybe ibuprofen to reduce the fever? It's an infection; I know that is the reason why I have this fever.

4-18. It's obvious now. I am shaking so much. It's uncontrollable. My arm is oozing, no longer bleeding anymore. Instead it looks disgusting. The pus is all blackened. Sarah knows I am one of hers now. She no longer shows any interest in me at all. She doesn't want to eat me; she doesn't want to touch me. It's like I'm not here at all. I want to be close to her, untie her…. I am one of hers… I shouldn't succumb, but what do I have left to lose?

The shredded pages of this journal were found in a music practice room in ARMC. Apparently, Landscombe purposefully or accidentally ignited a pipe bomb of his own construction. By the time a reaction team opened the door, the zombie, freed by the blast, had eaten most of his body.

3.7 Kathryn Stevens, journal

An active and retired schoolteacher, Kathryn lived in a farmhouse near Indianola. These diary entries were written after her encounter with some infected that broke into her house.

April 19. Cloudy. A front is coming in from the south.

I was nothing but a meal to both of them. And the way they snarled and lurched at me, the way that dark red blood oozed out of that woman's forehead and spilled down the shower curtain rod onto my hands. So warm and sticky. I wasn't sleeping much before, but it's far more difficult now.

It plays over and over and over in my mind. Every time the house creaks I jerk. At each little sound my mind clears, but my muscles tense, ready to take on another smelly, moaning devil. I see the balding blonde woman holding the rod sticking out of her eye socket. I hear the sound of my bathroom window break. I hear the soft thump she made on the grass. The memories are intense and scrambled.

Then the man. Even in my dreams my stomach tenses, and I deliver another kick that sends him through the bathroom door and to the edge of my bed. He jumped up quicker than I expected, but I blocked his grasping hand, grabbed his wrist and flipped him into a cabinet and then the floor, rolling him to his face and pinning him. I still feel him wriggling underneath me, snarling. Then I remember Uncle Jerry's desk clock as I gripped it and brought it down on the back of his head. Four increments of four, of course. Feeling the pattern relaxed me even as his brown-red blood and brains splattered my hands, arms, neck, face, and stained my already grimy clothes. It was my last pair of clean jeans—who has time to hand wash things four times?

I know I relive it even when I don't remember because I feel sore when I wake up, and I haven't felt sore from practicing since a month or so after I started taking taekwondo courses in the little dojo on the southside. My body grew used to the practices, but actual combat is much harder. Can one become accustomed to these constant spasms at every creak or whisper? I just need to start dealing with what's happening.

Maybe I'm at a loss. I know I can't let my OCD keep getting worse, but right now giving in to it is the only thing that can calm me; it lets me feel some sort of control, even as everything else is crashing down.

But just knowing that their bodies are lying mangled in the garden shed has me pacing. I'll wait until daylight to take care of them and board the window. I let myself ease into the clean-up. I picked up the broken pieces of the clock—four at a time. (I should find a good spot for that marble base, though. That could come in handy again.) I collected every bit of glass from the bathroom floor—four at a time. I wiped the blood off the tiles and windowpane and walls—that took two sets of four swipes. The fabrics in the bedroom were harder. I just stripped the bed and tossed those out the window. Then I tried to soak up some of the blood in the carpet. Now it just looks bright red. I took a rug from the linen closet and put it over the biggest spot. That would help for now. Then I went through the house and tried to re-board the doors. I'm not sure how they got it open – just the two of them.

April 20. Some showers over night. Today it is bright and fresh.

Two more army trucks just went by—They seem especially active today. Hopefully, they're starting to bring in some supplies. Wal-Mart and Hy-Vee are tapped out so quickly, and they are too long a trek without having a working car anyway. My canned fruits and vegetables are going fast. I don't even know if the stores have anything left in them. They must all have been completely raided by now. Funny how the things that were important to me are useless in times now: DVDs, CDs, toys and gadgets, expensive shoes and purses, a monthly hair color, etc. And when or if this all ends, how quickly will our lives return to such things? Will I have learned anything?

April 21: Sunny with a nice breeze from the NW.

I managed to get two good hours of sleep this morning. I'm not sure when. Checking the clock every time I wake up only makes the darkness move slower. When I did wake up my muscles were sore again. Writing it down helps a little, but not enough. I don't want to forget the other day—I should be proud of myself—I just want to be able to rest.

This time, it was 6 A.M. I took down the front door boards and stepped out to survey the area. I hadn't seen anything when I'd checked through all the upstairs windows. I took a slow walk around the house, making sure everything was in order and that no one was coming from any direction. Then I grabbed my shovel from off the porch and took it over by the tool shed.

I have been working on this hole for two days now. I think it's about big enough for the two bodies, but want to make sure. I don't want to risk throwing my back out because having to drag them back out of the hole just to make it bigger. I dug 'til sundown yesterday, taking breaks here and there and looking over my shoulder about every 16 seconds. This morning, I went back to collect the bodies.

They were covered in the stuff I'd pulled off the bed. When I pulled at the sheet, a cloud of black flies flew up. They were big and fat. I didn't want to look at their faces again—especially after what I'd done to the man. I managed to pull the shower rod out of the woman's head without having to look at her. I think I would rather not completely know what I'm capable of. Having to live with the dreams and the blood was reminder enough. I dragged them one-by-one over to the hole. I rolled them in, surveyed the area for a minute or two, and covered them up. I finished by 10 and went in to try to rest.

April 22. Another beautiful day.

A middle-aged man and woman with a teenage boy were speed-walking up the gravel road earlier toward town. I jumped when I heard their footfalls on the gravel. At least it wasn't snarling or moaning. I stayed motionless and silent as they passed.

The man and woman each had guns, but I still don't want to let on that I'm here. I had taekwondo, but what good is that against two armed people, younger and stronger than I am. I wouldn't put it past anyone to hurt a tiny 59-year-old woman anymore. And I'd had enough intruders to last a lifetime.

3.8 Leroy Blount, video diary

As the National Guard contingent was drawn down to deal with an escalating series of crises, students began moving around campus more freely. They could not get out of the perimeter, but they found inventive ways to spend their idle hours inside the wire.

LEROY: Alright you got it Jess? Yeah the third button... no the *third*... don't forget the lens cover."

[A young man is standing in front of a chain link fence topped with razor wire, presumably the containment fence around the Simpson College quarantine zone. The time of day appears to be late afternoon or dusk. There is a heavy cloud cover and the trees beyond the fence are swaying with the wind. Several figures loiter on the other side of the fence.]

LEROY: Here we are, coming to you live, once again, from zombie paradise. I'm Leroy Blount here at the northern fence with, as always, the lovely camera girl Jessica Maven.

[Camera swivels to a close up of a young woman's face. She also smiles, but there is a hint of trepidation in her eyes. She waves and turns the camera back towards the Leroy.]

LEROY: We're out here today to prove to Jess that these so called, 'Terrifying Zombies' are nothing to be afraid of. Then maybe she will stop waking me up at 12:30 and let me get some decent sleep. Bring the camera over here.

[Camera moves closer to the fence and a face comes into view. Its flesh resembles rotten meat but the most striking features are its eyes. Heavily dilated, they roll and come to rest on Jessica with a look of insatiable longing. The camera begins to shake slightly.]

JESS: Ok Lee. I get it, let's go back now ok? Hey! What are you doing?

[Leroy has lifted a large piece of concrete from the ground and is set to throw it like a shot-put.]

LEROY: Check this out!

[He hoists the cement into the air; it barely makes it over the wire then clips the zombie's shoulder. It begins to tip over, but rights itself.]

LEROY: Dammit. Wait. Here's another one.

[Leroy sees something and stands up quickly. The camera turns back to the fence where a fast zombie is clambering up the fence. It grabs a loop of razor wire and severs several of its fingers. Howling, it falls back to the ground. It gathers itself up and dashes towards the fence again.

JESS: [screams]

[recording ends]

3.9 Karen Grzesiak, diary

Internees reacted to their situation in a multitude of ways. Like many, Karen Grzesiak, a visiting musician, understood the virus through the filter of popular culture, but unlike most she almost immediately set herself to surviving. Testy and inventive, she hardly skipped a beat as the zombie apocalypse began in earnest.

My husband Eric and I were ordered to return to Simpson College's campus today. Before we came, Eric and I went to Wal-Mart to get some things. The shelves were pretty empty with no batteries, milk, or guns. When we showed up at Simpson, they gave us a room in a dorm (which for some reason they insist on calling a "residence hall"). I was confused until I overheard someone say that they were quarantining certain areas. I tried talking to some of the National Guard people about why we are being packed into this campus like a bunch of sardines, but they wouldn't talk to me. This made me mad, and I got in the face of a soldier. He looked about 12. I had his attention, but it certainly didn't do me any good. His superior saw what I was doing and ordered two other soldiers to "escort" me back to my facility. They treated me as if I were a prisoner, but I didn't do anything wrong.

An hour later two army medics came in and gave us a full and demeaning physical inspection. They told us we were clear. Do they think I am going to go around and eat them? They still treat us all like we have it anyway.

Also: No wireless Internet! *Arg!*

* * *

The room we are in is filled with undergraduate detritus including an aquarium with some of those South American tree frogs. One of the previous occupants was apparently really into them. It doesn't look like he read anything other than tree frog books. Tiny amphibian friends, I promise you this: I *will* keep you alive until your master returns.

Hm. I now see that it isn't an aquarium after all; it is a "naturalistic vivaria." Tell me more, *Guide to Tree Frogs!* (Give me a break on this. They lock us in from dusk to dawn. What else am I supposed to do?)

* * *

Eric spends his time in the building's computer lab, which has internet access. He doesn't like to talk about what he's doing. Online porn? Probably.[1]

You'd think in the twenty years since I graduated college, they would have come up with something better than beige linoleum as a flooring material.

Have you ever eaten an MRE? Eric says they aren't too bad. I think they *stink*.

* * *

Eric says that I'm "freaking out." He says everything will "be OK," but he is wrong. His wrongness drips from those words. Has the man ever actually watched a horror movie? I've read *and underlined* plenty of zombie books, so I know how this goes down. Doesn't he know that saying "everything is OK" is what someone says just before it becomes very, very clear that things are not OK at all? I'm getting ready. The zombie apocalypse is here!

Survival is going to be tough in a world that will be trodden with death and disease, but I have an idea. Being a bassoonist, I have a lot of tools for my reeds. Those damn things are so touchy and you must work with them constantly, so I have a nifty tool box full of dangerous weapons. Unfortunately, they're all hand-to-hand combat weapons. The most effective "weapon" I have would be my reed knife, which I have to sharpen on a regular basis so I can work with my reeds easily. It is wide but thin, making it perfect to sever a spine if necessary. I plan to use this as my finishing weapon.

MORTAL KOMBAT!

My other weapon of choice is not in my tool box actually, it's a part of my bassoon itself. Though the three largest parts work great for clubbing something to death (especially the butt of the bassoon), but the

---

[1] Actually, Eric Grzesiak was working with a team of computer programmers in an effort to overcome the firewall that had been imposed on Simpson's Internet connection.

parts I am particularly interested in using are the two bocals in the case. The bocal is a curved, long tapered metal tube that attaches the reed to the bassoon itself. Each bocal is a different size and I need to test out which one works best as a blow dart gun. Yes, I just said it. Blow dart gun. Oh, how my undergrad bassoon teacher would be proud of me in discovering a use for my bassoon in "everyday" life. They tell you that being able to play a musical instrument is a life skill, but you don't believe them. Well, *believe them.*

I can easily make darts out of pins. (I traded a pack of gum for a whole sewing kit. This is America's future? What a bunch of knuckleheads!) I just stick them through a piece of shoelace, and glue it to the pin. Tested this out earlier and the accuracy is great with my second bocal (the smaller one) but doesn't work so much with the 3. I told Eric about my ingenious plan and he just stared at me like I was insane. He asked me how I planned on killing zombies with little needles. He turned green when I told him I plan on using the toxins from my frogs' glands to make the darts poisonous. I can't wait to test these out. *I have pimped my ride! Poison* bassoon blow dart gun!

* * *

Thank you Internet! I know it sounds crazy that my frogs' sweat could kill someone, but 150 micrograms of poison from the Golden Dart Frog can kill an adult human in one minute. This means one milligram could kill around 15 adults. This poison is known as a batrachotoxin, which prevents the nerves from transmitting impulses, and leaves all the muscles in the body contracted. It sounds dangerous to blow darts at zombies with it, but as long as you use the right equipment and be careful about not touching the poison directly, I should be fine. Since this toxin freezes the muscles up, I can then finish the job with my handy-dandy reed knife AND retrieve my blow dart for future use.

* * *

Did you know that it is really time consuming to get a frog to sweat toxins? I wish I could just pick one up and squeeze. I kind of imagined they'd be like little sponges full of poison. Not so. The other problem is trying to NOT make my Golden Dart frogs become part of a Chinese dinner from heating them up with a candle.

After several hours work, I have about enough to cover the bottom of a cup. I really want to try this blow dart thing out, but if I'm ostentatious about it, someone will probably take my stuff away, doing me no good. As for my reed knife, I am so bored that I actually sharpened it to the point I can shave my arm hair without it even touching my arm. *Amazing!*

What's Eric doing while I'm preparing to go mano y mano against King Zombie? He's taking a poetry class. *Poetry!* Really. At this point he may be becoming the pretty boy that must be left behind so that the girl reporter can survive. Sorry, pal, it is becoming clear that you have a shortage of special skills. Nor do you have a Tom Selleck moustache. I am not going to march to certain death while you consult your sonnet notebook.

I saw my first true zombie today. That was fun, I guess. I'm confident I could kill one, but really, I want nothing to do with them. One of the guards shot it in the head as it was trying to scramble up the fence, and I mean *scramble*. I hope it doesn't always take a shot to the head though because that sucker was moving fast. Though I hate being cooped up, I am pretty sure I would not have stayed alive in Kansas City like I have in Indianola. Eric read some pretty harrowing stuff on the Internet before the firewall went up. Riots. Devouring. Streets red with blood. Etc.

I find it funny that my bassoon technically saved us from dying, and now I am using various items for it, or of it, as potential weapons.

Thank you, Simpson College, for inviting me to give a recital right on the cusp of Armageddon, and thank you Eric, for being enough of a moistened bint to accompany me.

* * *

Good news!! I got to test out my little bocal blow dart thingie this morning while there were some zombies hanging out by the fence. Fortunately, the National Guard were busy somewhere else, so I crept down, went out the back door, took a deep breath, aimed, and I got one. I don't quite know where, but it hit him. At first I thought it wasn't going to do anything, but after about five minutes, it just seized up and fell right over. I think it was dead, but I was not about to climb that fence to find out. It was amusing though, in a morbid way. Unfortunately, he probably would have eaten my brains by the time it kicked in and clocked out his central nervous system. Darn.

Eric's genius anti-zombie alternative to my blow dart system: get guns.

Well done, Dr. Horrible. You are the evil genius of my hopes and dreams.

On the evening of April 22, the National Guard was redeployed to Marion County, Iowa, in an attempt to re-establish the perimeter around Central College. When college residents awoke on the morning of the 23rd, they found the gates locked, but undefended.

Chapter 4: MAY

4.1 Radio Transcript

Although the quarantine system began to break down, live radio broadcasts continued. Some of the information on these broadcasts was useful; most of it was designed to be reassuring. Occasionally, as in the following entry, these broadcasts likely had the reverse effect.

ANNOUNCER: The orders from the state and federal government remain the same: A dusk to dawn curfew is in effect. Stay in your homes, lock your doors, and barricade yourself in with at least as much food and water as you can. Travel is extremely dangerous. Roadways are blocked; bridges are clogged or destroyed, and infected are concentrated very heavily on highways and streets. We have eye-witness reports of fighting in several locations including the streets of West Des Moines. [Static]

ANNOUNCER: We are receiving a live broadcast from the Governor's office.

GOVERNOR: Citizens and residents, I urge you to remain calm during this crisis. Very soon the National Guard will regain control of the situation here in the capital. From there we will begin sweeping outward to relieve towns and farms throughout our great state. In short order the federal government will begin airlifting supplies and reinforcements to us, at which time we expect to gain complete control over this situation.

Due to a number of factors, it has been necessary to make significant redeployments of National Guard and State Police resources. In every case where redeployment became necessary, security has been entrusted to local officials.

There is nothing to fear so long as you keep your head down and don't attract attention. Under no circumstances should you fire upon an officer of the law or a man or woman in uniform; they are here to protect you. There is [static] about the nature of the outbreak. Keep a calm and cool head when assessing whether someone appears to be infected or not. Bites, confusion, and lack of coordination could all be possible signs. I will continue to direct the containment and control effort from …
[Crashing Sounds – Gunshots]

UNKNOWN: Can't stay here.

GOVERNOR: What about the …

UNKNOWN: Go! Go, go go!
[Gunshots – Shouting]
[Static]

ANNOUNCER: We'll continue to broadcast updates every half hour as they arrive. As we said earlier… there's … as long as … you don't need to panic. The federal government is on the way.

The few subsequent communications from Iowa state government authorities that followed were taped before being broadcast.

4.2 Zoe Kinsley, diary

The redeployment of the National Guard resulted in chaos. The Indianola Police Department failed to assume responsibilities for security, and it was initially unclear what authority the college administration had to regulate the perimeter. Consequently, within a few days, a large number of people fled the compound in search of family members. Most of those who remained focused on developing some sense of organization, securing supplies, scouting the town, and strengthening their defenses, but some panicked.

Oh my God! I don't know what to do! Everywhere I turn people are panicking. I thought they were crazy. I mean, all this hype about a few deaths from an illness. But it's here. They haven't even canceled classes yet, but it's all around us.

They've left now. There are some in here. They can't get rid of all of them. Not many, but there are some. They hide, and people are changing. It's hard to know what to do, but they usually don't show up unless you're alone. At least that's what I've heard. This is the worst thing ever....

I just went back to my apartment, after class and the blood! BLOOD! Everywhere! I went to my room to get my things, namely pot, journal, and cell phone. And there she was. Sara was right there in the middle of the floor, but she was not just dead -- it was like she was eaten. EATEN! Who *eats* another person??? Who eats my best friend??

I avoided her body and all the blood. I got my things, and I didn't know where to go. I checked my phone. There was a voicemail. *She had called me!* She was scared and needed me and I wasn't here!

I smoked right there. I didn't think it mattered anymore. I smoked right there in the middle of my room over my roommate. Over my best friend's dead body. Then I went to the living room window and checked outside. I couldn't see anything going on out there.

I left out the back and went to the library, which is where I am now. I can't believe this is real. But it's everywhere! People's Facebook pages say it all. Siblings missing, warnings to friends – there's even a group you can "like" about not being eaten by zombies.

I even have one friend who posted that she'd been bitten. She was asking for help.

I'm sick. I'm want my grandma. I want to get out of here.

4.3 Photograph of combat outside ARMC

After the unexpected departure of the National Guard, defense of the school fell largely to the students themselves.

4.4 Sam Warner & Tony Reynolds, telephone conversation

The following phone conversation between Tony Reynolds and his boss, Sam Warner, was made after the departure of the National Guard. (The transcript was recovered from a recording in the national offices Warner Trucking Co.)

WARNER: Tony? Tony! Where are you? Are you okay?

REYNOLDS: No worries boss, I'm fine. I can't talk very long, but I'm in Indianola right now. My cell-phone is still working. [muffled] Back off man, I said you could use it after I finished!

WARNER: Thank God. Wait... is there an outbreak there?

REYNOLDS: There was. This thing is pretty much everywhere now. I just thought I should check in with you quick and see how you are holding up.

WARNER: We're doing fine, for now. The wife is trying to keep the kids calm, but we've boarded ourselves up in the house and are waiting for help to arrive. Luckily Lily had the sense to stock up on supplies when she first heard the rumors about the virus, so we're pretty set and should be able to hold out for at least a month. How are you doing? Are you safe?

REYNOLDS: Yeah, I think I'm pretty secure right now.

WARNER: So, where are you exactly? You're not just in your truck are you?

REYNOLDS: No. I managed to get into a Wal-Mart before it was locked down. I'm here with some townies, mostly Wal-Mart employees and their families. Not the most ideal situation, having so many people around, but I didn't really have any other choice.

WARNER: What are you talking about?

REYNOLDS: The things. They are all over the town. The National Guard was trying to contain the situation, but they didn't have a whole lot of luck. Some people got out in time, but those who didn't have been scrambling to get to a safe place. I got lucky and managed to get into Wal-Mart before the staff opened fire.

WARNER: Opening fire?! They were shooting at people?

REYNOLDS: People are pretty desperate, and I guess some didn't want to share the supplies with too many others.

WARNER: What's happening now?

REYNOLDS: We've barricaded the doors so that none of them can get in. We should be able to hold out here until this thing is over.

WARNER: Hopefully it isn't too long...I hate to think of you locked up with people crazy enough to kill people.

REYNOLDS: Honestly Sam, at this point, I would probably shoot someone to keep them out of here too. ... Listen Sam, you don't know what it is like out there. People are scared, and we can't be sure who is infected and who isn't. Why take the chance? ... Desperate times, man.

[Shouts in background]

WARNER: What's going on?

REYNOLDS: People have been arguing about trying to get over to the college, some think that it is safer over there. Others don't want to risk it.

WARNER: A college?

REYNOLDS: Yeah, I've seen signs for it. I actually think that's where the first outbreak around here happened.

WARNER: They have been locking down campuses all over.

REYNOLDS: I suppose it would make sense to cut off the college from the rest of the town, especially if that's where the disease is.

WARNER: Why would anyone want to go there, then?

REYNOLDS: The rumor is that the students and whoever else is there have turned the place into some kind of fortress. I don't

	know if that's true or not…I don't know how they could possibly pull something like that off.
WARNER:	If they haven't, it's really too bad about those kids. Their families must be losing their minds.
REYNOLDS:	What they should be worrying about is covering their own asses. They're no use to their kids if they're dead.
WARNER:	That's a little heartless, don't you think?
REYNOLDS:	At this point, it's every man for himself.
WARNER:	Are things really that bad?
REYNOLDS:	Don't know. [muffled] God damn it, fine! I am hanging up. Will you just leave me alone? Listen, I need to go, but I will call you later when I know a little more and to see how you're holding up, all right?
WARNER:	Sure, sure. I'll do the same if I hear anything you should know. Don't worry, Tony. We'll be fine. I promise, when this is all over, we'll go out for a beer at Puff's, okay?
REYNOLDS:	Many beers. Many, many beers. Take care of yourself Sam.
WARNER:	You too, Tony.

4.5 Chad Nguyen, debriefing

The first organized attempts to scout outside of the perimeter were haphazard affairs. Many small groups went off in search of friends and families, but two fairly organized groups went out in search of supplies. One of these groups moved east and north to determine the situation at Hy-Vee, Walgreens, and Wal-Mart. The other went south to assess the situation at the county courthouse before moving further south to Fareway grocery store.

This is the first recon expedition since the National Guard left and I'm not sure how to explain it so I'll just write whatever I can.

We left the fence line to see what was going on down on the square at the courthouse and it started out pretty quiet. The way there we never saw anyone outside but I could've sworn I saw a couple faces in windows that disappeared as soon as we looked up at the windows. They wouldn't come down when I yelled so we moved on toward the courthouse.

Then Terry stopped walking. I called to him, but he didn't say anything. He just kept staring so I went back to see what he was looking at, and I looked down Ashland, not ready for the body we saw. It looked like an older man, but one of his legs was missing, he didn't have on any pants, and his skin was scratched to shit. I tried to keep everyone calm, but it was clear that we needed to get to the courthouse quick. He'd started to bloat. His shirt was stretched tight.

We got there and called out. On top of the building a cop poked his head out and yelled at us, wondering who we were and if we were one of "them." I yelled back that we were from Simpson, and said he should let us in. After a minute a garage door opened, and we were told to get in quick. There were four cops there with their hands on their guns.

They closed the door, and after a bit they calmed down. We told them what had been going on at Simpson and asked where everyone was. That's when it became clear that our little outing would be disappointing. They seemed even more confused about the situation than we were.

They looked pretty shaken up. They didn't want to let us much past the entrance hall, but from the voices we heard, it was pretty clear there were families in there. I assume that they collected their families together and they're planning on using the courthouse as a fort or something.

At that point we decided that Fareway could wait, so we returned to campus to file this report.

4.6 Frederick Wish, Debriefing

Within a few days, the college organized an eight-man Simpson Perimeter Assault & Reaction Team (SPART), which was quickly nicknamed "The Spartans." Some of the members had military experience, but they included civilians with excellent stamina and weapons proficiency. The leader was Frederick Wish, an elementary education major who was a veteran of the conflict in Afghanistan.

They tasked our group with finding this one badass zombie motherfucker that no one seems to be able to pin down. There have not been any bodies, but people keep getting bit and claim that they haven't left the perimeter, so that can only mean that it is lurking somewhere around here. I didn't know if some of the people in our group were up for the task. We'd taken two casualties when a fast one got over the fence a few days ago. I didn't know the new guys well. I just hoped they didn't bug out when the shit started getting hairy.

So, in terms of personnel, I wasn't too happy, but in terms of equipment, we were in much better shape after a salvage team brought in a truly impressive haul of weapons that some militia nutcase had stashed in his basement. This was the first operation in which we felt like we were properly armed. Everyone had goggles and bandanas for blood spray, and we had shinguards, flashlights, gloves, and whatever other "armor" people felt comfortable wearing. Our eight-man team deployed with three shotguns, two scoped hunting rifles, a two-handed axe, and a ten-foot polearm. Our point man, Dolores, had a Glock .45 handgun with a tactical light.

We first swept the bottom floor of the ARMC, which was difficult in itself. It had been sealed up by the Guard, and no one had really been interested in exploring further since they found those two dead kids barricaded into a practice room (some kind of freaky zombie suicide pact or something). The ARMC has multiple doorways, floors, and staircases. We took our time. After we finished, we took a break before moving on to College Hall.

It's an old three story building. First, we were clearing the first floor (Admissions), going room to room. Everything checked out clear, not a soul in sight. It was time to move up stairs. The stairs were arranged in a square pattern. Dolores paused at the bottom of the stairs and directed her light up the center. Into view came a silhouette of a woman leaning over the railing on the top floor. We all paused. She appeared to be undulating back and forth.

The banister that the woman was leaning on broke. She, along with the wood fragments, came plummeting down the center of the staircase. We had to dodge to avoid being hit. She banked off a lower banister and landed with a thud. We slowly moved closer to her mangled body. Naturally, she was dead. There were fresh wounds in addition to the battering she'd taken on the way down. Much of her flesh was missing. We were standing there when a scream echoed from above. Well, maybe a screech. I'm not sure what to call it, but we've all heard it by now. It's a horrible sound.

All flashlights snapped up except for Gramsci. He's a pro. No combat experience, but he knew what his job was and he did it. He was tasked with watching our six; he just said, "Who pushed her?"

For a moment, I saw a face twisted in rage, violently rocking back and forth while gnashing its teeth at us. Our lights reflected in its eyes. As it shook, fresh bits of meat rained down on the ground around us. Kevin snapped out of it and took a shot. It was a weird angle and it was raining blood, so he missed.

It retreated out of view. It sounded like it was running on all fours. Some of the others had a worried look on their face and eye balled the front door.

Dolores started up the stairs. As we got to the top floor, we twice heard the distinct sound glass breaking. It came from a room directly to our left. We got into position and aimed our weapons inside. We saw the broken window and felt the breeze blowing through it. That bastard jumped.

We ran towards the staircase, and rounded each corner to head down the stairs. Then we saw the last thing we expected. It was bounding up the stairs as if to greet us. I mean, WTF?

We all fired, and Jackson tried to hit it with his pole, but it was fast – scary fast – the fastest one I've ever seen. Our firing was pretty erratic because of the way we were stacked up on the stairs, but I'm sure we hit it. It must have dumped every cc of adrenaline into its bloodstream to get up the stairs that fast. It jumped and latched on to Dolores. She wrenched around and they went over the banister. Another banister.

When they landed, the zombie must have broken its back. She landed on top and had the wind knocked out of her, but she got her sidearm up and under its chin even though she had a broken arm. She was pretty cut up, but she squeezed off every remaining round in her clip. She was pretty cool about it too. She had a good firing rhythm. By the time she clipped out, there wasn't really anything that you could call a head.

4.7 Sarah Beth Estes, interview transcript

Here a student with little to no experience in nursing or therapy attempts to interview the sole survivor of a botched salvage mission to Fareway grocery store on the south side of town.

ESTES: Can you say your name?

SCHACHT: I am .. Chris .. Schacht.

ESTES: I need you to stay with me. Here let's keep walking. Where is the pain coming from?"

SCHACHT: My head. My head hurts.

ESTES: Here we are. Chris, can you lie down on this table for me? Thank you. Do you remember what happened?

SCHACHT: I was running. And then I was running.

ESTES: What about before you were running? Were you with Kyle and the scouts?

SCHACHT: No … Yes. I was at home with the family and they came and got me.

ESTES: Your family is here?

SCHACHT: No … Yes. It's the Barkleys. They moved in when the guards were here.

ESTES: But they aren't related to you?

SCHACHT: No … No. They got interned here. He is a man, and he's a … a … a race car driver? She is a psychology professor.

ESTES: Alright, I'm going to give you an injection now; it should help you to concentrate better. You'll be fine in a minute. I don't see any wounds on you; did you see anyone outside the wire?

SCHACHT: Oh yes I saw the sick people.

ESTES: Were they chasing you?

SCHACHT: Yes, that's why I ran. They were following me.

ESTES: I see. Did you touch any of them? Did they touch you?

SCHACHT: No, I ran. I ran here. I was standing outside, Fareway? And I was on lookout with a few others. They gave me a gun, but I don't like guns.

ESTES: Did they touch you?

SCHACHT: Yes the gun touched me, but I tried not to touch it.

ESTES: No, I mean the ... the infected.

SCHACHT: I was faster than them; I ran here.

ESTES: Did you see what happened to those that were inside the store?

SCHACHT: They came out. They came out so fast. There were guns and noise, and the brightness, but they still came out. The zombies were everywhere. Windows smashing – they broke with the noise, and the zombies came running out. They went inside to find food. I stood outside to stand watch. We didn't see any monsters outside all day, so they went inside to get food. But they never came out; only the sick monsters came out. They were horrible, their skin was white as milk, and it was falling off of some of them. There was blood, oh there was blood. Their faces were covered in blood. Their arms were covered in blood. The yelling, the yelling. They were mean, and angry, and hungry. I ran. I ran fast.

ESTES: You said there was only a few of you outside, what happened to the rest? Did they try to come back with you?
[inaudible]

ESTES: Mister Schacht? Chris?
[inaudible]

ESTES: OK. That's enough for now. You rest, OK honey?

[recording ends]

4.8 Kelly Anderson, debriefing

Some of the internees brought important skills into the community. Kelly Anderson was an air marshal, who killed an infected man on a flight that landed at Des Moines Airport. She and several of the passengers were interned at Simpson due to the copious amounts of blood spattered around the aircraft cabin in the melee. After passing screening, she became the leader of one of the salvage teams, which searched the area around the perimeter for survivors and supplies.

I went out with my squad today. Each of us carried a backpack to put recovered supplies in. We also had two duffle bags for our group of six. After several encounters, we've been whittled down to a pretty hardened group. I'm surprised at how well some of these students hold up in the thick of this.

My second in command, Kitchi, had a near miss with death today trying to save some kid whose parents had turned. It appears that these monsters forget everything that they ever loved or cared for. The boy was cowering in the fenced in yard in a dog house. Kitchi heard some faint sobbing coming from the other side of the fence. He told us to wait for him to give us the all clear, and hopped over that six foot fence with ease and grace. I heard him talking quietly, trying to coax the boy out from his hiding spot. I don't know what he said to him, but he got him out. Kitchi came over and said that he was going to hand the boy over the fence. Just as I and Zebulon grabbed his hands we heard the crash.

The boy grasped my hand. I felt him trembling in fear. I could just barely see in between the cracks of the fence. These were the fast ones. They must have been trapped inside the house, but once Kitchi jumped into their back yard, they got one big ass hunger pang because they broke right through that double paned sliding glass door and headed straight for him. Kitchi is as quick and nimble a person as I have ever seen, but I didn't think he was going to stand a chance against two of them in close quarters. His preferred weapons were his blades. He carried several knives of varying lengths and shape, but his most prized weapon is his hatchet. It's good for close-in work, but the mess? Ugh. Not for me. He calls it his "tomahawk."

The male crashed through the glass first. Kitchi threw a knife. It didn't slow down much. Then he swung the hatchet flat side down with a crack right across the temple. Kitchi sidestepped as its momentum carried it forward crashing its head right through the fence. I fell backward looking right into its blood shot eyes. Can you believe it? That bastard was still "alive." It tried to push the rest of its way through so it could eat us, but it was useless. Kitchi had done some damage, but then Ike brought his shotgun to bear and blew dad's head to pieces like a watermelon.

Meanwhile, mom came out. This time, Kitchi threw a knife that looked like something out of "Blade." It lodged in her right shoulder. Once again he side stepped, and swung the hatchet into the side of her neck. Unfortunately, he didn't sever the spinal column. Instead, it lodged in her neck. It must have caught a vertebra. Blood sprayed out, but she was coming around to grapple. By this point, Nate was up on the fence. For once he didn't have his stupid video camera out. He dropped her with his shotgun.

By this time, some of Mr. and Mrs. Z's friends showed up. It was time to go. I ordered the others to make sure we had a clear path out of there. I turned and kicked what was left of Mr. Z's face out of the hole so I could see what was going on in the yard. I saw a teenage zombie come charging out of the house – maybe he'd been upstairs. Kitchi was checking Mrs. Z when I shouted at him that he had another one coming at him. Too late. He turned around just as the teen Z tackled him. I let go of the boy and raised my Glock with both hands, but I didn't have a clear shot. It was gnashing its teeth and growling. Droplets of blood were spattering on Kitchi's face. Not good.

Kitchi brought his knee up for a square hit and with one fluid motion twisted so that he rolled on top, pinning it as he sat on its chest. Nate jumped down and started bashing his head with the butt of his gun.

I turned to the kid. He was wide-eyed; his mouth was gaping. He could see it all through the hole in the fence.

Kitchi hopped back over the fence: blood and sweat running down his face and arms. The kid pulled away. He tried to keep me between him and Kitchi. I guess if someone was covered with the bloody remains of my entire family I'd react in pretty much the same way.

Then he took off. The kid just took off. We ran after him, but by the time we'd rounded the corner of the house, he'd found another hidey-hole. This was not a good time for a search. Zs were coming from every direction now – drawn by the gunfire and yelling. Part of me wanted to stay and find the kid, but I had to think about the unit. We broke contact and returned to the perimeter. After sunrise tomorrow, I'd like to sweep the area again.

Salvage inventory:

3 cans fruit (15 ¼ oz.)
3 cans beans (15 oz.)
4 jars preserves (10-18 oz)
1 can baking powder (10 oz.)
1 bottle cider vinegar (16 oz.)
1 bottle caesar dressing (12 oz.)
1 bottle olive oil (1 qt. – half full)
2 compact fluorescent light bulbs
4 screwdrivers
1 20 x 20 plastic tarp
2 butcher knives
1 tube children's toothpaste

4.9 Erin Broich, proposal

In mid-May, college salvage teams discovered that one of the silos at the Indianola grain elevator was half full of dried corn. Another silo contained thousands of kilograms of dried soy beans. These quickly became the staples of the diet inside the perimeter, but long range planning encouraged the college administration to investigate alternative sources of supplies.

Several plans about procuring livestock as a food source have been brought forward, and below is the description of the two plans that were determined the most plausible, as well as pros and cons to both:

1. **Raising livestock inside of the perimeter**

a.   Positive: A small herd of cattle could be obtained from an area farm and raised on campus. (Historically milk cows were kept on campus in an enclosure around College Hall). There is also the possibility of raising swine either with or instead of cattle. Both options would allow for a constant food supply to be available for all of those inside of the perimeter, and so would allow us to stay within the Simpson safe-zone for a much longer time period than was previously planned. As to raising the animals, hogs are capable of eating almost anything, including food scraps. Cattle can be raised outdoors, and so do not require much of a shelter.

b.   Negative: We have limited space and resources as it is, and both cattle and swine require great amounts of both. One hog that is 200-250 pounds would need at least 10-12 square feet of space, and on average would drink 2-4 gallons of water a day. Cattle require a delicate balance of food in order to grow properly, and are susceptible to many different types of diseases that can affect their growth and more than likely kill them. On average, cattle need 8 to 10 pounds of fiber for every pound they gain. Both species of animals need vaccines to fight off common diseases, and such resources and not easily at our disposal.

2. Scavenging nearby farms and obtaining existing livestock:

a. Positive: This plan would consist of us simply going out, obtaining what livestock we are in need of at the time, and bringing it back to the safe-zone. We would either butcher the animals at the farm or upon returning to the safe zone. Hogs could be easily gained if they are housed in metal hog houses, because the zombie threat would be unable to enter the building.

b. Negative: Gathering livestock could prove difficult, especially if zombies have scared off the cattle supply or contaminated it. Potentially, hogs would quickly die off of starvation, dehydration, or disease if kept locked up without proper care. Also, scavengers would have to exit the perimeter and take some vehicle, such as a pick-up truck, in order to bring back animals. This would attract attention and it would consume limited fuel resources. More problems arise when it comes to the butchering of the animal and cleaning the meat, especially if there is no one with experience to do so. Some of our students grew up on farms, but apparently none of them has experience slaughtering livestock, however several experienced deer hunters expressed an interest and willingness to apply their knowledge to cows or pigs.

Based on the information above, we ask the administration to make a decision whether or not we should raise livestock or simply collect it as needed.

If neither plan is accepted, we ask that the administration present a third option. Our food supply is very limited. At this point almost everything salvage teams bring in is consumed almost immediately. We are not stockpiling efficiently. We must either increase our salvage efforts or tighten up rationing.

4.10 Arthur Rembrandt, debriefing

The "road trip" to the airport was organized by two refugees who were assisted by a number of Simpson College students. Since the college administration would not authorize the mission, preparations for it moved off campus to the Station Square apartments and the adjacent parking lot. When the bus returned, the members of the expedition asked to be re-admitted to the community. As per established protocols, they were processed as refugees. Due to his injuries, Arthur Rembrandt was interviewed in the quarantine ward of the infirmary.

What can you tell me about your plan?
Calling it a plan is really generous. Thanks for that. ... We started earlier today, nearly at the break of dawn. A couple of those resourceful fellas found where the grounds crew kept snow plows for their trucks. It wasn't hard to outfit the front of the bus with it once we had Jim Kirk help us out. He knows a lot about this kind of stuff -- told me he was an engineer of some sort. He's a bit odd -- kind of looks like a hippie transported from Woodstock and aged 40 years, but I don't care much about all that. He knows his business, and we were ready before nightfall to get started this morning. We had some technical problems, but we managed to deal with them.

I know, in retrospect, it was a moronic idea to try and get to the airport. Hell, I knew at the time we were trying it. But we'd seen some planes that looked to be trying to land in the last couple of days and our hopes kind of took control of us.

What was the highway like?
Getting out of Indianola wasn't as hard as I thought. I pushed the cars out by Hy-Vee out of the way as gently as I could. The sound of screeching metal could attract the wrong kind of attention. But hey, it's not like the bus was exactly quiet.

Anyway, we finally got on 65/69 without many problems. On the drive up we saw a few roamers and even heard some gunfire, but that was it. I saw what looked like smoke from random fires scattered about, as well. I hoped they didn't spread too much. At least back in the fence there was some semblance of order.

We passed Wal-Mart on the way out. It was hard to tell if it was still inhabited. There wasn't an "alive inside" banner or anything. They weren't the friendliest to begin with anyway.

The highway was where I started having real, chest-tightening doubts. I went pretty slowly, about thirty or forty for the most part. I wasn't worried about the abandoned cars (they were pretty dispersed), but I was looking for debris. I was not interested in getting a flat out here.

I figured other people were the most dangerous thing we could find at a time like this. The panic, the fear, the anger. And we were a pretty big target, driving down the road like we owned the place.

I checked my mirror pretty often, the kind that lets you see the passengers. Everyone was staring nervously out their windows, their hands gripping their random assortment of weapons until their knuckles were white. They looked out at the scene around us with some kind of mix between awe and disbelief.

The stretch of highway between Indianola and Des Moines wasn't much, as highways go. At least it hadn't been. I had driven this route many times, taking snotty businessmen or annoying kids or complaining old people to various places here and there. It hadn't been remarkable in the least. Now every time I crested a hill everyone was rapt.

It seemed like every other mile there was a new smoke column somewhere in the distance. And if there wasn't, there was some sign of a fire that had already burned out. At least one crashed vehicle, abandoned houses, and what looked like the remains of bonfires off the side of the road that had been left untended.

The corpses were worse by far. Some were just laying on the highway or the side of the road with no explanation. Some showed signs of being hit by cars, what with their body parts being in wrong positions and pointing wrong directions. I figured a lot of these ones had been infected, wandering the road. Still others were the result of collisions with other vehicles. Clouds of flies buzzed around them.

Were there any of the infected along the highway?
Oh yeah. They were on the road too. There weren't many, but they would see the bus and try to get to us, useless as that was. Some of the kids wanted to shoot at them, Mitch was particularly persistent, muttering about his stats or something, but me and Jim knew it was nothing but a waste. Who knew how many bullets were left in the world? I had a little more than forty for my .38, and the .22 rifle I'd found had less than eighty to its name. I didn't want my nice gun to turn into a stick with a pipe stuck in it.

The drive continued like this for a long while; it probably felt much longer to me than it actually was, but I guess time flows differently in Hell.

What is it like in Des Moines?
We got to the highway 5 bypass, but there was what looked to be an SUV on subcompact collision on the onramp. We could have probably bulled our way through it, but I didn't want to risk a puncture. We decided to skirt through the southern part of town instead. Well, that was a mistake.

I could barely recognize the suburban areas I had driven through for years. There was trash everywhere, cars in strange places, buildings looked run down. Lawns were, of course, so overgrown that they looked like prairie.

Were there survivors there?

Even though we didn't see anyone, you could tell that there were still people around, and you could see barricades up on some of the side streets, but the businesses were shot. Totally looted and burnt out. I imagined the Guard was still out in force somewhere up here. Maybe they were crowded around the Capitol complex. Hopefully they'd left the airport alone, or abandoned it to defend somewhere less open.

We kept going west down Army Post Road. It would have been nice if there was still an army post on it. All we saw was more abandoned buildings. Most of the post had been converted to civilian use, but there were still some National Guard facilities there. They all looked deserted even though they had a nice and seemingly intact perimeter fence. Not good.

What was the airport like?
We rolled up on the southeast corner of the airport. The main entrance was clearly not going to work – it was a huge scrum of cars, so I decided to go through the fence. There didn't seem to be a presence at the airport, so I figured no one would mind. (Fortunately, the state budget never came up with the money for anti-terrorist berms. There was just a big fence, and it was no match for the bus.)

I shifted gears and gave the pedal all it was worth. This old faithful beast roared for me and smashed through the fence. I heard metal scream and the harsh sound of chainlink being dragged underneath us. Soon we left it behind, and I prayed the wire hadn't damaged the tires. I looked up and tried to spot what we were looking for: a ready to fuel jet, small enough to not attract attention, big enough to get us somewhere safer because staying in Iowa was looking more dangerous all the time.

Half the sky was black by the time I'd driven out onto the runways, trying to see an undamaged plane through the haze. Ideally we wanted one of the little puddle jumpers they used to ferry people out to big airports like O'Hare. That should suit us, but the smoke made it hard as hell to navigate. The control tower was out; it looked like something had sheered it off from the base. A direct hit from a plane? This smoke was enough to blind anything, I imagined.

We rolled up to a hangar. Jim, some of the boys, and the old pilot went out to check on it. I stayed with the bus and a few shooters, about a hundred yards off, keeping watch on the terminal.

At this point, a member of the medical staff intervened so that Rembrandt could receive medical treatment. The conclusion of the interview, if it was ever conducted, remains unavailable.

4.11 Mitchell Draigiau Kramer, journal

By May, many members of the Simpson community had slipped deeply into depression; however a few embraced the particular challenges of the zombie apocalypse with an almost unnatural fervor.

Zombie Journal : Zombies Offed: 12

Got back to the apartment today. I let Dana have my .22 and the little Beretta 9mm. Between us we have about 400 rounds of .223 for my Mosin-Nagant and 600 for her .22, as well as about 600 each the pistols. I'd like to have more, but quite honestly I was lucky as hell to stockpile that much before this all started. .223's been scarce all year, and now there are so many brains to destroy out there. Lucky I've got Baby. No reloads needed. She's attached to my belt in her sheath right now, and she'll be staying right beside me forever, if I get my way.

We were wandering around back inside the Perimeter when we heard a couple guys talking about some excursion up to the Des Moines Airport. They were going to try and get somewhere safer. There was even some old dried up pilot with them. I didn't think they'd find a plane, but I figured going with them and actually *doing* something was better than sitting behind a flimsy fence waiting to get eaten. Also, I thought I might up my score a bit.

Anyway, we found the guys in charge (kind of) and helped out getting some bus this one guy was driving ready. That thing is a fortress now. Me and another couple guys broke into a storage shed and found a snow plow. That bus ought to be able to ram through hard things and squishy things alike now. (Hard to score, but still satisfying).

Going to bed now, big day tomorrow killing things. Hopefully between Dana and me we can rack up triple digits.

Zombie Journal : Zombies Offed: ~102

Triple digits! Did I kick some zombie ass or what? Can't stop smiling. It's just like I'd always imagined it would be after that first zombie movie I saw, all those years ago. Cutting down hordes and all that.

I'll start at the beginning. We started riding the bus, just like back in middle school, at the break of dawn. The trip up there was tense, and I wanted to kill all the moaners we saw on the way. The driver and the pony-tail guy shot me down though, saying they weren't worth the ammo. Maybe not to you man, but I've got my stats to think about.

We finally got to the airport and to my disappointment there wasn't much but burning fuel and abandoned planes. Well, at least at first. The old pilot and the pony-tail guy and about three fourths of the group went out to check on a hangar.

Dana and I stayed at the bus since we had rifles. It was boring as hell. No zombies in sight. The driver wasn't real sociable. He just sat there writing on some clipboard thing when he wasn't nervously checking in all directions. He would also talk to the pony-tail guy on a little radio occasionally. Me and Dana and the other guys on defense just tried to shoot the breeze. There wasn't much to do besides look in every direction. I was eager though, almost like I knew what was about to happen.

One minute we were sitting there, warm and uncomfortable and bored. The next minute, something huge exploded about a mile or so away and shook the ground. I think it might have been a big fuel container -- maybe even a tanker truck . Either way, it caught somebody's attention.

The terminal was not a huge distance off. It was maybe 250 yards away. And we were between it and the explosion. I saw movement over there and looked through my scope. Then I laughed, because the zombies were coming. *All* the zombies were coming. It was *awesome.*

They must have just hurled themselves at the windows until they shattered, because there were gaping holes every couple yards in the terminal. And zombies were pouring out of them, literally raining out of the windows. The explosion caught their attention, and they must have seen us as juicy sirloins just standing on the tarmac waiting to be devoured. I am not going to be *anyone's* steak.

My Mosin was ready to go, practically shouting at me to use it. Before I knew it I was sprinting toward the zombie horde. About twenty or so were moving much faster than the rest. I had to distract them from the guys in the hangar so they could get out. I motioned and Dana started running right behind me, unslinging her .22 on the way. God, I loved that girl.

When I was about 150 yards from the first sprinter I stopped and went down on one knee. I set the butt of the rifle against my shoulder and calmly peered through the scope. I steadied my breathing. In, out, in, out. In. Out. CRACK! The old rifle smacked into my shoulder. It wanted to kill the Zs just as bad as me. The first shot blew the top of the lead sprinter's head apart and a red cloud settled on his comrades. I smiled and stroked the little plastic sticker I'd placed on the stock that read *"Zaitsev."* Then I went back to the serious work of killing zombies.

I let the rhythm build in me. Work the action, eject the spent cartridge, slide the action forward and chamber the next round, slide my finger from the trigger guard to the trigger itself, center the crosshair on where the next zombie's head was about to be, squeeze gently until the firing of the gun was almost a surprise, watch the target's head cease to exist, smile wider, whisper "headshot" to myself, repeat. Every five rounds I would grab five more from my cartridge bag and thumb them into the magazine. I had reloaded this thing so many times it was almost as easy as opening and closing my hand. I had a couple of faster five-round stripper clips, but those I was saving for an emergency. 15 sprinting Zs were nothing to worry about.

Dana was beside me and shooting rhythmically as well. Her .22 didn't kill them as spectacularly, but a good headshot killed quick and dirty nonetheless. She had a bit of a speed advantage over me, to boot. I heard that .22's just bounced around inside the skull once they got in. That was pretty satisfying, not to mention a fantastic way to destroy someone's brain.

Two other guys from the bus came up behind us, stopping and shooting, though not as effectively. Pantywaists. I was starting to lose my hearing by this point.

In twenty seconds we'd accounted for twelve of them. Three of the fast movers had tripped over the corpses of others and were slowly getting back to their feet. The remaining five were about 40 yards away and closing fast. Dana was busy getting a new magazine in her rifle.

She'd missed a couple of times through no fault of her own. That .22's scope hadn't been sighted right, even before all this began. It shot a little high to the left.

That left five, and I only had time for one more shot. You can't win 'em all.

My last .223 round tore through the leader's skull in a torrent of red. For a split second everything felt extremely still. Then I swung my rifle around on my sling, and I drew my Glock 17. It was a decent gun, kind of lacking stopping power, but I had nineteen round magazines for it, and its low recoil meant that I could pump out a lot of fire pretty fast.

I set my stance, my feet as wide as my shoulders and left hand set in a double grip. I sighted in on the closest zombie and fired two shots in quick succession at his center of mass. I didn't have time to waste with a headshot with a weapon like this. The shots tore into his chest and made him stutter and falter. It wasn't because of pain; I think I nicked his spinal cord. The zombies behind barreled through him and he fell to the ground.

The next one got two quick shots to the torso and one through the lower jaw. He stumbled and I got a spectacular view of his brains exploding as one of the guys with us nailed him with a point blank shot. The last two were close now, and I was running out of time to aim. I fired off three desperation shots, but unfortunately the runners didn't want to go down. Killing zombies takes luck, after all. Anyone who says differently doesn't know what they're talking about.

They were almost within lunging range of me. I holstered the Glock and changed my stance slightly, drawing Baby from its sheath. Its blade reflected all the fires, just begging to kill something. The 27 inch katana swung downward as I sidestepped the first zombie's charge. He wasn't ready for my rapid move, expecting his meal to stand perfectly still for him. The sword sliced through his shoulder and sliced his arm clear off. I stayed clear of the blood splatter. Wouldn't want to get all messy now, would I?

The last fully whole zombie closed in on me, but I didn't figure it would be smart enough to avoid the same trick I'd just used. I sidestepped to the right, crouching and aiming lower this time, slicing through all the tendons in its right leg. It dropped to the ground like a sack of… well… meat. One of our backups beat his head to mush with a tire iron he'd been carrying. I was about to turn and finish the first one I'd sliced when I heard the report of a Beretta 9mm behind me. I glanced behind me and saw Dana smile as she finished off the remaining zombies, her eyes on me.

We shared a tender moment and surveyed the oncoming tide. Slow ones were still pouring out of the terminal by the second. Thousands of people must have run to the airport hoping to escape. The shamblers were too many to stop and eventually they would surround the bus.

Dana and I kneeled next to each other again and started firing, able to take our time, finally. The two other guys joined us, trying to mimic our steadiness. One shot after another, careful and calm. They fell in heaps. Sometimes I got really lucky and bagged two at once. I was aware of the bus doing something behind us, but my concentration was so focused there was nothing more important than bagging another infected. By the time I'd muttered "headshot" a couple dozen times they filled almost our entire view. They were going to surround us soon.

We probably could have run, but there were probably some quick ones in the mix; if we stopped firing they would swarm forward and finish us before we could get far. We didn't know how many fast ones were still out there. I remember turning to Dana and saying, "I love you baby. You did good today." She smiled back at me, her eyes sad but understanding the situation. She nodded to me then turned back to the horde, keeping up a steady stream of fire.

Just when I thought we were done for I heard the roar of a diesel engine from somewhere to our left. The line of zombies in front of us just disappeared as our bus's plow bowled them over, smashing some of them to nothing. The door was already open and I could see people firing from its windows in all directions.

"Hah!" I shouted, "You picked up the spare!"

Then someone dragged me back onboard. Maybe I did resist just a little bit, but I wanted more kills, you know?

The zombies tried to swamp the bus but we picked up speed and got the hell out of there pretty fast. I think some more stuff exploded behind us as we left. I suppose that rules out the airport for any future kills. Still, got some good shooting in. Just sitting here recovering from all that activity and listening to everyone decide where in the hell we're going next. Who cares so long as I get some more kills? I want to finish what we've started. There's plenty more who need to meet Zaitsev and Baby.

4.12 Jim Kirk, voice recording transcript

Jim Kirk, an electrical engineer, also accompanied the airport expedition. As a recording, his account is difficult to follow, but what it lacks in clarity it gains in veracity.

JIM KIRK: Test...test...ok. I just popped in a new memory card and recharged the batteries so I'll just lock it into record mode.

ERIC UPSON: How long can that last?

KIRK: Oh four hours give or take, it will be plenty. I'll just clip the mic to my collar and that should be good.

UPSON: Why are you doing that now?

KIRK: Well, after yesterday's trouble I decided to start recording everything I could outside the wire.

[recording ends]

KIRK: Okay then. Here we are at Des Moines International. Cesar, our pilot over there, can't seem to find a functional plane. If there's one thing Cesar knows about, it's flying. He's not going to risk putting us all on a plane that has been torn up by a bunch of infected.

UPSON: Who are you talking to man?

KIRK: It's my recording device....That was Eric; he's riding with me. Quiet, shy college kid. A little effeminate, but that's probably just ...

UPSON: I'm right here dude.

KIRK: Sorry.

[recording ends]

FEMALE VOICE: Jim! Jim! Rick wants you to come check something out! He says you aren't going to believe what they found. It's over there between two fuel trucks.

KIRK: Alright. Coming. How do things look, Arthur?

ARTHUR REMBRANDT [via radio]: Looks good. Keep an eye on those fires, though, I didn't come all the way out here to blow up in a jet fuel blast, over.

KIRK: Well we're probably not going to be able to stop the fires but it seems like we're at a safe distance, over.

RICK STITCH: Hey, Jim, come take a look at this thing.

KIRK: This must have been quite a fight.

STITCH: No doubt. How many are there? Twenty? Thirty?

TONY LAMONT: It looks like they were clustered around this thing.

STITCH: What is it?

KIRK: Let's see.

[recording ends]

KIRK: We need to load that thing onto the bus.

STITCH: What about finding a plane?

KIRK: Screw finding a plane. We need to get this back to the perimeter.

[massive explosions]

KIRK: Holy shit!

[recording ends]

REMBRANDT [via radio]: Back to the bus now! Everyone! There's a shit ton of those things pouring out the terminal!

KIRK: Dammit. Alright EVERYONE BACK TO THE BUS! Leave it—no leave it. LEAVE IT, GODDAMMIT! … Rick, get Cesar and get back to the bus right now! GO! GO! GO! Holy Christ. Tony!

REMBRANDT [via radio]: Get back here man, Mitch and his crazy-ass girlfriend just ran out *toward* 'em.

KIRK: Rick! Shit. SHIT! Just fucking *carry* him!

[engine noise]

MALE VOICE: We are done man! It's game over, man.

KIRK: Paula, toss me that!

REMBRANDT: That kid …

KIRK: Here. Have you got it? Have you got it? OK. Go!

[engine acceleration]

REMBRANDT: We're coming up on them!

KIRK: Jesus H. [panting].

ARTHUR: Brace yourselves!

[gunfire]

KIRK: Watch out for Mitch! Don't shoot him!

[engine noise, gunfire, and screaming]

FEMALE VOICE: Oh, Jesus.

[multiple shouts and crashes]

KIRK: Open the door! Grab him!

MALE VOICE: He's not—

KRAMER: Oh, hey guys... Thanks. Thanks, but I was fine.

[recording ends]

In his after-action debriefing upon return to the college perimeter, Jim Kirk and Arthur Rembrant both corroborated one another's accounts that Mitchell Kramer's attempt to fight the horde with his katana ended disastrously. It apparently glanced off the skull of one of his intended targets and seriously injured his companion, Dana Thompson. Despite the intervention of the crew of the bus, Thompson and the two students who dismounted to provide fire support, Kevin McCullough and Curtis DeVetter, were all overrun. The crew on the bus did, however rescue Kramer who was put under psychological observation. Because of the obviously delusional quality of his account, college administration decided that he was too dangerous to remain inside the perimeter. Subsequently, he was regularly assigned the most dangerous patrol duties and was housed in a safe house outside of the perimeter.

4.13 USAF after-action report

This document was leaked by the Air Force. It debriefs the mission in which the town of Pella, Iowa, was destroyed using conventional explosives. Targeting was centered on the campus of Central College.

Date: May 31
Mission Date: May 30
Mission: Infection containment
Location: Marion County, Iowa

Methods: Concentrated conventional ordinance via air-strike on the compromised quarantine area of the city of Pella, Iowa, and surrounding outbreak zones. [See attached ordinance list].

Using conventional high explosive ordinance, numbers indicate that the quantity of infected neutralized was sufficient to contain the rapid spread of the disease. Census numbers indicated a population of around 10,000. Initial, conservative estimates at the time of the perimeter set up placed the number of infected around 15 to 20 percent. The National Guard battalion put in place was under-manned, or under-supplied, and allowed this manageable number to become 40 to 50 percent.

After authorization was secured with Executive Order 5690, precision munitions were employed to destroy and neutralize areas with high concentrations of infected. This enabled ground forces to pull back and attempt to set up a larger perimeter. However, it became clear that a perimeter of the entire town was impractical with the number of men they had at hand. Of the 513 men deployed, 153 were lost in the initial perimeter set up.

Satellite imagery estimated the number of infected in the target area between 7,000 and 8,000.

Further reconnaissance needed to assess infrastructure damage and effectiveness of anti-personnel munitions on the infected.

Chapter 5: JUNE

5.1 Paul Dule, journal

After the departure of the National Guard and the bombing of Pella, most Simpson residents developed a deep and abiding distrust of the federal government. During this period regular radio broadcasts continued, but most residents suspected that they consisted mostly of propaganda.

So much for World War III! I mean, how can you fight other powers when zombies are rampaging?

The National Guard has left us to wait out the storm in this makeshift base here at Simpson. Before they left, those bastards impounded my fucking computer! How typical is that? They can't manage to shoot slobbering maniacs that are trying to eat our brains, but they do a great job preventing us from downloading free internet porn. Thank you, defenders of American liberty!

I finally have it back after a group of nerds broke into information services where one of the supply closets was stacked to the ceiling with computers. It has been a couple of long months without Internet access or phones. The Guard set up some firewall on our Internet keeping us from accessing the outside world and they turned off the cell towers or switched the frequencies around or something. Unfortunately, given the piss poor computer science department being what it was (All dead now. No big loss), I seriously doubt that the nerds will be able to reset the system. That's even if they had the instructions with some nice pictures in crayon!

I hope someone somewhere is having better luck than I in spreading the truth about this shit.

Two days ago a series of explosions from the direction of Pella rattled everything. It happened at night and the undersides of clouds were

111

lit by the flashes. As far as I know there are no nuclear or coal power plants in that direction, which leads me to believe that the government is taking its usual search and destroy tactics and applying them to its own country. Welcome to Vietnam—USA edition! Rather than using some sort of humane way of rounding up the infected citizens and helping them die peacefully we "macho men" try a different route. "Let's bomb major cities and hope we manage to kill enough infected people to contain the spread of the disease. Meanwhile, we will have no regard for the millions of other completely innocent, defenseless folks who will either be destroyed and forgotten forever in the blasts of our tactical nuclear warheads or lose everything they owned and have nothing to live for." I guess if you are sitting in Cheyenne Mountain that kind of logic might make some sense.

A few refugees came in the other day looking for shelter and we, of course, did the right thing and helped them. Apparently, we're satisfied that a standard HIV test can determine the likelihood of you becoming a flesh-eating freak. So, some of the bio professors do that to see if they are clean before entry. I interviewed a few of them, and tried to get a sense of what was happening over towards Pella. At this point, my best guess is that the Central College campus was set up with a perimeter like Simpson, but for some reason containment failed. So, in response the government cleaned it in the best way they know how.

I do not believe we are in any danger of being hit directly. However, fallout from such large blasts can provide other issues such as filling the sky with poisonous toxins. In the end all of this could have been avoided if we weren't so hell-bent on controlling the world's oil supply and worked together as a species.

This is Paul Dule saying, FUCK THE WAR, LOVE THY NEIGHBOR.

5.2 Father Michael Sheraton, diary

Despite the Vatican's enduring position against euthanasia, many Roman Catholics initially accepted the practice as a legitimate final decision by the infected. Most preferred the option of "suicide missions" as a more theologically sound solution to the problem of the consciously infected.

Over the past few weeks, our salvage missions have gathered some supplies. On the 10th we had a head count and came up with 736 persons residing within our fence -- that's a lot of mouths to feed. There is also a constant stream of people wanting to reside within the perimeter. Two weeks ago, I was one of those people. Now, I'm a member of the Simpson community.

We have a quarantine system, and if any petitioners are infected, we give them a choice. It's the same choice we give to members of our own community. I am there when the final choice is given, whether it is outside or inside the perimeter. In the last two weeks, I have given last rites one hundred and fifteen times.

We present them with a choice: Either go on a suicide mission for the betterment of those in the perimeter or submit to euthanasia before this plague ends their humanity. Many refuse to hear it. They are given one hour to decide. I am on hand to help them make the decision. I have cried with many a person. I have saved many a soul. Most finally accept their fate. All have seen what this disease did to their loved ones. Many take on a stoic front and for the safety of others make their choice. We let them know, if they are still aware of their surroundings, they won't feel pain if they choose that route.

The things that hit me the most are their stories. They just have to tell me how they lived, how they loved. They need to tell me how their lives made a difference, about their families, what they did for a living, Many confess to me the worst things they've done. Many share stories of how they first fell in love. It takes a lot out of me. Euthanasia is a sin, but

I believe that I must be a part of these proceedings. I cannot deny people the chance to unburden their souls.

Everyone is given the opportunity to write a last will and testament. One woman asked of me a specific request. I have decided to honor it. She asked if she could record her story. Her name is Valerie Rash and she escaped Pella before it was bombed.

Ever since I was a little girl, I loved riding my bike. I would ride through Wonderland; I would ride my bicycle into the clouds. I would be a princess escaping from a witch and would ride into the arms of my prince. I always daydreamed while riding my bike. So one morning about a month ago, I was daydreaming. I was imagining what my new kitchen would look like once it was finished. I was on my way to work. I had 20 patients to see that day and was running late. My practice was in Pella.

As I was picturing my copper pots and pans hanging from a rack over the stove, I saw a convoy of National Guardsmen driving into town in their trucks and Humvees. It looked like they were headed to Central's campus. Now, we all were talking about the possibility of infections here in Pella, but I hadn't seen any cases yet. I rode alongside and asked where they were going. The Guardsman said that they were going to reinforce the perimeter around the campus.

When I got to my offices, the waiting room was packed. Usually Mondays are pretty busy, but that day there was standing room only. From the list of symptoms our offices received from the WHO, at least two from the waiting room were rather advanced in the stages of the virus. They were twitching, pale, sweating profusely. Those were brought back right away. If an infected was presented to us, our protocol was to isolate the individual behind locked doors. We put them in rooms. One was college-aged, so we called Central. Not ten minutes later, five Guardsmen, decked out in all their gear, with assault rifles no less, walked in and removed the infected patients. They refused to tell me where they were going, saying they were quarantining them.

By this time even more people had shown up. My colleague, a nurse practitioner, and I went through the room, sending those without temperatures home. Most didn't have temps but were insistent that they were sick. Those persons were the hardest to get rid of. The rest were

114

brought back into the exam rooms and I further tested them. Three more had increased pulse rates of 150 bpm (the normal is under 100). I was wondering how the virus could have spread so fast. Damn these kids and their lack of sexual inhibition.

Again the Guard arrived and ushered more out. It was close to sundown and the line to get in was stretched around the block. I had just gone into an exam room with a little boy I believed had whooping cough – because that was going around— when there were some loud noises coming from the waiting area. I went to the door and people were running around screaming. I pulled some people into the room with me and locked the door. We were in there, listening to screaming . One of the infected must have turned quickly. We called the college again, and several people dialed 911. It got quieter. We heard whimpering, whining, and what I can only describe as *eating* noises. Slurping and crunching and cracking. It was awful. The boy was hysterical. He kept yelling, "Where's my mom?" I gave him a sedative.

After about fifteen minutes, we heard gunfire. I yelled from behind the door, saying we weren't infected and that I was a doctor. There was a muffled response and I cracked the door. It was a Guardsman. He looked like he was going to shoot me, but then he lowered his gun. He told us to come with him. The waiting room was in shambles. There was a lot of blood and a few bodies. The boy's mother had forgotten her purse when her son was called back, so she'd gone back to retrieve it. She was lying slumped over some chairs; her neck had been torn out. I shielded the boy's eyes as we passed. He was nearly catatonic. I'd probably given him too large a dose.

We got in a humvee, the four of us. Myself, the boy, and a couple in their 50s, Matt and Cindy. The soldiers looked nervous. We were heading in the opposite direction of campus and this cloud of ash rising from that direction. I asked if Central was on fire. All he said was that they were too late to help.

The humvee joined three others heading out of town. You could hear the popping of gunfire behind us. There were cars driving out of town also. About ten miles north, at a farmhouse in the middle of nowhere, soldiers were gathering. It was clear they brought me because of my profession. An officer rebuked the men who rescued us for bringing all of us and not just me. I interrupted him, saying that I wouldn't leave without those I was with. He signaled to a man to bring me inside the farmhouse. The others were hustled away. The boy was coming out of it and started asking, "Where's mommy?" He'd be hysterical again soon. Cindy and Matt both had their arms around him. Matt was folding little origami cranes out of the bills in his wallet to keep him distracted.

The officer met me in the living room of the house. He told me the perimeter they attempted to establish around the college had collapsed. He said they were redeploying to create a perimeter around the whole town, and gave me the option to be transported to an airbase with other "critical personnel." I asked about the others. He wouldn't meet my eyes, but he shook his head no. I said that I intended to stay with them. His face creased. "It's your funeral," he said.

I was walking back to Matt, Cindy, and the boy when one of the soldiers came up to me. He told me to get as far away from town as I could because Pella was going to be bombed in an effort to contain the virus. My home, where I built up my practice for the last five years, and my house, where I expected to retire, were about to be destroyed. I was going to ask when, but he moved away.

I told the others. Dazed and confused, we walked across the field to the next farmhouse. No one was there so we scavenged for food and weapons. It's amazing how quickly you drop into "survivor" mode. I had just found a collection of civil war memorabilia when Matt said there was an old truck with a half tank of gas in the barn. I grabbed an old sword off the wall. Looking back, I'm surprised I had no thought of how I was going to use it. I just knew I needed it. We stayed there for a week. The boy, Henry, slowly came around to us, but he was severely traumatized. Matt and Cindy had grown kids, so they had good sense when it came to children. The first step was getting him to eat. Once we accomplished that, we were hoping that he would start to talk. We stayed up late into the night listening to the radio. It was clear that we would not be able to get back into Pella, but it was unclear what we should do next. I suppose you could say we were paralyzed.

Then, one night, when it was getting dark, the rumbling started. The ground vibrated under us. The clouds were lit from below, and the bombs fell. We ran and stood in the yard watched as Pella was bombed. It was like watching the fireworks at Tulip Time. Cindy started crying. I hugged Henry. We watched until it looked like most of the city was burning.

The next morning, we decided to get in the truck. Matt and Cindy had a farmhouse in Minnesota by a lake that was surrounded by woods. They wanted to go there and hide out until this mess was over. It was as good a plan as any. I had no place to go anyway. I didn't have any family left, and my friends, well, I really only had Amy, my partner, who I suspected had died in the bombing. Don't think I'm callous. I'm a realist. What could I have done? She was gone. We left that morning and drove north for about two miles when the car started chugging and smoking and died. Matt couldn't get it started again and after careful inspection said it was a cracked radiator. We kept walking north, but then we heard gunshots, so we turned west.

We walked for days like that. We didn't stop at farmhouses as we went by. We especially avoided those that were boarded up. Luckily we didn't encounter any infected. We walked until we found an abandoned sedan, and then we drove again. We'd gotten pretty turned around on the little gravel roads, but within ten minutes we came in sight of a major highway.

We saw that it was impossible to traverse with the amount of cars abandoned on it. We'd heard some broadcasts from Simpson on the radio. It sounded fortified. I wanted to take Henry somewhere safe, but Matt and Cindy wanted to head north to their cabin.

We actually played rock-paper-scissors for the car. I lost. Even though this probably screwed us, it was a heartfelt goodbye. We had gone through a lot together. We wished each other the best. I hope they made it to their farmhouse.

It took us two days of walking to get near Indianola. We saw some other groups and a few vehicles, but we kept our distance. I still had my sword. It was ridiculous, but I kept it. We carefully began weaving our way through town. As we came around a corner, we saw a mob of infected. They saw us. We ran. I had Henry by the hand, but with his cough, he couldn't breathe so well. I vaulted Henry up on a branch and pulled myself after him. One of them grabbed at my leg and scratched through my skin with his bloody, gnarled nails. I jabbed it with my saber. I jabbed it again, harder. I was trying to get its eyes, but I didn't seem to have much luck, so I just started whacking at it. I don't know what kind of damage I inflicted, but it dropped and lay still. Fortunately, the other ones were slow. They just gathered around the base of the tree, reached up their arms and their clawlike hands and moaned. We climbed higher.

We were up there all night. I didn't think about the scratch until the morning when I finally looked at it. It was inflamed; I suspected I had been infected. My thoughts were only of Henry. I had to get him to the perimeter. It was only a few blocks away, but three of them were still beneath us. I started yelling for help.

I yelled until I was hoarse, but it didn't seem to do any good. I was trying to figure out how I could kill one of them without dropping to the ground when the rifle fire began. It was a good marksman. Two of them were down with headshots before I could even figure out where the shots were coming from. The third started moving around, so it took three shots to drop it, but then that was it. A six-man team swept up underneath the tree and told us to come down. "You're safe," they said.

They found the scratches right away; I didn't even have to tell them. I'm sure they're pretty practiced at catching warning signs by now. They aren't letting me in. I'm already starting to twitch. They took Henry and promised to take care of him. I didn't say anything about his cough for fear they'd keep him out. I was given two options: euthanasia or die killing the infected. I will go out strong. I wonder how many I will take with me.

Dr. Rash was sent on a mission to Wal-Mart to deliver a message to those forted up there. A reconnaissance team observed her approach. She walked up to the doors and said something. The door cracked. Then from the door came a fireball. The patrol guy said it was the craziest thing he'd ever seen; he said it was like a DIY flame thrower or something. She was engulfed in flame. I'd like to think she died quickly, but I know that can't be the case. I said a prayer for her. Then I reported Henry to the infirmary as a community health risk.

5.3 James R. Lawson, interview

Spec4 James R Lawson, a member of the original National Guard unit that erected the perimeter around the college, returned in a Humvee accompanied by three other Guardsmen.

Can you tell me what happened in Martensdale?

After we pulled out of Simpson, our mission was to suppress the infected. The whole AO looked like a wasteland. Some houses had been lit up, and there were bodies ... and ... *pieces* of bodies. We began going down the main street, fanning out in fire teams, and looking for anyone alive. I have never seen anything like it. Like hell had just come up to the earth.

Can you describe what you saw?

Well... *Jesus*... People had been just *torn* into pieces. I mean, arms separated from bodies, faces half gone... There was blood everywhere. ... Have you ever been in a slaughterhouse? I have. I worked shifts at IBP in Waterloo for two years. This was worse.

Benson called out that he found a survivor, a young woman spattered in blood who couldn't stop shaking. She just kept repeating something over and over without ever finishing the sentence. Then a man came running out of a building across the street. Benson called out, asking if he was okay, but the man didn't stop. He ran right at Benson.

What happened next?

Um..., by the time we knew what was happening, the man had... He bit off Benson's nose and part of his cheek... He had his arms around Benson. He sort of, like, hopped up on him like a frog and knocked him over. And Benson... he was yelling—*screaming*. Benson was kicking around on the ground trying to get this thing off of him and there was just blood everywhere and...

Someone shot the guy multiple times; I'm not sure who did the shooting—I know I was frozen. Benson probably took a few slugs too. His Kevlar caught most of them, I think. ...What happens to you when your nose is bit off? Does it kill you?

I went to Benson; it was clear he was going. His eyes drifted in and out of focus. Blood was all over his face—it was bubbling on his lips. It was bubbling where his nose used to be. I think he was trying to say something, but I'm not sure... I don't know... I took his hand and he would squeeze it so tight.

And then?

And then... Then while I was kneeling trying to help him is when everyone opened up. Full auto. I mean, no fire discipline or anything – just panic fire. Maybe lighting up the guy on Benson called out the crazies, because the guys just opened up in every direction.

I don't know what happened to the woman. It got kind of hard to distinguish targets. They just pumped rounds into anyone they could see. If you weren't wearing camo, you got lit up.

We retreated, or withdrew, or whatever. Someone was dragging me along. I wanted to bring Benson, but they just dragged me along. Then, we just started to run. Ty opened up with the 50 cal. on the Humvee.

That didn't help the LT. He went down as some kid that couldn't have been more than eight came out of nowhere and latched onto his leg. I kicked it off him and tried for a headshot like we were trained to do. That's when I realized that my M16 was still on safety... I hadn't fired a shot the *whole time.*

5.4 Physical Processing Form

In addition to physical inspections of refugees and members of salvage patrols, the college instituted a strict policy of regular physical examinations for residents. Many hated this intrusion, but between these exams and the census, the spread of the disease within the perimeter was halted, and the infected within the perimeter were eliminated.

Check ups MUST be performed every 12 hours.
Report all "Red Flags" immediately.

FLAGGED:
Yes   No

Name: Date:
DOB: Gender:
Housing:
Status:
Occupation(s):

Visual:
Pallor:
1 2 3 4 5
Muscle Ticks:
1 2 3 4 5
Bleeding Gums:
1 2 3 4 5
Fine Motor
1 2 3 4 5

Vitals:
Blood Pressure:
Heart Rate:
Body Temperature

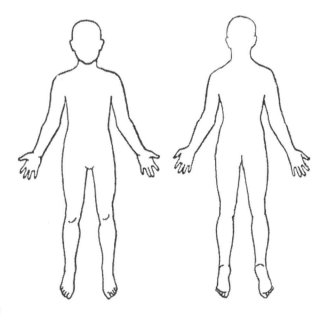

Inspector (Print & Sign):

5.5 Patrol and Search Doctrine

The first disorderly groups left the protection of the Perimeter in search of friends, family, and supplies and suffered heavy casualties. Within a week, an effort to increase cohesion and order was made. This procedure is the result of that effort by individuals with former military service/knowledge.

DEPLOYMENT: Two squads of six. Squads separated into Lure Squad (LS) and Entry Squad (ES). Team CO directly commands Entry Squad, Team XO Lure Squad.

The SPART remains on standby to carry out rescue operations whenever teams venture outside the wire.

SQUAD BREAKDOWN: LS consists of three 2-man teams of riflemen. Each member has a sidearm as well as a melee weapon available.

ES consists of two 2-man teams of with close-quarter weaponry (shotgun) and one 2-man team of riflemen. Each member has a sidearm as well as a melee weapon. ES is equipped with the best armor available, as well as flashlights.

MISSION DOCTRINE:

Stage One: Preparation
Prior to starting any excursion beyond the Perimeter the commander and XO will be heavily briefed on the operational area. Any possible threats will be evaluated based on old data of the region including prior observations and refugee reports. The CO and XO will be extensively briefed before briefing their respective teams. The specific targets of the operation are to be clearly marked and memorized by every participant. Two contingency targets will be included in this briefing due to risk of unforeseen circumstances. All participants are to mark themselves as

residents of the Perimeter by tying the standard bright green cloth to the upper right arm, marking themselves as friendlies while outside the fence.

Stage Two: Infiltration
While en route to target all hostile Zs in the operation's path are greenlit to engage if they classify as (moderate to light) density. If an area is too high density, the operational path will be re-routed. This is up to the CO's discretion. All COs should make it a point that ammunition is not to be wasted while in this stage. One bullet fired should mean one kill, and all participants are to strictly follow their weapon training doctrine.

Stage Three: Visual targeting
Once the target area is visible through binoculars or a rifle scope, the situation is to be assessed. This is where the discretion of both CO and XO is put to most use and good decisions are vital. The plan may change based on different circumstances, but once all intelligence is gathered and the threat identified standard operations will proceed.

Stage Four: Lure
Lure Squad will advance from a direction far from Entry Squad and attempt to draw a large portion of the Z force present in the area off. The XO must carefully plan the stages of his egress in order to avoid being surrounded. Both teams should have a general agreement on how much time is available before they are scheduled to rendezvous at a pre-agreed location. Standard lure operations would entail each two-man team leapfrogging backward, drawing hostiles away from the target building or buildings. Generally, the LS is to move in a large circle and end up back at the target area for rendezvous, though this may change based on the situation.

Stage Five: Entry
Entry Squad will give LS enough time to draw the majority of hostiles away and proceed toward the target building. The perimeter of the building will be cleared first. This entails checking every window, outbuilding, and vehicle on the premises for Zs. Once perimeter is secure

and there is a general idea of the hostiles present inside, the team will split up. The rifle team will remain by the front door to cover the street against hostiles. Breach team one will enter through the front door, using the standard room clearing tactics taught in weapons courses, while team two does the same through the back entrance to the building. Every single door, closet, crawlspace, and nook of the building is to be thoroughly searched for infected. Once the ground floor is clear one of the riflemen will proceed to cover the back of the house and both close quarter teams will clear the top floor(s).

Stage Six: Supply
Once the target is clear, while under cover of the riflemen, the two close-quarter teams will begin gathering anything of worth into the standard storage bags provided to salvage teams. The CO should have received a briefing prior to the mission on which things are of the most value to the Perimeter. If a large but extremely useful object is discovered, it is to be left but mentioned in the after-action report so that a larger mission can be scheduled to retrieve it with appropriate manpower or even vehicles. Once the house is empty of most valuables it will be marked with a circle of red spray paint on the door in order to avoid it on further missions in the area.

Stage Seven: Exfiltration
When LS and ES recombine the load should be as evenly distributed as possible to keep from hindering movement speed. Squads will return to the Perimeter along the predetermined path, engaging any Zs on the way that are necessary. When returned to the Perimeter all individuals will be thoroughly checked for bites and non-Z wounds and treated as warranted. All participants are to file after-action reports with extensive coverage of the mission area, Z activity, supply availability, and any insight on the situation.

5.6 Photograph of David Ward

The lack of firearms forced many students to improvise weapons. One hopes that this photograph was intended as a post-modern commentary on Grant Wood's "American Gothic" rather than a preparation for actual combat. Ward will be badly served by his welding mask as long as the polarization plate remains in place.

5.7 Kelly Anderson, salvage team report

The following report was filed as a result of an altercation with those in control of the Indianola Wal-Mart. By late June, supplies were running low and getting harder to find. Increased competition for resources made scavenging homes and stores complicated. The Indianola PD's unwillingness to help Simpson survivors left security and supply allocation up to Simpson inhabitants. Efforts were made to trade with "Fort Wal-Mart," but attempts to deal with their leaders went poorly.

We went out today on another search for supplies. The number of people on my patrol has increased to eight due to the need for extra security and eyes to watch every possible corridor from which a zombie attack can come from. Also, we've increased our use of melee weapons in an effort to conserve ammo. We were patrolling the eastern side of town looking for supplies in some of the abandoned businesses and residences. Kitchi was once again in my squad as second in command.

Part of our mission these days is to spy on the Wal-Mart compound to determine how well they were holding out or whether they had been overrun by zombies. I split the team in two and gave Kitchi the second group. This goes against normal protocol and common sense, but he has shown his ability to lead exceptionally in the past. Kitchi was in charge of finding any useful weapons material in the industrial park south east of Wal-Mart, while I and three others scouted the hill overlooking the store. We were supposed to meet up at a designated area in an hour. Two of the individuals with me were recently assigned to the squad. I thought our mission would be a relative cake walk since we were going in familiar territory that was pretty regularly cleaned out by Wal-Mart's defenders.

We stuck to the fences to avoid the open areas where we could easily be ambushed by zombies. The only things to watch out for were any zombies lingering in back yards and in the houses. I'd already seen my fair share of zombies crashing through glass doorways. Residential houses line the hill overlooking the Wal-Mart compound. We were about to cross a street when I saw some zombies walking slowly through the yards. There were three of them and four of us, but I didn't want to rely on the greenness of my new members. I ordered my squad to get behind some overgrown shrubs in the yard until I could figure out how to get into one of the houses that could overlook the privacy fence.

I didn't have a chance to make a decision because a minute after we were crouched behind the shrubs a black H2 Hummer sped up the street. The zombies were immediately attracted to it and started to stumble in its direction. I saw a figure with a metal baseball bat lean out the back window just before the vehicle passed us and heard a metallic thud as it drove by the zombies. The Hummer continued up the street followed by the remaining two zombies. The third one lay in the street with ooze coming out of its head. We ran across the street and into a house. It had been partially fortified at some point, but it was empty now. I'm not sure exactly how empty houses looked different from those that were still occupied, but by this time I could definitely tell. One person watched the door as the rest of us went from room to room searching for any sign of zombies.

Once the house was clear, I looked out a back window at the Wal-Mart compound. Their perimeter looked to be intact and I could see armed guards walking on top of the building. They had stacked shipping containers around their perimeter. Several vehicles sat in the parking lot. I'd seen enough to know that they were doing fine at the moment.

Someone downstairs shouted that we had company. I rushed down the steps to the front of the house and peered out the curtains of a window. It was the black Hummer. It had stopped in front of the house and six men piled out of the vehicle. They had an assortment of handguns and shotguns, with one guy who looked to be in his early 30s holding a metal baseball bat.

The man with the bat called, "Why don't you come on out?" He was wearing a fancy-looking maroon, pin striped dress shirt and black pants. Not the kind of thing you see people wearing anymore. His dark hair was slicked back, too. Gordon Gecko.

I scanned the area to see that they weren't followed and we walked out into the yard. He asked what we had in our bags. I told him it was just some food we found in some houses.

He said they didn't take too kindly to people walking around their area, "dead OR alive. " He pointed to the bags and told us to hand them over, along with our guns. His buddies gripped their weapons tighter.

I asked him how we were going to survive if we didn't have any food. The bat guy stepped forward and said, "life's a bitch and then you die."

One of the new guys to our squad started to raise his gun. The bang echoed through the street. He was thrown backwards; his chest shredded with birdshot. He lay there trying to catch his breath.

The leader was rubbing the crisp lapel of his suit jacket. He said they valued life and if we did too we'd hand our stuff over and leave. We didn't have a choice. We threw our packs and guns down on the ground between us. Four of the guys walked forward to collect them. Just then we heard primal screams coming from up the street. The gunshot had attracted the zombies. I didn't know it yet, but it also alerted Kitchi.

A shot went through the Hummer's windshield. Gecko and two others hopped in the Hummer while the other three rushed to get our bags. More shots rang out from down the street. The men with our bags looked confused. I was too, with screams coming from one end of the street and gunfire from the other. Brian lifted his gun and drew down on them with his rifle. They'd taken their eyes off us. Bullets started to ricochet off the ground. The zombies were in sight now. Four fast ones loped toward us. Another bullet went through the windshield on the driver's side and struck the man behind the wheel in the chest.

The pinstriped leader climbed behind the wheel, pushing the man out the door. He barely gave his guys a chance to get in and gunned it. One of them was still running after it as they went around the corner. Pathetic. I picked up my glock and looked down at my wounded man. He was pale and having difficulty breathing.

He said, "Do it. I don't want to be one of them. Please. Do it. Make it quick." Idiot. He was wearing a motorcycle jacket. He'd been hit with birdshot. It was very unlikely he was seriously injured. The boy had seen too many war movies. Still, I admired his priorities: better dead than undead. We dragged him into the house as Kitchi's squad joined us.

The zombies swarmed the man who had been shoved into the street. I'd thought he was dead. I'm not sure how seriously injured he was, but it didn't matter anyway because they were on him. His screams would likely bring every zombie on the east side to our location. We picked our targets and took them out in two volleys. Not all headshots, but we're getting better.

Conclusions: Wal-Mart and its inhabitants are deemed hostile. Gang members have no discretion toward survivors. They have no problem stealing from other uninfected humans. I suggest we stay clear of them unless violence is our intent. Any hostile action toward our squads should be returned in kind for self-defense and the preservation of our security.

5.8 Disposal Team Protocol

One of the most unpleasant tasks assigned to college residents was dealing with the disposal of dead bodies. After the campus was cleared of human remains, disposal teams began clearing the areas immediately adjacent to the perimeter. Assignment to the disposal team was usually considered a punishment, but it was critical to the overall health of the community.

BODY REMOVAL
1.) Make sure it is dead. Poke it with something. If it moves, decapitate it with a shovel. Even if it doesn't move, decapitate it. Better safe than sorry.
2.) Determine the pre-death status of the corpse. Was it a zombie? Look for bloody gums, gray skin with dark veins, and skin lesions.
3.) Load the body and the head on the cart.
4.) Take the load to your designated disposal site.

BURN DAYS
1.) Transport bodies to municipal swimming pool for cremation.
2.) Assemble entire Burn Day Team before you leave the perimeter.
3.) Advise/enforce all community members to remain indoors.
4.) The chapel bell will toll ten times in commemoration of the fallen on Burn Days.

HYGIENE
Required equipment: Thick Gloves, Coat, Mask, Goggles, and Shovel. Disposal Team members will be issued 1 extra water and 1 extra soap chit. They must use these for cleaning purposes.

ETHICS
Bodies of the fallen or the infected should not be mutilated or stripped of valuables. If you engage in either of these unseemly activities you will be put outside the perimeter.

5.9 Meshach Jacobs, interview

Refugee processing was a difficult and demanding process. Consequently, the mental health of the teams working the gates into the perimeter was regularly assessed.

Please state your name and age.
Meshach Jacobs. 67.

What work you are doing in the Perimeter?
I'm a dog handler at the gates.

How did you come to that position?
I came into Indianola in late May. I had my dogs with me then and I wouldn't leave them outside the wire so I holed up in an abandoned house. Then some hotshot discovered that dogs could sniff out the sickness. So, me and my boys had a secure position, since those two will not allow anyone else to handle them. They like people and zombies equally poorly, but they bark at Zs. They bark a lot.

How do you feel about the refugees and our processing of them?
I suppose it has to be done. Don't want something getting in here and ruining it all. I don't deal with all that, though. But the families... It's tough to watch sometimes. It's not like anyone deserves what's happening.

Would you allow those feelings to keep you from doing your job?
Hell no.

Why's that?
Well...no one can *approve* of sending someone off to die. But it's got to be done. As bad as I feel for them, I am not willing to put all the other lives on the line. There's a fair amount of unpleasant people in here, but there's decent folk. I'm glad I don't work *in* the processing center. I can't

imagine having to tell someone that they only have two options left, and both lead to death. And I couldn't stand telling some kid that it's time for dad to die. It's bad enough splitting them apart at the fence. Breaks my heart, but I know why we do it. At least I'm not the one pulling the trigger.

So you approve of decisions regarding refugee treatment?
I don't get involved in politics. I'll just stick to my dogs and my job. Nobody cares about an old, almost-blind black man. As long as I do my job, they let me alone. And that's how I like it.

Do you have any opinions on some of the major issues facing our community? The refugees? The lack of resources? Perimeter expansion? Whether to allow so-called "useless people" inside the perimeter?
I'm not interested in going into any of this, but I think any sensible person can see that there's no such thing as a useless person.

Well, thank you for your time, Mr. Jacobs. You're free to go.
Free to go where?

5.10 Fornication License, application

The final element of the college's system to prevent the transmission of the disease within the perimeter was the issuing of fornication licenses. Fornicating without a license became a major crime, which could result in expulsion from the perimeter.

Name: Date:
Date of Birth:

Gender:
☐ Male
☐ Female
☐ Other

Marital Status:
☐ Single
☐ Married
☐ Divorced
☐ Engaged/In a committed relationship
☐ Widowed
☐ Separated

Sexual orientation:
☐ Heterosexual (straight)
☐ Homosexual (gay/lesbian)
☐ Bisexual
☐ Other

You may apply for fornication rights with up to four (4) individuals.
1._____
2._____
3._____
4._____

How many times in the past six months have you had sexual contact?
- ☐ None
- ☐ 1-5
- ☐ 6-10
- ☐ 11-20
- ☐ More than 20

With how many partners did this occur? _____

In your lifetime, how many sexual partners have you had?
Describe your relationship with each.

_____
_____
_____
_____
_____
_____

(Attach extra pages if necessary.)

Do you have a history of STDs? If so, please provide details.
- ☐ No
- ☐ Yes

_____
_____

When was your last STD test? _____
When was your last HIV test? _____
Have you received the HIV vaccine?
- ☐ Yes
- ☐ No

WOMEN: When was your last pap smear? _____
Are you pregnant?
- ☐ Yes
- ☐ No

Are you on any form of birth control?
- ☐ Yes
- ☐ No

If yes, what type?

MEN: How often do you use a condom during sexual intercourse?
- ☐ Always
- ☐ Never
- ☐ Usually
- ☐ Rarely

READ THE FOLLOWING AND SIGN

I understand that this license, if I receive one, is to be used solely for sexual interaction with those listed on the card. I agree that all of the individuals I plan on having sexual encounters with will sign as well. I understand I am a mandatory reporter of any bites, strange behavior, or otherwise unnatural activity from any of my sexual partners. I also understand that once such symptoms and/or habits/behaviors are noticed, I must cease sexual contact with all persons and reapply for a license. In the event of an un-terminated pregnancy, I (or my female partner) am continuing sexual activity at my own risk and the risk of the unborn child. I understand that if I go against any of these rules, am untruthful or secretive about who my sexual partners are, or otherwise contaminate this system, my license will be revoked.

Signed (applicant) _____

Date:

Signed (partner/s)

_____

_____

_____

_____

Signed (witnesses)

_____

_____

- -

For Licensing Agents and Personnel Only
- ☐ Approved
- ☐ Not Approved

5.11 Paul Dule, journal

Despite these precautions, the infection of college residents remained a very real threat. Most of the inhabitants of the college worked towards an ideal of collective security, but others remained staunch individualists – even when they stood on the brink of losing their humanity.

Fuck me! So I was actually working as a contributing member of society, unlike those administration dicks who sit in Hillman, and it happened. I was clearing bodies that had become tangled in the razor wire on the perimeter fence and something ripped on one of them, and blood spilled all over me. I spat it out and doused my eyes with water, and this is bullshit! This is not how it's supposed to be! I can't turn into one of the walking pus-bags. Who will be able to spread the truth about what has happened to the world? Who will save everyone from the lies that are sure to come once the government is back on top again?

Fortunately, no one saw it happen. My team leader had stopped to take a leak and the other jerkoff was fussing with something around the corner. I dropped my gear and ran down to the creek so that I could clean myself up.

If the team leader or my CA even just slightly suspect me of hiding an infection, I will get The Choice: execution or a long walk into zombieland. Well, fuck that!

We are supposed to submit to a physical every twelve hours, so I need to play off that everything is OK. There's no break in the skin, so I should be OK. I don't know how much of that shit I swallowed. Maybe I didn't swallow any of it. How much is enough?

If I flip to team Z then fuck it. Every one of the retarded survivors living in this dump deserves to die. They are a bunch of incompetents.

Maybe as I turn I'll take them all out! For now I'm cool.

So, hey, if you are reading this: FUCK YOU. I'm going to eat your fucking face!

5.12 Kathryn Stevens, journal

After leaving her farmhouse due to a lack of supplies, retired schoolteacher Kathryn Stevens applied for sanctuary at the college. After the quarantine period ended, she was housed in Kresge Hall where her informal taekwondo lessons soon became one of the most popular "courses" on campus.

June 20. Hot and still.

Tara, one of the girls I am roomed with, came to me the other night. Tara is a little more stand-offish than the others. For one thing she is not around much other than on lockdowns and after curfew. She always spent a lot of time with her boyfriend before he started showing suspicious symptoms and was hauled off to quarantine for observation. He had to be killed the following week when he reached Stage 2. Because of the time frame, everyone had realized he had become infected through sex.

Tara and I were the only ones in the room the other night when she asked if she could talk to me about something really important. She looked so nervous and unsure. I told her of course, and we sat down on the futon that serves as Janet's bed and a kind of couch when we're not sleeping. I began to be a little worried when she made deep eye contact with me and made me promise not to say anything to anyone about what she was going to tell me, that she would take care of everything. I agreed, urging her to clear her mind and just say what she needed to. Her eyes welled and tears fell out of them.

She whispered, "I'm pregnant."

It was silent for nearly five minutes. I just hugged her and let her cry.

When she calmed down she told me what she knew. Her period is two weeks late and the last time she'd slept with Aidan was nearly four weeks ago. I asked how she knew she was sure and she told me she was always on time. She started sobbing again, but forced herself to talk. She said how she was already upset about Aidan having been infected and killed, and now she was worried about the state of their baby. She wondered if it would be infected, too—and how long it would take for a zombie baby to eat its way out of her. I was surprised she was telling me all this—because now I either had to report her or have her report herself and that would only mean she would be killed, too.

Thinking she understood this, I asked her what she planned to do.

She looked up at me and said matter-of-factly that she would have an abortion; she couldn't have a baby, and certainly not an infected baby by the guy who cheated on her. She was sure people would understand and agree with her. That was it—she would just have an abortion. She didn't seem to understand that unless she was incredibly lucky, she was infected too.

And how do you bring that up with someone who, although making a difficult decision, thinks life might be able to continue as normally as possible? She had calmed down again by now, feeling the decisions were all over now. I put my arm around her; she relaxed into my shoulder.

I told her I thought she was missing something, and it wasn't going to be easy to hear. She leaned away from my arms and looked at me with confusion, but trust. "Tara," I told her, "there's a good chance you are infected too."

She just kept looking at me. Slowly her eyes unfocused and she was looking through me. She opened her mouth to speak a couple times but nothing came. After a minute she stood up, pulling me with her. She linked arms with me and we walked slowly out the door, down the hallway, and outside. We headed toward Carver. It was silence the rest of the way. When we got in the building she spun and caught me in a tight hug. She said I should go, that she'd be okay and tell them everything. She turned and went in.

I came home and sat in silence for an hour before going back to check on her. They said she'd been taken to quarantine about a half hour earlier, and that it didn't look good for her but they would not know positively until her tests were finished.

I have killed zombies; they're inhuman. Inhuman, unthinking, remorseless...they're things. I never felt like a murderer until now.

Tara Hallbrand was found HIV-Z positive and chose euthanasia, but she committed suicide before treatment could be administered.

5.13 Student Weekly Planner Page

This is a page from a daily planner during the calm of early summer. After the situation stabilized in mid-June, classes resumed as part of the "summer special semester," which was almost immediately nicknamed "Z-Term." Weekly and daily schedules provided Simpson residents with a sense of normalcy and purpose. New classes were offered taught by various members of the community that shared practical survival skills along with those that allowed for stress release and maintaining health.

MONDAY, June 21:

        Unarmed Combat Class 8-9

        Lunch 12:30-1

        Water treatment lab 9:30-12:30

        Z Ethics 1-2

        Poetry 2-3—peer reviews DUE!!!!

        Fence patrol 4-5

TUESDAY, June 22:

        Counseling strategies 9-11

        Lunch 1 – 1:30

        Conversational Spanish 1:30 – 2:45

        Melee Weapons Class 3 – 4:15

                bring kitchen and classroom utensils

        Yoga 5 – 6:30

WEDNESDAY, June 23:

        Unarmed Combat 8-9

        Lunch 12:30-1

        Teaching shift 9:30-12:30

        Z Ethics 1-2

        Lunch 12:30-1

        Poetry 2-3

***Escape and Evasion Forum @ 8
>>Dragon is guest speaker!!!!!!!

THURSDAY, June 24:
Counseling strategies 9-11
Lunch 1 – 1:30; Conversational Spanish 1:30 – 2:45,
Melee Weapons Class 3 – 4:15
Yoga 5-6:30???
Art Workshop 7-8

FRIDAY, June 25:
Unarmed Combat 8-9
Z ethics 1-2
Teaching 9:30-12:30
Poetry 2-3
****CARDIO! 6-7:30**NO SKIPPING!!**

SATURDAY, June 26:
Yoga 9-10:30
Work Refugee Center 12-2
Fence patrol 4-5
Scavenging and Foraging Tactics Forum @ 6

SUNDAY, June 27:
Church @ 10
Sunday School teaching 10:15 – 11
Cards w/Aslynn, Devon, and Shelby @ 7

5.14 Adam Floyd, audio tape

Although the college administration organized the defense and maintenance of the college, some believed that their refugee policy was indulgent and their anti-crime efforts were too lenient. The most outspoken of these critics was Burke Wolf.

ADAM: Hello and welcome to another installment in my ongoing quest to meet with the members of the Simpson internment community. Today, the 29th of June, I'm meeting with...?

TESSA: Tessa. Tessa Murphy.

ADAM: Tessa, what brought you to Simpson?

TESSA: Well, I'm an alumna, graduated in '05. Was on campus because I had lunch with one of my old professors. Really, it's as simple as that.

ADAM: And when the outbreak occurred?

TESSA: I didn't even know there was an outbreak until I was pulled from my apartment in Des Moines and shipped back to Simpson. I don't know. It's crazy isn't it? I mean, zombies? What's next?

ADAM: At least they don't sparkle.

TESSA: Oh, thank God! I'm so glad other people hate Twi—

[Gunshot]

ADAM: What the hell was that?!

WOLF: [on bullhorn] We must not become like these beasts!

TESSA: What's going on? What's he saying? What are all those people doing?

ADAM: There's something up outside the chapel. What's the main guy saying?

WOLF: We must know who our enemy is! We must have the true leadership this community needs!!!

[Shouts and cheers]

TESSA: Sounds like some kind of rally... Who *are* those guys?

WOLF: This man we bring before you…he failed to understand the simplest rule: Don't become the enemy! Don't become *the Other*. And he was not bit, mind you! He did this *himself!* He did this as one of us. He relinquished his humanity through his betrayal of our community.

[Crowd rumbles.]

TESSA: What…?

WOLF: Here he is!!!

ADAM: What is that?

TESSA: No—*who* is that. He's pulled someone out of College Hall…see? What's over his head? Is that a…a sheet or something…?

ADAM: …Something.

WOLF: This man forgot what it means to be *above* the beasts! But what he did was worse than the acts of the infected. He *raped and murdered* within our walls! He has taken our *community* and the protection of these walls for granted. Will these actions be *ignored*? Will they be *allowed*?

[Crowd roars. Shouting.]

WOLF: NO! *This* is how we deal with those who become animals while we strive to *preserve* our humanity!

ADAM: Where are they taking him?

[Crowd roars as screaming is heard and a loud thumping sound.]

ADAM: Oh God…this isn't a rally…

TESSA: What? It's a lynching?!

WOLF: Who wants a *crack* at this BEAST?

[Individual shouts of approval and anger ring out.]

ADAM: They're just taking turns now, different people with a different weapon… Who do they think they are? Is anyone going to stop this? We should go down and—

TESSA: Are you crazy? What do you think they'll do to you, huh? Those guys on the steps … [softly] Holy herpes…

WOLF: If he wants to live like one of those *animals*…then I say we kill him like one!

TESSA: [Short, choppy breathing.] Did… did they…

ADAM: …yeah…

TESSA: We...we need to get out of here...

ADAM: ...yeah... Um, where do you live?

TESSA: [softly] I got put in Barker.

ADAM: Okay, c'mon—get your stuff; I'll take you over there. We'll cut south of the library.

TESSA: Don't take this the wrong way, but do you ... is your F-license full?

Chapter 6: JULY

6.1 Zombie Biology Study, video transcript

Immunity to HIV-Z remained poorly understood, but survivors quickly noticed that zombies appeared to ignore certain people. The number of people with inborn genetic immunity is so comparatively low (3-4% of the overall population), that it was difficult to detect patterns in the midst of chaos, especially since zombies still eagerly devoured everyone. Zombies only ignored people with a substantial amount of the virus in their bloodstreams. Consequently, the Biology department began conducting experiments. Since these required the consent of human subjects, they were vetted by the Institutional Review Board. As time passed and the situation grew increasingly desperate, the experimenters became secretive and no longer sought the approval of the IRB.

[When the recording begins, the camera is pointed toward the ground, focusing in and out on a pair of dirty work boots. The lens lifts to a woman standing alongside a chain link fence enclosing a 10m x 10m area in the quadrangle north of the Carver Science Building. She is in her thirties, and has short dark hair. It is dawn, but a few people have gathered to watch. Something lashes around inside the fence. Snarling noises cut in and out. She flinches a little.]

DOLING: Okay, are we ready? You'll work in all the background info later, right? Okay. Go. [Pause.] Hello. My name is Amy Doling. I am a professor of biology at Simpson College in Indianola, Iowa. Today is July 12. We are continuing our study of HIV-Z. In particular, we are examining zombie targeting priorities. It is now widely reported that certain people who have come in close contact with the infected are ignored while others are violently and relentlessly assaulted. This study proposes to isolate the factors that cause zombies to ignore certain humans.

[Camera focuses on subject within the fence. A young, infected man is connected by a heavy chain around his neck and wrists to a recently planted utility pole in the center of the fenced-in area. Camera zooms. His eyes do not seem to focus on anything. His skin is gray and covered with blemishes. He runs and stumbles when the chains pull taut. He falls frequently, seeming to forget he can only go so far before choking himself. Half a second later he is back on his feet, trying a different direction. His constant movement makes it difficult for the camera to follow him closely. His clothing is torn and there are patches of dried blood. His wrists and neck are rubbed raw by the constant chafing of the shackles, but no blood flows.]

DOLING: Our subject is 21-year-old Simpson College student Matthew Davis. He asked that his family be notified, should this study be made known to the public, that he volunteered for this project. He loves his family very much and wanted to help them in the only way left to him. Davis was bitten in an off-campus attack during a refugee-recovery mission at approximately 1 P.M. on Sunday, May 9. He reported the incident upon returning to campus.

[Doling stands next to the door to the enclosure. Davis sprints toward the camera. The chain straightens and he is yanked back from the neck. Doling flinches. He recovers and scrambles on all fours in another direction. Doling returns to her original position.]

DOLING: We have established this containment area for the subject and have been studying him since he returned to the campus. He agreed to 24-hour surveillance and thorough study. We have thoroughly documented the subject's progression. In an effort to determine the variable attraction of zombies to humans, we asked for volunteers from within our community.

[Camera pans to a small group together. They look warily toward the fenced zombie. A couple look shyly at the camera, smile slightly, then turn full attention back to the fence.]

DOLING: We have taken extensive biological information on each of our volunteers. All subjects have been on the same diet the past 3 days. It consists entirely of corn and soya recovered from the grain elevator supplemented by one liter of water fortified with citric acid.

[Camera focus widens as a young woman steps next to Doling. She is about 5'7" with cropped dark blonde hair. She smiles slightly then looks at the ground. Doling reads from a large notepad.]

DOLING: The first test subject is Jennifer Benson. Jennifer is 21. Blood type: B Positive. Allergies: mold and dust. To the best of her knowledge, Jennifer's ancestors primarily originated in Scandinavia and the British Isles. Family history of diabetes on the father's side. Consumes alcohol, but none since before the outbreak. Non-smoker. 10th day into cycle. No sexual activity since early April.

[Two men with shotguns and body armor move to the gate while Doling releases the padlock. The gate swings open and both men move slowly inside the fence. The rise and fall of their chests show they breathe heavily. Davis moans and screeches as he futilely tries to reach the two men. They stand on each side of the gate and keep their guns ready. Benson, after taking a deep breath, enters the compound.]

[Davis dashes at them, repeatedly choking himself. His howls cut in and out as he strains the neck brace and cuts off his air supply. Benson is visibly nervous. She stops and stands about 5m out from the zombie's reach. Doling's voice cuts in:]

DOLING: Our volunteers should be perfectly safe with the armed guards and heavy chain. We have previously introduced stimuli to the subject and he has yet to damage the chain no matter how aggressive he gets. [shouts] It's alright, Jenn. Just take a few steps forward.

[Benson hesitates, and then takes two small steps toward Davis, who is now totally focused on her. He snarls and gnashes its teeth. He bites down on his outstretched tongue and dark red blood spills out of its mouth. He takes no notice, and keeps thrashing. Both eyes are bloodshot, but the left has popped blood vessels, making the even smaller whites of the eyes a dark red. Doling speaks just over the howling.]

DOLING: This is the standard reaction the infected subjects have toward humans. Note its mounting aggression and focus. It is no longer generally aggressive – it is now focused on an individual. There is a clear loss of pain sensations. It does not seem to notice or care about the way it chokes itself by straining against the heavy chain; nor that it has just nearly bitten off its own tongue [shouts] Alright, Jenn, that's fine. Come on back. Well done!

[Camera zooms out. Benson walks slowly at first, not turning her back, and then takes off for the gate. The armed men pull back outside the gate as well. Davis remains animated, but they no longer hold his attention. He returns to making leaps toward random parts of the crowd. The camera follows Benson. She is visibly shaken: crying and looking weak. She nearly doubles over before collapsing to her knees on the ground. Doling approaches her, whispers in her ear and pats her on the shoulder.]

[recording ends]

DOLING: Our next volunteer is, Nick Veneris. 21. O-neg. Allergies to latex, shellfish, and cat dander. To the best of his knowledge, his ancestry is entirely from Greece, but there is a family legend about a "Cherokee Princess." Um, heart issues on the mother's side. Last alcohol consumption was in late May. Non-smoker; last sexual activity was also late May.

VENERIS: Yup. Over here. [camera pans. He is about 5'8" with dark cropped hair, a hoop in each ear, 5 o'clock shadow, and a solid, muscular build. He gives the camera a wide smile and friendly wave.] Hey, what's up? Let's mess with some zombies today, huh? [He grins again and claps his hands a couple times. He turns toward the gate and struts inside the fence followed by the armed guards. The zombie grabs at the air and keeps running at them and choking himself.]

DOLING: Okay. Move a little closer, please, Nick. Just a couple steps, take it easy first.

[Veneris seems to have lost a little of his confidence as he takes only small, slow steps. Camera zooms in].

DOLING: Oh here…Yes. This may be what we're looking for. This is definitely not as strong. What do you think?

LLEWELLYN MORSE: Yes. It definitely doesn't seem like he's as strong a focal point as Jenn. Let's get him a little closer though. Could be a fluke. [He projects his voice] All right, you are doing well, Nick. A couple more steps now, you've got plenty of room, no worries. No, you know what? You just move to your left. Tyler and Simon, why don't you guys take a step or two back and move to your right a little?

[The three move accordingly. The movement excites Davis; he increases movement and aggression again. It kicks and grabs, but follows the two gunmen, taking no notice of Veneris, who is now closer. He strains its neck and lets out a high-pitched moan and bats the air trying to get to Tyler and Simon.

DOLING: Okay, Nick. Now, just inch your way toward it. Take it nice and easy. No need to get too close. Nice and easy. [Veneris makes exaggerated steps toward the zombie. Again, it takes no notice of him.] Great. Well done. Let's get you out of there. Come on out.

MORSE: [Quietly] Couldn't he just get a little bit closer? A wee little bit closer?

[Veneris backs up, turns, and walks slowly to the gate. He glances over his shoulder twice. The gunmen follow him out. Veneris is absolutely beaming. The crowd is buzzing with excitement. The only identifiable sound is the zombie's high screeching.]

DOLING: Alright! Alright! Let's calm down.

[Veneris walks towards the crowd with his hands up for high-fives. One person slaps his hand, but the rest shy away. He looks confused. The camera pans back to Doling.]

[A man about 6' tall comes from off to the side to stand next to her—the camera operator has to zoom out to fit him in. He has shaggy blonde hair and is well-built with a friendly face. He purses his lips and gives the camera a small nod before looking absently back to the crowd. Doling scans her notepad.]

DOLING: Daniel Peterson is 27. Type A. Slight anemia. Family ancestry is largely northern European. Peterson's maternal grandmother was a light-skinned African-American. Last alcohol consumption was June— moderate—, smoker. Let's get started.

[Peterson moves to the gate. The guards enter first and take their positions. The gate clangs noisily behind him. Peterson moves slowly and stops . Again, Davis' excitement swells. His chain pulls and he is snapped back by the neck. He scrambles on the ground for a moment before leaping forward. Without prompting, Peterson takes three steps forward. Davis growls and claws ravenously at him. After gathering himself up for a mighty jump, he springs toward Peterson. The force of the leap tears his hand through its restraint. The fingers shred and break. Peterson jumps back; the guns come up. The crowd gasps. The muscles or tendons on the arm appear to have been severely damaged – it sways uselessly].

MORSE: The neck is still good. Stay in, stay in.

DOLING: Again, subject does not seem to notice any pain. He continues to throw himself against the chain around his neck trying to reach any of the three . We've already observed a severe loss of cognitive skill and reasoning in our observations. [sighs.] The subject has even more trouble staying balanced due to the arm injury. It doesn't seem to be able to compensate for or understand this.

[Peterson takes four steps in. The arm swings back and forth as it strains against the chain. It snarls and yelps in between chokes that cut off its sound. The camera zooms in again, getting what it can of a close-up of the zombie's neck.

DOLING: Ugh. Yeah, I see. Complete loss of sensation. If we could just tie all these things up by the neck they'd kill themselves.

[Davis's head begins to loll. His eyes bulge. It stumbles and then leaps again at its prey. The chain jerks; the head snaps forward, and the body lands on its back with a thud. The mucus-like blood seeps out of the mouth, nose and eyes, but the chest continues rising and falling. The crowd bursts into a symphony of cheering, groaning, and chatter.]

[Camera zooms out. Doling stares dejectedly out at the body. She takes a deep breath, and then chucks her notepad at the ground.]

DOLING: [She balls her fists, bringing them to her temples. She stands like this for a moment] Now we've got to get *another* one of those things. Dammit.

[Doling picks up a shovel from off camera and strides into the enclosure.]

MORSE: Hey! Hey, what are you doing? It's not dead!

DOLING: Double-tap, Morse. Never forget to double-tap.

[Doling neatly decapitates Davis. The shovel slices off his head directly above the neck shackle.]

[recording ends]

6.2 Dolores Ceiba, journal

Throughout the summer, scavenging crews went out daily to search of needed supplies. Many of these crews developed a sense of professionalism and unit cohesion. This was exceptionally true of the SPART (popularly known as "The Spartans"). Frederick Wish, an Afghanistan war veteran, was the first leader of the team. By July, Dolores Ceiba was his second-in-command.

We didn't get sloppy. We weren't in a rush. Z just got lucky, and we just got fucked.

A green scavenge team on the southside had opened up a cellar full of them, so we went out at top speed – we used the truck and everything. It took us no more than two minutes to get down there, but they'd already pulled down at least two members of the team. The rest had fled to a house where they barricaded themselves into a room on the second floor.

We went into action like clockwork. We didn't even need words any more. We all knew what to do. Clearing the house didn't take more than six minutes. They'd bunched up at the door of the bedroom, so when we came in the front door, they stumbled and tumbled over to us in a nice little train. Bam! Bam! Bam!

One of the scavengers had been bit. He was freaking out too much, so Roy took him out – a knockout blow, not a killshot. We value all human life, right?

The other one was chewed up pretty bad. She was unconscious. Doubtless she was infected, and would not recover from her wounds sufficiently to pull the mission option. So, we put her down. Not in front of her team. Roy did that one too – after they'd exited the house. They were a little weepy, but one of them remembered that the first vic had a sweet can of beans in her pack. Fred went back in to get it. Ted was backing him up, but that kid – that nasty little skeeve – just sprang out of some overgrown bushes and latched on to Fred's leg.

Our armor was pretty good, and Fred had on lace-up boots, but somehow that kid got his little needle teeth into his lower calf. Fred didn't have time to react, before he knew. I about pulped that kid with my boots alone.

This was enough for them inside the wire. Rules are rules. Two options: euthanasia or a suicide mission. As far as they were concerned Fred had already died. He was totally out of it. Thousand-yard stare. He just wanted to get on with it. He just wanted to run the mission as quickly as possible. He knew how fast a Z4 bite could take you.

We were pretty sure that Wal-Mart had fallen, but we didn't know how it had gone down. It was possible that there were still some salvageable goods there. But, considering the size of the target, the unfriendliness of the survivors there, and the mob of zeds that usually lingered in the area, we had steered clear: Perfect suicide material.

He was supposed to go alone, but I promised the gate crew that we could all get hooked up with a fornication license tomorrow, so they let me slip out five minutes after him. I'm not sure I needed to promise the sex, but I needed to hurry, so I didn't stand on ceremony.

He knew that I was following him as soon as I left the perimeter. He was just waiting for me in the middle of an intersection a few blocks east of campus.

I did not want to talk about it. I just wanted to be there for him. So, we walked to the grocery store together. I waited outside in the bed of an abandoned pickup while he went inside.

Ten minutes – ten long minutes later, he came out with a crate marked "Old English Bratwursts" hoisted on his shoulder. He smiled and told me that there were at least ten crates of processed food in one of the rear offices. To his eye, it looked like either a civil war had broken out between factions inside Wal-Mart, or that the surviving defenders had endured a lengthy siege inside the building after Z breached their doors. He wanted to look around some more, but he realized that the muscles at the corner of his eyes had started to twitch.

I told him that I thought it was stress or lack of sleep. He wasn't having it. He told me to do it. I drove a .45 slug into the back of my best friend's head. He was a good soldier. He would have been a better elementary school teacher, but that was not to be.

153

6.3 President's Council, minutes

The President's Council was known for harsh decisions that often ignored basic human rights. Much remains unknown as to the various "special directives" issued by the Council. Many say the Council was the only reason the perimeter survived. The following is an excerpt of the minutes from a meeting addressing the coming of winter. The two main speakers are the Academic Dean and the Dean of Students. Other speakers appear to be different building captains. From the discussion it is difficult to know exactly how the political system operated.

PRESIDENT: On to the next line of business: our plans for the future. As we all know, it doesn't stay warm forever in Iowa. What will be our action plan when winter comes? How will we deal with the problems we will face, if we stay here? Steve, how about we start with you?

ACADEMIC DEAN: Well, the Cold Weather Study Group, after careful consideration, advises that our best option would be to vacate the Simpson perimeter before harsh colder temperatures come around. They believe it would be best for the community as a whole to move to a warmer climate. With supplies dwindling as we speak, the situation is only going to get worse with the coming of winter. If we move to a new area, we'll have warmth and new foraging opportunities. I'm basing this on several factors. First, the news reports we accessed when the internet was temporarily restored and the radio broadcasts we've been picking up indicate that the military has carved out a series of large safe zones along the Gulf Coast. Second, it appears that the survivors at many good schools like ours are moving south in anticipation of winter as well.

KRESGE HALL: What about the Mexicans? Isn't there like some sort of giant horde of Mexican zombies down there?

WALLACE HALL: What exactly is your particular problem with *Mexican* zombies, Hank?

ACADEMIC DEAN: Clearly, the zombie population in Texas may be a problem, but I still think we're better off in the south. We don't know that there is not a giant horde of Minnesota zombies that we are going to need to deal with up here.

DEAN OF STUDENTS: So, you're just going to make a run for it? How are you going to manage and move a large number of people out in the open for *hundreds of miles* while defending them against the infected? What's our current population? 700? It would be chaos. Who knows how many would die?

ACADEMIC DEAN: Our foragers are well-drilled at this point. They could form a mobile perimeter. Everyone has been getting some weapons training, so if something got through the guards, I think the people in the center could cope.

DEAN OF STUDENTS: You don't know how many are out there. We have no idea what's between Osceola and the Ozarks. What happened to St. Louis? We don't know. What happened to Kansas City? We don't know. There could be millions. Missouri could be a deathtrap.

ACADEMIC DEAN: I understand your concern, but I don't think we have another option. We either die trying to get to another place, or we die here when we run out of supplies.

BARKER HALL: I agree.

DEAN OF STUDENTS: I think this is sensationalism. I know supplies are running low, but we have enough to make it through the winter if we tighten up the rations. Everyone is forgetting something: If we go south to a warmer climate, we are going to face the same type of zombies we are facing here right now. They'll be active and they'll be hungry. However, if we stay here through the winter, the cold and the snow will slow them down. Possibly, they will even freeze to death. When they start to slow, we can pick them off, refortify the perimeter and secure the area.

MARY BERRY HALL: We could even expand the area.

DEAN OF STUDENTS: It's true. With a refortified perimeter, secured area, and slower zombies, we can start to build back up. Salvage teams can range further from the compound. There may be farms that are stuffed full of supplies out there -- we just don't know about them because we've been staying close to home. Augmenting the food supply will allow us to get through the winter. If zombies die from the extreme cold, we may be living smack in the middle of the biggest safe zone in the continent.

ACADEMIC DEAN: How do you know the zombies will be slowed down? How do you know they will freeze to death? Maybe they will just speed up. We've never seen a cold zombie before. Weren't the zombies in Fareway locked in the freezer or something? It didn't seem to slow them down.

CARVER HALL: Erm. They should slow because the cold will affect their muscles. They won't have as much energy to move. If the zombies exhaust the energy in their bodies trying to keep themselves warm, they will freeze to death. Alternatively, they might starve to death more quickly.

DEAN OF STUDENTS: *Do* zombies starve to death?

CARVER HALL: From what we can tell they are infected human beings. They aren't some new kind of creature that does not metabolize. They need to feed; their blood needs to circulate.

ACADEMIC DEAN: Do we know that? Do we know that they need to feed? Have we seen them starve?

MARY BERRY HALL: Right. Is blood black? What's that stuff that pours out of their mouths?

CARVER HALL: Probably regurgitated meat that they are unable to digest. That's the working hypothesis.

ACADEMIC DEAN: Look. I admire science. Science is a wonderful thing, but I'm not confident that the old paradigms work anymore. It is possible that we are dealing with things that don't need to metabolize and that don't need to circulate their blood. We are in the middle of a zombie apocalypse – about as far from science as you can get. We just don't know what these things can do; that's why we need to get *away* from them.

MARY BERRY HALL: It may be possible that they could keep warm. They could huddle together. They could take over abandoned buildings like snakes in hibernacula.

KRESGE HALL: If they huddle to keep warm, we could take out their shelters with bombs or something. Right?

MARY BERRY HALL: I hear all of this talk about moving to a warmer climate and refortifying the perimeter, but these don't deal with the source of the problem: *Zombies* are the source of the problem. Both of the options you all are putting on the table are flawed. Neither running off to find some pixieland in Missouri or having us hole up on the campus are going to solve the problem. The only thing that will solve the problem is extermination. I've read the math model. We've *all* read it. It may have some problems, but it doesn't sidestep the real issue: We must counterattack and we must counterattack now. We should immediately and aggressively start eliminating the infected. We shouldn't just expand the fence, we should reclaim our fucking planet.

DEAN OF STUDENTS: So, are you suggesting we should stay here and just run around killing zombies with no actual plan for the future?

MARY BERRY HALL: Killing zombies is the future, and if we don't kill them, and kill them all, then there is no future.

SAE: I agree. Let's see winter as an opportunity. When the zombies slow down, we go kill them.

ACADEMIC DEAN: But we don't know if they will slow down.

MARY BERRY HALL: Then we will die trying to restore humanity. There are pockets of resistance all over the place. The shortwave tells us that much. If we kill thousands of the Z's, we'll be helping them to survive. We'll be protecting our species by fighting for it instead of getting ready to die in a hole or taking off on some hare-brained voyage across America. I'm ready to fight, and if necessary I'm ready to die, and the people in my house are behind me.

DEAN OF STUDENTS: How certain are you that these "numerous" pockets even exist? Occasional radio broadcasts are not exactly evidence of thriving civilization. We may well be the only community over 500 left in this whole state.

PRESIDENT: OK. Clearly we need to continue to discuss this. Let's take the following actions: Professor Morse, if you all could get some more reliable ideas about behavior by next week that would be great. If you can come up with some ideas about how they react to cold that would be ideal. Maybe some patrols have encountered them in walk-ins or something. Is anyone who went to Fareway still with us? No. OK, then. Check the patrol logs.

CARVER HALL: OK. Do we need to run anything by the ethics board on this?

ACADEMIC DEAN: I don't think that will be necessary at this time.

CARVER HALL: OK, then.

PRESIDENT: Chris, I'd like you to put together an action plan for a reconnaissance in force towards Osceola. Three vehicles, ten shooters.

BSC: Done.

WALLACE HALL: Maybe I could make a rubric.

PRESIDENT: Fine. You do that. Maybe we can make a definitive answer on this when we have more information. Next topic: refugees as a potential food source.

6.4 Public Health Service, poster

To help prevent the spread of HIV-Z through sexual contact, and in order to reduce chances of unplanned pregnancy, the Council had art classes design posters to keep the message in plain sight.

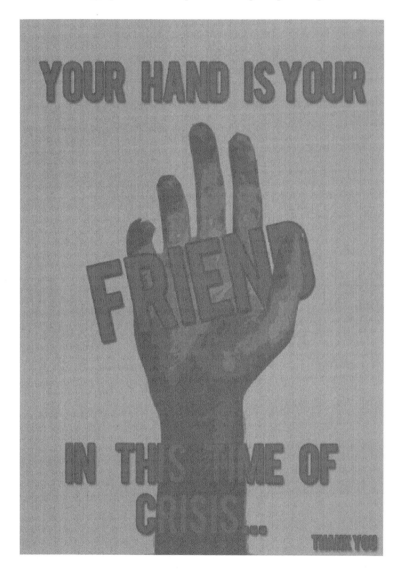

6.5 David Shleswig, radio communication

The following is a two-way radio transcript between David Shleswig, and ground control at Simpson College. After being bitten on a salvage operation, David chose to use his skills as a hot air balloonist to go on a long-range reconnaissance mission towards Des Moines.

GC: Man, I never thought anyone would be taking off in a hot-air balloon from the football field.

David: It'll be a tight squeeze, but we'll get her up there.

GC: Is everything seem okay? I see you looking around a lot. What are you checking out right now?

David: We're good. I'm going to attach the envelope and fire up the burner. [To another group of people:] Come on guys, the envelope is ready to go.

[10 minutes pass.]

David: Inflation completed. I'm ready for takeoff. Release tie down.

GC: Houston, we have liftoff.

David: I'm going to fly at a lower altitude so I can see the ground with my binoculars better.

[One minute passes.]

I found a wind current headed North at about thirty miles per hour at elevation of about 800 feet.

GC: Good. Good. Right where we wanted you to go. Can you see anything?

David: Yea, yea, I'm flying over Indianola right now. It looks like a ghost town. I'm out on the north side of town now. Whoa, whoa, I see some people on the roof of their house. It looks like a family. They've got a ladder up there with them. I can see some Zs on the ground around them. Damn. The little girl is pointing straight at me. They… they're waving. They're waving at me.

GC: What's your estimate of their location, Dave?

David: They're on the north-south street that runs along the west side of the golf course. I forget what it's called, but they are three houses north of the stream on the east side of the street.

GC: OK. I'll tell dispatch. We can get a rescue team out there.

David: They're pretty frantic. [Shouts] Hey! Hey! Calm down! Stop jumping around! Shit! Did he fall? I think he fell.

GC: Repeat. Who fell?

David: The guy. The dad. I think he just fell off the roof.

GC: Are you sure?

David: No, there are too many trees, but I swore ... Hm. I don't know. I guess not. I hope not.

[Three minutes pass.]

David: I hope he didn't fall.

[Two minutes pass.]

GC: Where are you at now?

David: I'm almost out of Indianola.

[Twelve minutes pass.]

GC: Hey, Dave, I'm sure he's OK. It's not like some guy who is about to be rescued is going to just fall off his roof, right? That would just be dumb.

[Eight minutes pass.]

David: I see some deer.

GC: Repeat. You see what?

David: Deer. I see some deer. Three or four of them. They're just eating some grass in what used to be a cornfield. They don't even notice me.

[One minute passes.]

David: There's a farmhouse here. It looks inhabited. Everything's boarded up, but it doesn't have that abandoned look. ... You know, "the look."

162

GC: Yep. I know. Where is it?

David: Some gravel road. I'm having some trouble knowing where I am with no map. It's a long way. Too long to scout out. ... It looks like there was some kind of fight there. There's a burnt out pickup and what look like some bodies.

GC: Recent?

David: Hard to tell from up here. No crows or buzzards though.

[One minutes passes.]

David: It's inhabited for sure. There's a garden. I can see dirt. Someone's been weeding that garden.

GC: Roger that. Good for them. I think competition at the State Fair is going to be a little weaker than in past years.

David: Yeah. Maybe they can bag a blue ribbon.

GC: Can you see any of Des Moines yet?

David: Yea, yea, I'm looking north right now. There's a lot of smoke. The big buildings all look more or less intact.

[Two minutes pass.]

David: You know; it's weird. I haven't seen a zombie for the past ten minutes. Maybe they are under the trees or something, but it doesn't seem like there are that many of them around even as I get closer to the city.

GC: Maybe there aren't many zombies because there weren't that many people to turn into zombies.

David: Yeah, but you'd think that there would be some idiots out wandering around.

GC: Yeah. I wonder if they can detect food sources from a distance.

David: It's hard to know. I saw some bones and skin from a couple of dead cows a little while ago, but it was hard to tell if zombies ate it or if it just died and got picked over by carrion birds and coyotes.

[One minute passes.]

David: Hey! Whoa!

GC: What?

David: A truck! Someone's driving around in a truck.

GC: What kind of truck? Is it military?

David: I don't think so. It's camouflaged, but it doesn't look military. It looks like something a hunter would drive. ... It's definitely been souped up. It has a giant bumper on the front. ... It's been modded to be a zombie crusher for sure.

GC: Can he see you?

David: I don't think so. The angle is wrong. I'm looking down at his roof.

GC: Where's he going?

David: West along a gravel road.

GC: Can you tell how many people there are?

David: No. Sorry. Hey! They're stopping. They're stopping by a car that ran into a ditch.

GC: Do they see you now?

David: I don't...Hey! Yeah! They see me. They're waving too.

GC: People just love balloons, I guess.

David: I guess so. Yeah. It's two people. They're dressed top to toe in motorcycle gear. They look pretty well equipped.

GC: I'm getting optimistic.

David: Well, I can see more of the city now, so you can forget about that. It's clearly worse than it was when the bus came up here. I'm west of the airport now. It's about what you would expect from their report: totally schwacked. The neighborhoods around it look pretty shot. There's debris all over the place. A lot of houses and buildings are burned out.

GC: Any sign of life?

David: It's hard to know. There could be people down there, I suppose.

GC: Any zombies?

David: Uh, no. No zombies.

GC: That's kind of weird. I imagined them just be sort of standing around waiting to eat someone.

David: I guess they got hungry and went in search of a meal.

GC: Or maybe they're all dead. Maybe the military came in and killed them all or something!

David: Perhaps, but I suspect they were eradicated by a strike force of killer Easter Bunnies and machete-wielding fairies, myself.

[Three minutes pass.]

David: Okay, I see something … little black figures running through the trees.

GC:　What? Little what?

David: They look like… Wait, they—… They're monkeys.

GC:　From the zoo?

David: Or the Great Ape Trust, maybe?

GC:　Special zombie killing monkey commandos?

David: Probably. You know fairies are unionized. They probably charge too much for this sort of thing.

GC:　Damn Teamsters. I thought this was a right to work state.

[Four minutes pass.]

David: OK, Ground Control? I see Jordan Creek.

GC:　The big mall?

David: Right. This place has been *ravaged*. The whole place is a mess. Overturned cars, all kinds of debris. … Some trucks are parked in front of the mall entrances. It looks like half the place is burned. … Hey! Hey! I see some of them!

GC:　Some what?

David: Zombies! Zombies! Five or six. Shamblers. I bet there are still some survivors in there. Or … in a car or something. The entrances I see look pretty barricaded. Who goes to the mall in a zombie apocalypse?

GC:　Well, who stays at school?

David: Wow! There's more. I see several dozen at least.

David: Hey! I see two people on the roof! Hey! I can land, I can save them! The roof definitely has enough area!

GC:　Think rationally, David. You're infected. If you pick up all those people, you're going to put those people in more danger than they are in now. Anyway, how many people can fit in the basket?

David: I could let them have the balloon. I could stay.

GC: And then what would they do? Float to Nebraska? Come on, man, keep it together.

David: OK. You're right. It would be too much of a risk. The wind would probably take me over the edge anyway. I'm gonna fly up to higher altitudes and find a wind current that will push me Northeast towards downtown. I'll report back when I get close.

GC: Do you still see them?

David: Yeah. They are not happy. They are not waving.

[20 minutes pass.]

David: Okay, Ground Control, I'm flying along I-235 right now. I'm very close to the downtown area. It's worse than I thought. Zombies are everywhere. All the buildings are—are just devastated. Windows are broken... Hey wait. One of the buildings has some people on top of it.

GC: Damn. I guess surviving isn't as hard as I thought it was.

David: Crap. Another building is in the way. I can't see them now. I lost my line of sight.

[One minute passes.]

GC: Still there?

David: Something's happening.

GC: What's going on?

David: It's the temperature gauge—something's wrong with it. It's reading at a normal temperature, but the temp tabs have changed colors. How did I not notice this?

GC: What does it mean?

David: The temperature is over the max continual temp; the fabric of the envelope is being destroyed.

GC: What? The envelope?

David: Dammit! *Dammit!* It's ripping!

GC: David! David—

David: Come on! Come on!

[End transmission.]

6.6 Grant Johnson, journal

The Indianola Police department was well fortified in their stationhouse, a few blocks from the county courthouse and the college perimeter. After the first encounter it became clear they were no longer around to serve and protect, as they took several hostages, and killed others in salvage teams that strayed into "their territory." Grant Johnson is the only prisoner of whom we have any record. Others are presumed to have been eaten.

July, 10

Now, when I can't get the thoughts out of my head, I come back to this journal. In some ways, it is the only thing keeping me sane. The officers at the Indianola Police Department have me locked up in this cell for most of the day. At least they let me keep this journal, but the isolation is getting to me. Writing is all I have.

I hate them. They are using me to save ammo until I get bitten. Then, they will pull the trigger and not think twice about it. It might be easier to give myself up. Just let myself be devoured by those flesh eating beasts, but, when I'm out there killing, bashing their skulls, and the blood is splattering, instinct takes over. My face tightens, jaw clenched, eyes focused. I can barely hear "What a wonderful world" playing over the loud speakers. The officers play it to mess with my mind when I'm doing my "work." I tune it out. Sometimes I picture those zombies as the cops. I've wanted to kill them ever since they took me hostage. I never understood how the cops, upholders of the law, could be so unjust. But, I have to control myself; if I lash out at any of them, they will surely kill me. Maybe, I can survive this. I am not sure if I want to.

July, 13

I haven't seen the cops in three days. One of the wives brings me a little food and water, but she won't make eye-contact with me.

July 14

They are back. Apparently, they were at the courthouse, which is where the sheriff's department is. From what I gather, the IPD and the Sheriff's deputies have parted ways, but I don't exactly understand on what grounds. Still, I don't see anyone springing me out of here.

Apparently, they had a big meeting because they received some sort of radio message from somewhere. Whatever it was scared the bejeezus out of them, and they are making hurried plans to head south to Osceola. Stupid Cops! I could have thought up a better escape plan with half a brain. We probably don't have enough supplies to even get down there or have enough firepower to defend ourselves against all the infected. We are not even sure how many are out there! These are probably some important things to consider before we walk into living hell out there. I hope they have. The only thing I can control is my thoughts. I have to stay focused. I can't lose it.

Unsurprisingly, this whole zombie apocalypse business is really making it harder for me to overcome my PTSD from Afghanistan. Still, I think this journal has really helped. Thank you Dr. Kleinzfelter, wherever you are.

July 16

We are getting ready to head out for Osceola. I think the police chief has gone around the bend. Apparently, he decided that we should go south, but the sheriff is staying put. This should be some road trip -- 30 miles through infested territory. I can't believe this. I have been trying to keep my head low, trying not to be noticed. This waiting is sickening me. I'm sure the cops will put me right out in front. May God, if there is one, protect me or give me a quick and painless death. We leave at night tomorrow.

July 17

Today was hard. We made it outside of Indianola, but not without sacrifice. Since we are moving the whole operation we are a big group. Six cops, two friends, fifteen family members, and me. Because they've been eating the food they stockpiled in the police station, most of them haven't been out and about, so they are pretty soft. That's why it took them three days to get to the courthouse and back. They do not know how to handle themselves.

A fast one picked off one of the kids. They didn't see it coming. He didn't have a chance. Hearing his screams affected me greatly, but I think it affected the others even more; watching one of their kids get his jugular slashed out by a dirty, naked, blood-spattered old man has got to be disturbing.

By the time they killed it with gunfire, the kid was dead. Still, the chief didn't hesitate to shoot him in the head. "He was bit!" the chief yelled. What a dick.

Still, the way that the rest of them reacted made me think there was a little bit of human still left in them, but I wondered how could they not be affected by what they were doing to me? I am a human, too. I don't understand. At least, some of the wives and girlfriends seem to think that what they are doing to me is wrong. Still, they don't actually seem prepared to do anything about it. I should just take it as it is. It is comforting to know some people care and understand, even though they can't do anything about it; caring and understanding, those words seem alien in a world like this.

Did I mention that I'm on a leash now? That's why I haven't run away.

July 18

We walked about five miles today, not too long but the most difficult five miles I've walked in my life. We walked even with Highway 69, but kept out of sight at the edge of the woods. Once we got out of town, we stopped seeing zombies, but the chief seemed to think they were everywhere, so we've been sticking to brush as much as possible. It has slowed us to a crawl.

Then, suddenly, there were two of them. Farm kids, I think. It was hard to tell since he was missing half his face. Then another three of them stumbled out from behind some trees. The chief shoved me towards them.

"I can't fight them all by myself," I yelled at the officers. The kids were totally freaked out. Women were screaming. I kept swinging my bat, but these Zs were tough – dehydrated. It was like beating a piece of jerky.

The cops waited for the order from the chief to fire. They backed away, as the zombies closed in. Their mouths were gaping with hunger for flesh. "Shoot, Shoot," I screamed. The first shots weren't fired until they were about arm's length from the police. As I looked back, I noticed the police chief standing behind everyone.

I looked down, and I noticed his son wrapped around his legs "Keep me safe, Keep me safe, daddy." Finally, one of the women came up to help me. She had some sort of golf club. It wasn't much of a weapon, but it shamed the cops into getting involved. They shot some of them and used their billies on the others.

Then I heard a scream from behind us. Another one had been attracted by the commotion – a fast one. It had jumped on what looked to be someone's mom. They both went down with a great deal of screaming.

Everyone ran in different directions. This was my chance. They were too busy with their own survival. The chief didn't even run after his own son.

I kept moving and realized that the boy was running parallel to me.

A tall Z with long arms stepped out from behind a big oak tree. The boy shrieked, but it had already zeroed in on me. I couldn't get the bat around in time; there was too much undergrowth. It lunged for my body. Its gray, withered hands almost caught hold of my shirt, but I jumped backwards. Swinging the bat furiously, the metal crashed into the face of the moaner's mouth. The left half of its lower jaw separated from the skull. Black ooze began to pour over the ground. It kept coming toward me. One more powerful, slicing blow cracked the top of its head, but it was still coming.

I swung the bat low, and hit a kneecap. I was getting exhausted.

It gurgled. Black goop flowed out of its mouth. It was dragging itself towards me. I smashed the dripping bat down as hard as I could. I heard the bones crack. I beat him with all my strength, sending blow after blow to his skull.

I approached the boy curled up on the rock. He was sobbing uncontrollably. "It's okay. They are all gone now. It's okay," I tried to console him. Then, behind me, I heard the shlack of a round being chambered in shotgun. Turning around, I saw the chief.

"Get away from my son, homo."

He called his boy over, staring into my eyes the whole time. The boy clambered over to him, and they picked their way back through the woods. I watched them until I lost sight of them. Now, I am all alone. I'm writing this in an abandoned farmhouse. Hopefully, tomorrow will be a better day.

6.7 Wesley Smyth, sermon

Following this sermon, there was a movement to put the Chaplain outside the perimeter. It was argued that he was a traitor, did not understand the situation, was too dangerous as an idealist, and was not offering the comfort that a chaplain should.

Chapel Reflection
Date: July, 21
Chaplain Wesley Smyth
Preaching Text: Matthew 25: 34 – 40

Then the king will say to those at his right hand, 'Come, you are blessed by my father ... I was a stranger and you welcome me ... when, Lord, did we do this to you? ... when you did this to the least of these who are members of my family, you did this to me."

Do you know what the sin of Sodom and Gomorrah was? Do you know what so offended God? Most of us don't know the story of the two visitors to Sodom and Gomorrah; we simply accept the Sunday school tales told to us when we were way too young. The depravity that raised the ire of God was a lack of hospitality. Two visitors – angels from God – having visited Abraham and Sarah, continue on their way. Abe warns them not to go; however, they are determined to do so . . . sound like anyone you know?

They arrive and decide to sleep out in the courtyard of the town – like our parking areas and abandoned house – but one of Sodom's inhabitants, Lot, warning them that it is not safe, takes them into his own home. That night, the home is surrounded by everyone in town – not a person is missing we are told. The crowd demands to see the visitors in order that they might "know" them.

Now, the Hebrew word that is used, here translated as "know" is the same word that is used to describe the knowledge that people share in marriage – it is the knowledge that is carnal and complete, this knowledge is intimate, physical, and leaves nothing to the imagination. The crowd demands this knowledge of the two visitors.

Surprisingly, Lot offers his own virgin daughters to the crowd rather than the two visitors. Now, we are not going into the social analysis of how this could be a serious offer. The crowd refused this offer and began threatening Lot. The two visitors "drew him back into his house and caused a darkness to fall on the eyes" of those in the crowd.

The next day, after Lot and his family escape, God rains down the fire. Preachers and Sunday school teachers have used this story as an example of how God's anger is invoked for dissolute living and as a text against same gendered relationships.

The desire of God is hospitality. Welcoming the stranger is essential . . . it is inherent in everything that God has commanded of Israel . . . it is to be first nature to these people that God has claimed . . . the stranger is to be welcome and cared for. Hospitality is indispensable: to be faithful is to be hospitable. Welcome is how we participate in God's unfolding, grace-filled passion for this world.

This theme is resoundingly present throughout the first testament of our Bible. Micah talks about showing mercy, living justly, and walking humbly with God. Even as a remnant in captivity in Babylon, Isaiah and Jeremiah both speak to this critical welcoming move. In a land with little by way of easy living, hospitality is singularly significant to survival!

It will serve us well to note that this is one of the ingredients missing when Jesus comes to Israel, according to the Gospel of John. In the very first chapter, John writes that the Word, Jesus, came to his own people and his own people reject him. Together – the world and his own people – "knew him not" (John 1: 10-11).

Throughout his entire public work, there is one characteristic that remained consistent: Jesus draws no lines in the sand, saying you're in and you're out. Those who remain "out" in Jesus' world are those who draw such lines, those who maintain distinctions, those who exclude and diminish. Jesus is quite critical of the leaders who mislead – of leaders who chose to protect their own interests. Jesus is quite critical of all those who will have nothing to do with the powerless, the stranger, of all who take advantage of those in need! Welcome according to Jesus goes to the last who shall be first, the lost who will be found, the least who are to be fed, the lonely who will be comforted, and the loser who in Jesus receives the whole world!

Listen to him: "when you did this to the least of those within my family, you did this to me." Now we might try to parse the language and argue that Jesus, when speaking of those in his "family" is restricting the welcome and hospitality. This is a self-serving parsing. If we are going to restrict our hospitality, then we must ask to whom it is to be restricted and I suspect that Jesus would start with those doing the restricting, us.

First, for those who seek to live with Jesus, who is in the family? How can we keep anyone out on this basis, for Jesus is God's love for the whole world, it is for the sake of the world that we encounter this Jesus. His blood is shed "for you and for all people" according to his words at the final supper he has with his followers.

Second, for those of us in survival mode and who seek to restrict entry of the stranger AND who do not follow Jesus, what is just for us? How do we make decisions about those we welcome? Are we willing to apply the same standards on our own population? Do we simply justify our position based on quarantine decisions that are now determined by us? It was arbitrary and capricious when the fence went up and the quarantine was imposed. Now we are inferring some sort of privilege because we are "already in?"

In either case, what is it that makes us human?

In either case, what does survival "trump" when it comes to values and faith?

In either case, the future is bearing down on us! I, for one, will choose to stand with Jesus and welcome those who are seeking shelter, those who are heavy laden, those who are lost, those who are losers, those who are last and least. My arms are open – as open as Jesus on the cross.

Amen.

6.8 Photograph, Robin Whitford

As the siege continued and ammunition ran low, Simpson residents fashioned melee weapons from the materials available.

6.9 Alexi Levi, journal

Most of the firsthand accounts that survived are diaries of those inside the 'safe zones'. When the Simpson perimeter closed on July 26 those seeking refuge were turned away. Many waited outside the fence hoping against hope, to be allowed in. Others attempted to fortify buildings outside of the perimeter.

I have lost track of all time. I don't know the hour or the day (number or day of week) all I know is that it's July, it is hot, and the zombies have started to turn us against one another.

Why can't they just let us into the perimeter? Wouldn't it make more sense to have a bigger population? More people mean more man-power, more scavengers to go seek for food and resources and more people means a better chance of survival all the way around. Why can't they see that? O.K. I do understand the repercussions that come along with letting more people in. But I think it's possible to expand the perimeter. And why did they not think of that in the first place? Did they honestly think that there were only going to be a couple hundred survivors?

I was working on shoring up the boarded windows on a house that I share with ten other survivors. One of my housemates has a granddaughter who is (was?) a student at Simpson. By the time Raging Granny, as she prefers to be called, made it to the college, the administration had decided to stop admitting refugees lacking in "special skills." Marilyn has plenty of special skills – she can sew; she can cook; she can do some carpentry. I'd say that her ability to fight her way from Ontario to Indianola in the middle of the Great Panic shows the possession of some special skills, but the turned her away. She doesn't know if her granddaughter is still alive or even if she's inside the perimeter, but she set up a safe house from which she can "keep an eye on her." It sounds pathetic, but I've seen her take out a slowboy with a hatchet blow to the head, so I'm glad her special skills are working in my favor.

The house we live in is just outside the perimeter. Over by the north gate, there were about a hundred refugees there, hoping that somehow something would change. I'd done the same for a couple of days, but then it became clear that the Simpson crowd were real hard cases, so I'd gone in with a few other people to make a "perimeter" of our own. Everyone else is out foraging.

The day was normal, well as normal as you can get these days, and everybody was pleading with the guards at the gate to let them in. Some were families yelling about their children needing protection. "At least take the children," they said. It was heart wrenching. Well, to me at least. The guards did not seem moved at all, but they all had on mirrorshades, so it was hard to tell.

By midday the sun was scorching and the humidity was punishing. People began to go a little more nuts than usual. I thought at one point that maybe there was a zombie attack, but I was wrong.

A father, begging to be let in, hoisted his infant, still wrapped in blankets, high above his head and threw his baby over the fence. The guards watched its slow arc through the air. They did not move. The baby hit the ground with a soft thud and nothing else was heard from it: not a whine or a scream. One of the guards picked up the bundle with one gloved hand, examined it, and then talked with his buddy. They looked at the baby, then at each other; one shook his head while the other threw it back over the fence.

The refugees erupted with anger and fury. After the baby was thrown back, people just went nuts; some started to climb the fence until they got to the razor wire where they would fall back with deep gashes in their hands. Some took their shirts off to try to get by the wire. The guards were yelling at them to stop, but they didn't. Before the Fall, you heard a lot about "shooting to wound," but anyone who is a survivor knows that's bullshit: Unless you are a crack shot or shooting at a stationary target, you've got to go for central body mass. These guys knew the score.

The first shotgun blast blew a climber right off the fence. I'd like to think they switched to birdshot or something, but I don't think they did. He fell back into the crowd.

People started shaking the fence. I saw one man start climbing about fifty feet away from the commotion. He got to the top without falling off or being shot and when he got to the razor wire I saw him grit his teeth and squeeze his eyes shut to protect himself. When he tried to swing one leg over the top he slipped and his leg became entangled in the wire, shredding his pants and flesh. His hands slipped out from under him and he went face first into a couple loops of the razor wire. His bottom lip got snagged, and then torn almost completely off. The man screamed, stuck there, his blood shimmering.

The alarm must have been raised because about twenty armed and armored Simpson people came out of nearby buildings. They had a mix of guns and melee weapons. Several of them ran over to where the guy was hanging. One of them had some kind of spear, which he used to push the guy back off the fence.

I don't think this is going to work. I need to find some new neighbors.

Chapter 7: AUGUST

7.1 Operation Hawkeye, radio communications

Tim Reynolds was the field commander charged with coordinating the convergence of the three main caravans in Des Moines as part of Operation Hawkeye. In this discussion with Lt. General Marcus Stafford (likely based at Offutt Air Force Base, which is just south of Omaha, Nebraska), it was decided to shift the strike on Des Moines southwards; Indianola became Ground Zero.

MARCUS STAFFORD: Sitting Bull actual, this is Kickstarter actual. Sitrep.

TIM REYNOLDS: Sir, Tango Fox Alpha arrived at 8 Arapaho 1400. To facilitate, Tango Fox Bravo has been immobile for 20 hours. Our perimeter remains fairly porous. Lead elements of Zulu Hotel are approximately 8 hours north. We need to make a decision.

STAFFORD: What about Tango Fox Charlie?

REYNOLDS: They are twenty klicks due west. Instead of punching through the suburbs, I would prefer to route them around the southern edge of the city. They could cover that distance in a day.

STAFFORD: Can you still converge on 9 Arapaho?

REYNOLDS: It is 20 klicks south. We're essentially foot mobile. We need to ferry injured civs on our vehicles, so we only have a few technicals fully deployable.

STAFFORD: Liaison reports 9 Arapaho leadership as suspicious and competent, cagy but desperate. I'm not expecting that you will be welcomed as conquering heroes.

REYNOLDS: We live in an age of diminished expectations, sir.

STAFFORD: What is your ETA at 9 Arapaho?

REYNOLDS: 36 to 48 hours.

STAFFORD: Proceed at the pace you deem appropriate. We need to get this right.

REYNOLDS: Do we know why they moved the ZED yet?

STAFFORD: There are known knowns and known unknowns. This is the latter.

REYNOLDS: I wonder what the unknown unknown is.

STAFFORD: That's unknown. … What's your rad count?

REYNOLDS: Well within the margin, sir. It hasn't gone up for a week. All things considered, sir, I think I preferred Anbar.

STAFFORD: It had its positives.

REYNOLDS: I'll inform Tango Fox Charlie to re-route south. We'll be Oscar Mike in two.

STAFFORD: Sat imaging shows several minor roadblocks on your MSR. None look substantial, but they could be ambush sites.

REYNOLDS: Roger that, sir. I'll dispatch the technicals to clear them.

STAFFORD: Don't let any of your civs start thinking about staying at 9 Arapaho. Once ZED is activated it's a killbox. It is difficult to know the attitude of the people at the college about the plan. Reveal as little as you can. We need at least some of them to remain in order to concentrate Zulu Hotel.

REYNOLDS: Roger that.

STAFFORD: Transmit sitrep in two.

7.2 Llewellyn Morse, audio recording

These are audio files recovered from the records of Dr. Llewellyn Morse. Many consider the tests he performed cruel and unusual, but they did provide extremely valuable knowledge about the progression of HIV-Z.

Entry 1: Pain
Test subject 107-Z, stage five. The subject displays a distinct attraction to me. His eyes are fixed on me and he is struggling to break free of his bonds. I will now use a power drill with a 1mm bit. I will begin drilling through his deltoid muscle now.

[Drilling sound. Moans]

Subject has no apparent reaction to pain. Subject's eyes remain fixed on me. Conclusions: by stage five, the pain receptors provide very little feedback to the brain or the brain does not register the feedback from the nerves.

Entry 2: Flame Aversion and Flammability
First subject, 59-Z, early stage four. I will observe if the infected attempt to avoid fire. After, I will also perform the same test on a stage five. Administering test using an acetylene blowtorch.

[Distressed moans]

Subject shows distinct resentment toward flame.

[The moans grow more distressed. Screeching]

Subject 59-Z appears to feel pain, but is not highly flammable. The skin retains too much moisture.

[Angry growls and hisses]

Subject appears to understand I was the cause and is not happy with me. She seems to be showing more of an effort to try and bite me. What a scrapper.

The second test, subject 124-Z, advanced stage five. Administering test using the same apparatus.

[Moans]

Subject seems to have no aversion to flame. He does not seem to recognize it, nor does he feel pain; not unlike subject 107. Flesh burns easily the skin seems dehydrated.

[Fire extinguisher discharge]

Now, where did I put that ice pick?

[Recording ends.]

7.3 LT James Bradley, journal

Despite efforts to maintain operational security, at least some of the military personnel accompanying the refugee caravan kept a personal journal.

The CO was looking at me oddly today. I think he suspects how I feel about this operation. I know it's the survival of the human race and all that... but how human are we if we sacrifice hundreds (thousands?) of unwilling people? They have to die for the good of all? I'm pretty sure that's come out of the mouth of every tyrant who's ever lived. How valuable is the greater good if we can't hold on to the lesser?

If only those idiots hadn't picked up the ZED at the airport. I know they had no idea what it was for, and I know it's too late to do anything about it. I still feel like there's something I should be able to do. I want to serve my country. Well, what's left of it, anyway. And I won't be remembered as a traitor.

Survival is the most important thing. Live to fight another day. We have to be alive to fight, and this plan's probably one of the few ways we can survive long enough to do so. Intellectually I know this is the only way it can work, but the rest of me hates every ounce of it.

Twin Cities after the lines fell: The Old Man, rallying and gathering soldiers and civilians, motivating them and keeping them strong. Practically for nothing. Only ten percent of the battalion showed up at the rally point.

We killed hundreds of them, but the rest tore the cities apart. When *everything* is on fire, where should the fire-fighters go? It moved too fast to build a firebreak. It spread too widely to carve out a working safe zone.

So much for that metaphor. Now we have a new plan: we're bait. At least that part is working. They hunger for our delicious brains. They've followed us all the way. The big, bad Zulu Hotel. People see us and think we're salvation, but we aren't. We're just bait. They join us and then they become bait too. We're a bunch of red wigglers. A sad little convoy of broken, beaten down people. Everyone is so tired here, and we can never stop long enough. We never get enough food, enough water, enough sleep, hardly enough time to think.

If we are the new Israelites then where is Canaan? Where's the safe place? Somehow, I just do not imagine Arkansas as the land of milk and honey, but I guess at this point I'd settle for the land of running water and toilet paper.

Now, we're bringing that chaos down on every group of survivors in our path. People who haven't done anything to us: people who only want to survive. We're taking their chance away from them, and they don't even know it. After the Twin Cities, I have difficulty thinking this will be different. Sweet Jesus, please let this work. Don't let us fail again. Don't let our people die because of our incompetence.

7.4 Llewellyn Morse, autopsy notes

Summary of Clinical History:
Subject is a 34 year-old male. Apparently mixed ancestry. Copper colored pigmentation. Black hair. He contracted HIV-Z from a bite on arm, and reached S3 in under 20 hours. Prior, he had no severe medical problems. When he came into my possession, he suffered from severe fever of 109 degrees and shortness of breath. He soon started having hallucinations and violent out bursts. Within four hours he had reached S4.

Description of Gross Lesions:
External Examination: The body is dehydrated, but as a salvage team leader, he was well nourished. The bite is clotted with a thick black substance.

Heart: The heart is average sized with a normal shape. It also seems to have filled with the same black substance, which is fluid in this case. The epicedial fat is diffusely firm. The patient's heart is filled with the thick substance as if it filled his blood.

Aorta: The same black substance is present.

Lungs: The right lung weighed 640 grams and the left weighed 710. It is black. However this man had no history of smoking. Opening it I discovered the same black substance. Despite this the lungs were healthy.

Gastrointestinal System: The esophagus and stomach are normal in appearance sans the black substance. The stomach contains approximately 800ml without any substances in it. In the stomach are pieces of meat, they are partially digested and are presumably human in origin. The pancreas has a normal lobular cut, but all organs are tainted with the same black substance. The liver weighs 2850 grams and is pitch black. Gallbladder is normal sans black substance.

Reticuloendothelial System: The spleen is large weighing 340 grams and when it is cut open it is pitch black. The lymph nodes are also abnormally swollen.

Genitourinary System: The right kidney weighs 200 grams, and the left weighs 210 grams. Both appear to be normal. They both are stained black.

Endocrine System: The adrenal glands are swollen; they weigh 12 grams on the right and 14 grams on the left. Cut open it is stained with the same black substance. The thyroid gland is swollen as well. Weight 15 grams. The bullet went through and through. It entered through the frontal lobe above the left eye and exited out the right side of the parietal lobe.

Extremities: Both legs and calves showed signs of muscle tension and dehydration.

Clinicopathologic Correlation:
This subject died of a gunshot to the back of the head. This shot was administered by me with a .38 handgun at close range. Between initial infection and stage five zombification, the subject's blood developed the dark substance that now stains his whole insides.

Summary and Reflection:
 HIV-Z puts the body through rapid and extreme changes, dehydration, an overload on your endocrine system, and whatever psychological effects take place. It is 100% communicable as well. We know it caused by HIV-Z but, what drives the zombies to attack and/or eat humans? What other physical or cognitive skills do they have? These questions will have to be answered with further experimentation.

7.5 Burke Wolf, speech

After the death of Frederick Wish, Burke Wolf became the leader of the SPART. He subsequently exerted significant influence on the President's Council. There, he consolidated his power, led the faction advocating the closure of the perimeter to refugees, as well as securing additional supplies and preferential treatment and housing for his followers in the SAE house. After the death of the President, Wolf made repeated attempts to increase his political influence inside the perimeter. The renewal of communication with the federal government as part of Operation Hawkeye and the subsequent rumors surrounding the ZED device led to his attempt to seize absolute power.

Here we are. At a turning point in the course of the life of our community. This has been our home during these trying times. It has provided food, shelter, and support when all but God has abandoned us!

We are a white fleck in a sea of black. A glimmer of hope in the darkness and despair. While the infected have claimed men, women, and children, this Perimeter has become our savior!

[cheers]

Our liberties we prize and our rights we will maintain!

[cheers]

But a different kind of infection now threatens us. The stink of corruption has corroded our leaders. Thorius, Albrecht, May, Walden, Gammon [spits]. Those we once trusted with our lives and charged with the responsibility of preserving the stability of our community have turned on us [confused mumbling]. Yes! They plan to use us as bait for

187

a horde of the undead. This sacred place, this bastion of humanity, and all its people; they want us to be like cattle in a slaughterhouse!

[angry shouts]

My fellow soldiers. My family. None of us has ever once hesitated to defend the Perimeter from the infected and from criminals alike. But over in Hillman … over there are plotters who would sacrifice us to the infected. They are ready to stab us in the back! They are traitors to humanity, and they are among us!

[shouts]

There's only one punishment for treason. There's only one thing that can be done. It isn't pleasant, but it is necessary. Everyone here has given so much, and in return, the Perimeter has provided a beacon of hope in these dark times. Can we, after everything we've given, after everything we've lost, simply knuckle under and submit to their dark design?

[shouts: No! Never!]

Are we willing to concede our home and our future – this city on a hill – to a group of corrupt and selfish bureaucrats?

[shouts: No! Never! Fuck them!]

Then we must act. We must act to save ourselves! We must act to save the innocent! We must act to save humanity! We have one chance, just one chance, to tell our enemies that they may take our lives, but they'll never … take our freedom! They cannot resist us; they cannot silence us!

[cheers]

7.7 Governing Council, minutes

Wolf laid his plans to launch a coup before the regular Governing Council meeting. (It is unclear how the President's Council transitioned into the Governing Council after the disappearance of President Byrd). Wolf represented the SAE house.

DEAN OF STUDENTS: As you all know we have been given fairly precise instructions by the military on how to handle this device, and the decision we make here will likely determine the fate of every individual inside the Perimeter.

BSC: Considering what we know, I say we do what we were advised to do, evacuate the perimeter and activate it so the military can destroy as many infected as possible.

SAE: Oh and are you going to stay behind and see it through Jeff? Is that going to be you in the chapel, waiting until there is a sea of infected so you can activate ZED? Is it? Listen, we have survived on our own for months and now you all want to lie down for the government? Where have they been? What have they done for us? Do we even know who the president is? We have no obligation to them.

DUNN: Calm down now. The government, the U.S. government, is not plotting to get rid of us. There are simply too many survivors here. I mean, we may form a substantial portion of the population of the United States at this point.

SAE: Remember Pella? It's *gone.*

DoS: None of us have forgotten Pella, none of us will. But we need to decide what we are going to do here, with *our* community. We need to think about the long term.

ATO: Whatever happened to the cold test stuff?

CARVER: The lack of electricity makes refrigeration very difficult. We've been trying some experiments on *parts* of zombies, but we haven't come up with anything definitive at this point. Sorry.

ATO: What about the scouts we sent south?

BSC: Heavy Zs down there by the looks of things. According to the Sheriff, IPD headed down to Osceola a couple of weeks ago.

ATO: Do we know what happened to them?

BSC: No. No we don't.

DoS: That doesn't matter. We've run the numbers and it looks really unlikely that we'll be able to feed everyone through the winter. Unless we want to start eating one another, we are at a critical juncture.

SAE: Cowards! None of you have any clue about the world outside the Perimeter, I do. I know what's out there and thinking that it's miraculously going to be better than in here is the definition of stupidity. If the radio transmission is right, we are going to have thousands of refugees, and if there are that many refugees they are going to be gunned up and desperate. How much respect do you think they'll give us?

DoS: You need to get yourself calmed down. You are just the military advisor.

SAE: As your *advisor*, I *advise* you to get your *head* out of your *ass!*

KRESGE: Hey, now. Burke...

SAE: What, what exactly would you do? Who do you think has been enforcing law and order in this place? Me, that's who: me and my men. We defend scavenging missions; we kill these things, and we actually back up our threats with action! I understand our situation and I'm telling you, we need to get the ZED *out* of the Perimeter. Let's put it on a truck and take it to Winterset. It's the only way we'll have a chance.

DUNN: Scouts have confirmed that thousands of refugees are headed our way. What do we do when they arrive? We've already got hundreds of refugees stacked up against the wire. We can't just tell them to go away.

SAE: We have a good system here and if they are so determined to head south, let them do so. They do not need to stop. We know Indianola. We can defend this place as long as the perimeter is intact.

DoS: Is it really that easy? Are you really so selfish?

SAE: Don't lecture me, and don't try to hide behind your false sense of authority. They are threatening our well-being. We've made some hard decisions about refugees. It meant that some people had to die, but we acted because more people would live. Our people. I see how this is different, but I do not think the moral imperative to protect my community has changed. We need to stay, fort up, and survive. I will find a way ... *we* will find the way to hold out through rationing and enforcing rules if we can be led by someone who has the will to power.

KRESGE: Well, *mein fuehrer*, I don't think you could lead your way out of a wet paper bag.

SAE: You can hide behind your false ideals, but I'm the only one in this room that gives a damn about the people of this Perimeter.

DoS: Don't hide behind "the people." You are speaking for yourself. I say we put the matter to a vote. All in favor of cooperating fully with the government plan and preparing to evacuate, say aye.

DUNN: Aye.

ART: Nay.

CARVER: Aye.

ATO: Aye.

[gunfire]

[screaming]

Wolf's coup attempt was unsuccessful, and it was messy. Most of the members of the Governing Council were killed or mortally wounded when he and his men opened fire on them, but he proved unable to consolidate his power across campus. Even though he showed a willingness to use violence against those he perceived as his enemies, Wolf proved reluctant to bring the other buildings into line with force. Consequently, the campus simmered in a sort of cold war with Wolf and his followers (including the SPART) controlling Hillman Hall and the western half of campus, while the rest of the campus attempted to resurrect something resembling democracy. Since Wolf controlled the water tower, it is likely that he anticipated the rest of campus to capitulate quickly, but the eastern campus retained control over the cisterns that had been constructed to collect and store rainwater.

7.8 Photograph: Keith Bryan and Robin Whitford

After the bloody attack on the Governing Council, there was a brief flare of violence. Eight people died and dozens were injured, driving the two halves of campus further apart from one another.

7.9 Llewellyn Morse, audio recording

As the chaos in the Perimeter mounted, it became more and more difficult to experiment effectively. Furthermore, with the annihilation of the Governing Council, Morse no longer had to be distracted by oversight or medical ethics.

Entry 16: Sensory Depravation
I have decided to move on and begin researching other phenomena with zombies. I am curious to how these creatures track us humans. I know eyes and ears are our primary sense organs, I have seen zombies who do not have eyes still track a human, and zombies without ears still locate their prey. I am going to rid a fresh subject of her senses and see if she can still track me.

[recording ends]

This is Dr. Morse. I am here with subject 85-Z. She has been restrained and I will be ridding her of her senses. Sealing nasal cavities.

[drilling and hisses]

I will now remove her gag so she may breathe.

[Violent and raspy hisses]

I will now puncture her ear drums.

[hisses]

Now, just to be sure, I will plug the ear cavities with putty. Now I will begin to remove her vision.

[hissing becomes violent]

[sizzles and pops]

[recording ends]

Entry 17: Sense Deprivation, continued

I have left subject 85 alone in a room so as to have her forget me as a target and I can start fresh. I will begin my testing. I am entering the room and approaching subject 85, she doesn't seem to have noticed me at all. I am approximately three meters away from the subject. I will move in closer.

[Sudden, loud screeching]

Good God! How did she know I was there? Did she just wait for me to get close enough to her? No... She is fully S5. I wonder if I move to the other side, will she follow me? ... I am once again about three meters away she hasn't moved from the spot where she stopped. I will move in slowly.

[violent screeching]

She found me again! How? Perhaps if I stay the distance I am away from her? What is it, about one and one half meters? I am going to shuffle and see if she follows. ... I am now exiting the testing chamber.

[recording ends]

85's ability to track me without her primary senses perplexes me. When I am three meters away she has no sense of me in the room, but as soon as I am one and one half meters away she attacks. As if something gives me away. She has been blinded, deafened, and her nasal passages have been closed off. Many questions still remain to be answered, but for now I will feed her and test her another day. I need to construct tests to determine her receptivity to electrical fields and air pressure changes.

[recording ends]

Entry 18: Respiration

Two weeks ago I asked one of the scavenging crews to fetch me a vacuum pump. It took several days, but luckily they came across one in an abandoned repair shop. I am delighted to have an opportunity to make use of it. I have developed an ingenious way of suffocating a zombie without wasting water or putting myself in harm's way. I have developed a strong table bolted against the wall. The table has a hole in the middle and swings open. I place the restrained zombie against the table with his neck in the hole and lock him in. I then take a strong, thick glass container, to which I hooked the vacuum pump to, and place it over the zombie's head. And from there I will pump out the air from the container. This device has been made in order test whether or not zombies need to breathe. I will begin the project when I have finished preparing the vacuum chamber.

[recording ends]

I have completed the vacuum chamber and obtained a participant, subject 88-Z. I have restrained Subject 88 and I am preparing to start the vacuum pump. Beginning vacuum pump. … I am observing from a different room so as to be able to dictate what is happening. The pump is very weak since it is not designed for this kind of work. It may take some time.

[recording ends]

10 minutes have passed and I can tell the pump is working. His face is beginning to expand a little and his eyes are bulging.

[recording ends]

It has been 15 minutes now his left eye is really protruding. He seems to be struggling, gasping for air.

[recording ends]

It has been 20 minutes. His eye looks like it is going to burst. But it appears he has stopped respiration. I am going to turn off the vacuum.

[end machine noises]

I repressurized the chamber. His face has been stretched out significantly, but it remains elastic. My hypothesis is confirmed: Zombies need air!

[recording ends]

* * *

Entry 25: Food preferences
This is Dr. Morse. I am testing a very perplexing question: Do zombies prefer humans over all other meat? To do this I have two rooms with glass doors. In one room, a medium sized dog. Basset Hound. Nice doggie. In the other, a human – a criminal. He hoarded food or something. His file says he is 19, but he refused to talk to me. He even spit at me. Outrageous behavior from a student. I'm glad I gave him a C- for that class. I should have failed him: the ingrate. I've placed two S4 zombies together in a room. Subjects 99 and 100 are siblings, so this should be especially interesting. Here they go!

Good... they don't seem to know if any prey is available. Revealing prey.

I have restrained and gagged both him and the dog.

[moans]

100 has discovered the prisoner. 99 has joined him. Reference: Do more tests on their communication.

[moans and muffled pounding noises]

They haven't even taken interest in the dog. Do they really prefer human flesh? Why? Is it just because he's bigger? Is it because a dog is more capable of defending itself? Extensive additional testing is needed. Now that supplies are running low, new subjects should become available fairly regularly. What I really need is someone with immunity. We know immunity exists, but we don't know if there are any physiological effects. I really need to cut someone open.

[recording ends]

197

7.10 Photograph of Keith Bryan fighting zombies

Unfortunately, in the chaos surrounding the coup, safety protocols collapsed and the infected went unidentified. Whitford and others turned inside the perimeter.

7.11 Kathryn Stevens, journal

Kathryn Stevens proved remarkably resilient. A resident of Kresge Hall, her outspoken opposition to Burke Wolf's fascist tendencies played an important part in keeping the eastern half of campus independent.

August 15. Sunny and very warm.

The perimeter has fallen. After Wolf made his power play, regular patrols of the fence line ceased in some parts of the campus. He seemed content to keep order west of C Street, and the building militias did the best they could over here, but some areas – like Buxton Park – got very little attention.

B Street, which runs to the north end of the park had some solid barricades up. There's no way a vehicle could have breached it if they were intact. But somehow, for some reason, they were removed and this morning a huge yellow school bus blew through the fence. Everyone heard the sound. I got to the window in time to see it smash the gazebo to kindling. Then it smashed into the base of the fountain.

Someone shot right through the front windshield. Then, he got back up. Zombies.

It was bloody chaos. All of the poor souls who were camped out in the buildings north of the wire poured out. This was their big chance to get inside. Of course, the tumult attracted plenty of zombies too. They had become thin over the course of the summer. Our salvage teams had whittled them down over time, but in the past couple of days, it seemed like new ones began arriving.

The building militias ran to seal the breach. I could swear that I saw President Byrd running into the melee with a machete in both hands, but I recognize that's ridiculous. He died at least a month ago.

Discipline, practice, determination. That was what I needed.

They moved slowly. They all seemed to be in stage five, but there were a lot of them. The ammunition was pretty much gone by this point.

We'd need to take them hand-to-hand. It was an almost overwhelming proposition, but we were ready. We had drilled for this.

We did not move into them; they came to us. Some were slightly faster than others. It was important that we did not attempt to rush them. We had to hold a line. Cut them down as they came to us.

When it became clear that we were running out of ammunition, we tried out various different ancient and medieval tactics, but nothing was well suited for zombies. The Greek phalanx was attractive, and plenty of the kids had seen some awful movie named "300," but we found that spears do not work well against zombies. They get stuck. They are hard to handle, and it is almost impossible to get the brain.

The Roman legion approach also seemed promising, but it had shortcomings too. The shields were too heavy, the short swords were difficult to kill with, and it required really excellent drilling.

So, we adopted a roughly medieval approach. We had a mix of weapons and we tried to hold the line. The shooters sat on rooftops and in windows. They'd pick off selected targets. Ideally, they'd take out the fast ones, but hitting a moving target, particularly a ravenous adrenaline-soaked target, is very difficult apparently.

In the calm before the storm, someone (I think it was a history professor) came up with the idea of using two lines of cars to create a sort of funnel. The shooters would try to keep them off the cars while we waited at the end of the funnel. This way we would not get flanked.

It took a couple of hours to get the cars into position. It was midday and it was hot. I stood under a tree and kept watch and I was still sweating. Some gunfire came from west campus. I'm not sure if they were firing at zombies or refugees. Whenever a group of zombies would appear, everyone would pick up a weapon.

The funnel worked until nightfall. It was a crescent moon, so it was difficult to see much. It was almost impossible to coordinate our defense. Besides, everyone was exhausted. So we gave it up. We yielded the field. Everyone retreated into their respective buildings, and the zombies came in.

7.12 Karen Grzesiak, journal

The ultimately unsuccessful efforts to contain the perimeter breach lasted throughout the day on the 16th. Afterwards, the buildings on the east side of campus attempted to reestablish control over key buildings, but several structures, including Dunn Library, were abandoned. The stiffest fight was for Pfeiffer Cafeteria.

8.16

Everyone is in a panic now, and Eric and I are terrified as well. Things have gone from bad to worse. First, there was the exclusion policy, then food and ammunition started to run out, then we heard rumors about evacuation, then there was the civil war. What a mess.

Now it is worse. This morning a yellow school bus drove right through the north fence and zombies just poured in. I have a hard time believing that it was all just an accident; I think that they were angry that we didn't let them in the perimeter and decided to take our protection away. I wouldn't blame them though. I would be tempted to do the same.

Now we are bunkered down in our building. We're quiet. Quiet enough to hear them outside. Moaning. Gurgling. I need to calm down.

8.17

We are in the infirmary. My fears came true last night. Eric and I went with a group trying to see what the situation was in Pfeiffer. Most of the food is stored over there.

The zombies were on us in an instant. The first thing I realized was that one was attacking Eric. I had to get that thing off of him or he was going to die. I ran my reed knife right up its neck and then used the bocal to stab it in the eye socket. It started clawing at me instead of him. I don't know how many times I stabbed it or how effective my efforts were. It stopped attacking Eric because Sarah Beth blew its brains out.

At this point, adrenaline must have kicked in because I was all of a sudden aware of everything around me. There were three zombies moving toward us and with no hesitation, I stabbed the closest and fastest zombie with my bocal nailing him directly in the nose; I could feel it push through to soft tissue. I just kept going and slashed at the next one with my knife. In retrospect it is easy to criticize myself. Lacerations aren't going to do much to a zombie. But I was lucky – my knife sliced right across its face, through at least one of the eyes and the bridge of the nose. That disoriented it enough for Sarah Beth to take it out. Crack shot, that girl. A regular Annie Oakley.

Still running on pure fear, I grabbed my semi-conscious husband and moved as fast as I could with his arm slung around my shoulders and one of my arms wrapped around his waist. We didn't have any time to lose. Then I felt something grabbed my shirt and yank really hard. I thought we were goners, but right as this happened, I heard several gun shots and the zombies that were chasing us were now scattered around on the ground. That black gunk was everywhere. It was spattered all over me.

About ten men came running from Wallace. They grabbed us and pulled us into their building.

I don't know how true this was last year, but I can state with some assurance that during a zombie apocalypse *guns save lives.* If this ever ends I swear to God that I will become a lifelong member of the National Rifle Association. Charlton Heston, you rock.

8.18

Somehow, Eric didn't get infected. He got some scratches, but mostly he was shaken up. I guess layering worked. It's for more than the cold of winter, it's also for the zombie apocalypse.

7.13 Amanda Robinson, eulogy for Meshach Jacobs

After the fall of the perimeter, the chapel became the main fortified position on the east side of campus. This eulogy was offered there at the end of August. A week after the perimeter fell.

I'm sure all of you know who I am. Who I am does not matter on this day. I know we lost many of the people here in that battle: many good people, who gave their lives trying to keep those beasts away from us, people trying to keep the perimeter safe. I weep for all of them.

I remember meeting Meshach for the first time. He was taking his turn patrolling, even with that awful eyesight of his. I asked him if he needed anything and he turned to me, looked me in the eye, and said he didn't need anything from an uppity white woman who thought she knew best for him. I was shocked. It wasn't the best of first meetings, and I must admit, I was angry at him after that and refused to speak with him. I thought he was a hateful old man who survived by being hard, nasty, and hateful.

But, there were times when I saw something good in him. I always caught him keeping an eye on the children in the compound, making sure they didn't wander too far, or see too much of the evil outside. He taught all of the girls and boys things that would be useful: How to start a fire, how to use the stars to navigate, how to set up snares for food. He was patient, but he pushed them hard. He knew just when to give praise or encouragement. It reminded me of how my father was with my kids. I still didn't like Meshach much, but at least he kept the kids occupied and happy. I gave him that much.

That day, the day of the battle… I thought I was going to die. Worse, I thought I would watch my children die. I saw many horrible things after the collapse; we all did. But I saw great things, too. Meshach was one of them. He had no doubts that he was going to die, but he wanted to die doing something good.

I had lost track of my kids, my twins, Shelly and Brian. I was running around with my machete. I was screaming for them, hoping to be heard over all the mess of noise, crying at the thought of losing them. They dragged me into one of the buildings, kicking and screaming, telling me it was too late, to keep myself safe. I felt like I was going to be sick, that I would be best served to take a bullet to the brain now, rather than live without my angels in this god-forsaken world. That's when I heard shouting of a different sort.

I stood and looked out the windows, my heart stopping. There was Meshach, standing on top of a car near the building, passing the children up to others through the windows. I have no idea how he could do it. Here was this old, almost blind man.

When the last child made it to safety, he did not try to climb up after them, he just hefted his spade and made ready to fight. He looked like some ancient warrior, tall and strong and proud, fighting against impossible odds. It was like a scene from the *Iliad.*

He saw me sobbing, cradling my crying, fearful children, and do you know what he did? He smiled at me. We just looked at each other.

I did not know much about Meshach Jacobs. He was an old, mean, bitter man. He had been hurt by the world a thousand times over. But, in his final hours he did something that will live on in our hearts to the ends of time. He gave us our children. He gave us life. He gave us hope. Even though he was so angry with the world, with everyone and everything, he found the ability to love, to care, and to give his life for those who could not defend themselves.

Meshach Jacobs was a true hero. In a dead world, he remembered old values. He could have run and saved himself, but he refused to let himself fall into the grip of selfishness and greed.

There are more dark days ahead. I wish us all to face them like Meshach did: standing tall, strong, proud. Knowing good and doing it.

Chapter 8: SEPTEMBER

8.1 "The Scalp Song"

Burke Wolf resurrected the early 20th century college fight song in an apparent effort to raise the morale of his followers (who he had christened the "Knights Exemplar." The lyrics did little to quiet rumors that the inhabitants of west campus resorted to cannibalism in order to overcome the food shortage.

A scalp, a scalp, a scalp to hang up on the trophy wall! The foe, the foe, the wretched foe was taken to a fall! Victoria!
Round the glare of mighty fires dancing figures great and small, will hoot and yell, as warriors there assemble at the call.

Jah, Jah, Jah, Jah, Jah, Jah.

We'll broil, we'll broil, we'll broil them on the grid-iron 'til they're done!
Their hides, their hides, their hides we'll tan as covers for our drum!
A banquet! Hollow skulls will serve as drinking cups to toast the victory won,
then to our tents at rising of the early morning sun.

Hi, jah, jah, hi, jah, jah.
Hi, jah, jah, hi, jah, jah.
Hi, jah, jah, hi, jah, jah.

8.2 Photograph

Immediately after the collapse of the perimeter, different buildings fended for themselves.

8.3 Grant Johnson, journal

Some Warren County residents remained completely unaware of the factional struggle on campus or the approach of the caravan from the north. Grant Johnson was lucky to find one of these isolated survivors.

It has been a while since I have been able to write my thoughts and what has been going on in my life. Too many things have been happening. After the IPD abandoned me, I was stuck alone, out in the open. I knew I had to find someone to rely on. Someone who could help me survive. I walked for ten days searching. I stuck to the woods, as much as possible. The cover of the trees hid me from the infected lurking through the fields. At night, I slept up in the trees. Well, at least, I tried to. It was incredibly uncomfortable, and I was constantly waking in fear that I would fall to the ground into the outreaching hands of a horde of zombies. I had dreams about that type of scene a lot. I saw my body being ravaged, my limbs being torn from my body, and my intestines being devoured.

By the end of the second day, my body was exhausted, my ribs began to show, and my breathing was deep and slow. My arms and legs felt like they couldn't move any longer. When I felt like I couldn't take it any longer, that is when I saw it. I let out a sigh. A farm was about a quarter mile into a field from the woods I was standing in.

This was no regular farm. I knew someone was in there because there were some deadheads walking around the house. They wouldn't do that if they didn't want something in there. The house was boarded up, fortified with all types of things. A sheet of metal from a grain bin covered the front door.

I stuck low to the ground, and I got as close as possible. Then I saw the curtains move. I saw a face, and the woman's eyes saw mine. Her jaw dropped, and she quickly closed the curtain. I waited for a few minutes in anticipation. I heard a noise. The grain bin door was shifting, and the infected started to make a ruckus. I saw a huge woman emerge with a rifle in her hand. She started cursing the zombies and flapping her arms.

At the same time she jabbed the rifle toward the back of the house. When she saw that I understood, she went back inside and loudly slammed the door. The zeds compliantly started pounding on it.

It took me three hours to drag myself around to the back of the house. When I saw the door start to open, I pushed myself up onto my weak legs, and I began to run as fast as I could. My body tired quickly, and the 100 feet seemed like 100 miles.

The zombies were still gathered in the front of the house, but I didn't slow down. She swung the door wide and I collapsed inside her hall. I heard the sound of a heavy bolt being thrown.

Betty Cranston thought she was the last person on earth. She was surprised that there was anyone – much less a whole college – still in operation. Batteries for her radio had run out in June. Her husband had left her to seek help in Indianola two months ago. He never came back. She survived off her large well-stocked pantry. She always believed in buying in bulk, but the food was already running low. I've been staying here for a week, and, thankfully, there has been enough food here to revitalize my body.

Last night, the infected surrounding the house disappeared mysteriously. We don't know where they went, but it gave us time to gather grain from the bins. I threw some in my mouth and started chewing. She laughed all the way back to the house where she pounded a handful of them into flour using a mortar and pestle.

I spent most of yesterday pounding dried corn into meal, which Betty baked into something passable using cast iron skillets and her dutch oven. Tomorrow we'll go out.

We walked all the way to the highway, and we didn't see any sign of the infected. It's eerie. It gives me this weird feeling. I like it, but I don't like it at the same time. The absence of the infected puts me on more of an edge than when they are actually around. We went back to the house and baked more bread. The grain elevator is half full. Betty and her husband slaughtered and cured several of their hogs before the infected feasted on the rest. I'm curious about what's happening out there, but not that curious. I think I've found my winter quarters.

8.4 Cindy Tanner, journal

Task Force Alpha, which formed the core of the caravan that arrived in Indianola on September 28, originated near Duluth, Minnesota. Cindy Tanner accompanied the group, with her entire family. Her lack of first-hand interactions with the infected at this late date is striking.

August 15.

All in all, as I think back, we reacted pretty well when things fell apart. We didn't panic. We didn't pack all of the children's favorite toys, jump in the car, and head to grandma's house. We were certainly scared, but we never lost it.

Some people did. When we joined the evacuation caravan two weeks ago, we saw the results. Thousands of cars jammed the interstates. Pushing them all out of the way was too time-consuming. We ditched our minivan before we even left the city limits.

Even though we've left the protection of our house, I feel lucky to be evacuated. We had reached our wit's end. All the food was gone. Information on the radio was sketchy and contradictory. We were really at a loss until that beautiful humvee came rolling down the cul de sac looking for survivors. We have been walking southward for about a day now. I have no idea where we are going, and I don't care, as long as my family is still by my side. We were lucky we made it out alive, and we were lucky they were there to save us.

August 17.

We have mostly been walking through a desolate landscape. Oftentimes, the highway is wide open and there isn't a car on the horizon, but sometimes, especially when we are moving through a town or a crossroads, wreckage fills the highway, making our trip even more difficult. At least I'm not towards the outside of the group, I hear gunshots from there periodically. I hear the men yelling orders and people screaming. I cover my children's ears. I don't want them to be exposed to those horrors. I know what they are shooting at. I am reassured whenever I see one of the Toyotas tearing along. They drive *towards* the shooting. They are protecting us. They're leading us to a safe haven; I just know it. A place where my family can live in peace.

August 20.
We have been looting every small town we pass by. I know it is wrong to steal, but the supplies are necessary for our survival. Clearly, I'm not the only one. Most of the towns are pretty picked over. Sometimes we go hungry, but so far we get enough to survive. Others haven't had such luck. We have passed through Hinckley, Pine City, Rock Creek, Rush City. We are staying in North Branch tonight. It is actually fortified and intact. The leaders of the caravan are trying to talk them in to coming with us. We are getting closer and closer to the Twin Cities. I hope it isn't as bad as I think it is.

August 22.
It is worse. It is more horrible than I could have imagined. Every bridge over the river was blown in an attempt to contain the infection. Even though we are skirting the city center, the devastation is evident. We have been forced to go around the city, and bridges have even been blown out on the outskirts, as well. We had to abandon many vehicles. The crowd is moving a little faster now, but I feel closer to the outside. I feel less protected. Lizzie clings to my side closer now. I can feel her fear. Tiger insists on riding on Roy's back. Encounters with infected have become more frequent, as we make our way around the city. Men with firearms have been coming through the crowd grabbing other able men to replace holes in the outer perimeter. My husband has been taken from me. I hope he is okay. My grip on composure is fading.

August 23.
I have become accustomed to the blast of rifles and shotguns. Yesterday a helicopter came swooping overhead. Its rotors were thunderously loud.

August 25.

We made it past the Twin Cities. It has been desolation for awhile now. Our supplies are starting to run low, and my kids are starting to complain about hunger. I try to console them, but it is hard to promise them anything. I still don't know where we are going. I don't know when we will get the chance to settle down. I've heard from people around me that we aren't going to stop again until Des Moines. But, for how long are we going to stop? How long are we going to keep going? Are we even going anywhere? I have to stay strong for my kids. I have to keep faith that we will make it. Maybe, our salvation is in Des Moines.

August 27.

We had to move very quickly today. I'm not sure what was happening, but there was a great sense of urgency. They even used some of the trucks to ferry people down the highway. What's the rush? They don't tell us. "Keep going, keep going, help is on the way," that's all they say.

[text missing]

September 22.

Thank God, Roy is alive. He's shaken up pretty bad, but he is still alive. We were passing by Ames, and we were hit by a wave of fast zombies. Roy was among the ones on the side where they struck. I don't know how long the infected remain in the fast phase. I can't help but think that these were people who had held out for months and months. Then, with the caravan just over the horizon, they got infected, and they came after us. Are we in for the same pitiful fate? Will we be devoured a few miles from sanctuary?

We made it to the NE side of Des Moines. We're camped on the middle of the interstate near a deserted amusement park. The kids stared at its skyline until darkness fell, but they never mentioned wanting to go. That's over for them now. My heart is breaking.

September 26.

For the first time in weeks we all ate our fill. On a hilltop, just east of the city, the military had prepared a safe place for us to stay. It had tents and clean water. There was even a shower. You couldn't stay in it for more than three minutes, but it was *heaven*. We also finally get the chance to rest. I never thought the taste of food and water could be so satisfying. My children are finally happy for once, and my husband smiled today. It was the first time I saw it since we left our house. They are taking good care of us.

September 27.

It was too good to be true. We are packing up again, heading south. People tell me that we're staying here because the leadership was waiting for something from the government. I'm very upset, and I'm not excited to hit the road again. I don't know when we will get to rest again, but I hope it will be soon. Fortunately, all of the tents are coming with us. They went on to a couple of horse-drawn wagons tended by some Mennonite-looking guys in blue shirts.

September 28.

Hopefully this isn't false hope. We have bunkered down in Indianola. We are camping near the perimeter around Simpson College. They did a lot better than St. Olaf. That place was a charnel house. Somehow, these people seem to have their act together.

8.5 Anne Howard, journal

The deteriorating situation at the college encouraged many long-time residents to at least contemplate joining the caravan.

I've remained locked down in Mary Berry since the perimeter collapsed and the swarm of refugees came in, some zombies tagging along with them. I've only ventured outside a few times, but I haven't seen anything of Carrie, Megan, or Michelle since that day. They may be alive…but it's probable that they are dead. I keep thinking about how I wouldn't mind dying. I'm just so exhausted. There's no rest anymore, even when I'm asleep. I keep having nightmares about crushed zombie heads, and I keep thinking of Kyle.

Kyle died from a blow to the head. It wasn't a fight with a zombie. It was a fight over drinking water. I thought that there was hope that he would live and he would wake up from the coma. He didn't. I'm not sure what he died from. A blood clot on the brain? Malnutrition? It's not like I could run a feeding tube into him.

We took Pfeiffer back, but they were in there for a couple of days so we don't know what food has been contaminated. No one wants to eat it. I don't want to find out that zombies like soybeans by being the first person to contract HIV-Z from tofu. Our food supply is running out…we can't stay here much longer.

A huge caravan of people arrived from the north, but they are not staying. They are not exactly friendly, but they know how to survive. They are well organized. It's hard to know how many of them there are. They formed up into a sort of circular defensive position in the old Hy-Vee parking lot, but they have patrols constantly going in and out, so it is difficult to make an accurate estimate.

They have outriders on some vehicles, horses, and they appear to be well armed. Some of their equipment even looks new. We've encountered smaller caravans coming through, asking for shelter, but never one close this size. They aren't asking for shelter either. A few of them came over to the wire to make trades. I managed to talk to a few of them, asking about their journey and how it is they have made it this far. Their stories are frightening, yet hopeful. One man I talked to told me the caravan found him just before his home was overrun by a horde of zombies. A woman I talked to said she barely escaped a zombie attack that killed her entire family, and wandered aimlessly until she stumbled upon the caravan.

One thing I heard more than once that really stuck out was about the caravan's encounters with farmers. I really didn't think anyone was left away from the perimeter, but they told me that fortified farmsteads are actually pretty common. Unlike city folks, who are usually very eager to join up with the caravan, most of the farmers prefer to stay in place. The farmers that came out of hiding spoke to the caravan leaders briefly, all of them obviously armed. The story was usually the same. They had hidden away any of their food and supplies and the caravan had no chance of finding them, so they might as well keep moving and don't try any funny business. So, the caravan left them all alone and moved on.

The refugees also told me about some of the homes and abandoned farms they had raided along the way. Most of the food was spoiled. All the gas has been siphoned off, and guns and ammo are long gone. From the sounds of things, there is not a lot left around here.

Despite this, they seem well equipped with at least twenty operable vehicles, which they use to bound ahead during the day. The vehicles clear the road ahead, remove roadblocks, and set up camp while everyone else follows on foot. One of the women said they needed to abandon a couple of vehicles in Des Moines for lack of fuel, but they still seem in much better shape than we are. The real jewel in the crown is a solar-powered water purification system mounted in the back of a pickup. I know what I grabbed when the zombies came down on me, and it didn't have anything to do with water filtration. At least someone in this group has his (or, more likely, her) head screwed on right.

Some of our people have decided to join them. I think I might go too. One of the stipulations for leaving with the caravan is that you must bring your own food supplies along with you. Given the rationing, I'm not sure that anyone has stored that up.

It seems like extortion, but at least instead of stealing, which it seems they could easily do, they are offering a peaceful solution. Of course, they might turn on us when we get ten miles down the road. They could slit our throats and take whatever we'd brought with us, but I guess that's a chance I'm willing to take. Jenna is convinced that they are cannibals. She thinks that's how they've survived. I knew *The Road* was a bad idea for the first-year reading assignment. They know what it takes to stay alive. I could be like them. I could be cold and hard. I can survive. I'm an expert at surviving. What is left for me here?

Leaving is a big risk, but staying is an even bigger one. I will admit that I feel a little guilty. It's like I'm abandoning Simpson, while others are choosing to stay. I found safety here, but the only option is to go. Simpson is broken. It's like a sick dog that should just be put out of its misery. There is no hope here anymore, no future, only death and destruction.

8.6 Nick Veneris, journal

The lower floor of Dunn Library was quickly overrun after the bus breached the perimeter, but the second floor was comparatively easy to defend. Only one open stairwell needed to be barricaded. The inhabitants contemplated abandoning the building, but when a series of zip-lines were installed connecting it with several of the neighboring buildings, the decision was made to hold the building – in part because the roof provided an outstanding observation and sniping platform.

September 14
After I busted my knee on the zipline, I decided to sit tight.
We always keep at least one shooter and two spotters up here at all times. We don't actually take many shots though. Ammunition is too sparse. Instead, we've gone medieval.

Zs are real suckers for bloodcurdling screams. The fast movers are a little cagy sometimes, but I have yet to see a slowboy who can resist a good scream. Falsetto is the best of the best. We've tried other techniques like whimpering, pleading for mercy, and frantic profanity, but the bloodcurdling scream is absolutely their favorite.

We play it like this:
1. Prepare some good, heavy piles of stuff on the north side of the roof. We've done this with everything that hasn't been nailed down, so by this point, we've started knocking loose bricks out of the walls.
2. Janet screams her head off from a second floor window.
3. Sly and the Family Z stagger over. They cannot resist her siren call.
4. Janet pulls her head in.
5. We drop whatever we've got on their heads.

Admittedly, we do not have many KIAs. Their heads get pulped up pretty good sometimes, but it is hard to hit a swaying target smack on with a brick, and that's what you need to do to crush the brain stem. The only one I ever got for sure was deeply, deeply gone: Its head just exploded like an overripe watermelon when my brick hit it. Still, it is satisfying and it gives us something to do. Unfortunately, the stench is almost overpowering.

September 17
Last night we saw a satellite breaking up in the upper atmosphere. In the dark of night it was magnificently bright. I guess if we have really gone medieval it would be a harbinger of doom like a comet. Maybe that's the right way to see it. Are satellites falling because no one is tending them?

September 22
Apparently, some giant refugee caravan is heading towards us. I'm glad that there are more survivors, but I'm concerned about what they want.

September 23
Burke and his cannibal fascists made a play for Mary Berry at dawn today. I guess he wants his office back. I think it was supposed to be an inside job, but something went wrong and the barricades were still up when he and his fireteam got there.

The people in Mary Berry started yelling at him to go away. Naturally, this attracted some Zs and infuriated the separatists. They noisily tore apart the barricade and got inside. I had plenty of clean shots while they were ripping it apart, but I didn't take them. Killing another human being … I just don't think I can do that. The infected are different – they aren't really human any more. Not really.

It was hard to tell exactly what was happening. Someone in Kresge started taking shots, but it looked to me like he was aiming for zombies. That's not how Burke's crew took it. They started firing on Kresge and on us. That lasted for a minute or two and then they got inside.

I'm not sure exactly what happened during the next five or six minutes because I was keeping my head below the parapet. I didn't want some trigger-happy westie to blow it off because he thought I was shooting at his Dear Leader.

The Zs were really piling up when I snuck a peek. There were more than I'd seen in months. They were jammed up at the door. I don't know what happened inside the building; there was plenty of screaming and hollering, but there was no gunfire. I know they have internal barricades in the stairwells. They probably deployed those, but they were designed with zombies in mind, so Burke's men would probably be able to take them down. However, their ability to do so would probably be hampered by the mob of Zs closing in behind them.

Two guys were holding the door with maces or something. The pile of bodies was getting big. They were gradually being forced inside. We took a few shots at the crowd of Zs. Someone in Kresge started shooting again too.

Then something happened. The defense just collapsed. It was like water going down a drain. The zombies just poured in. I saw Becca in a window on the third floor. She was shouting something to us, but I couldn't understand it over all the noise.

Then I saw Burke jump out of a second floor window on the east side. He landed wrong. Most of the Zs had gone inside by now, so he started to drag himself, but then some slow boys noticed him. He knew he'd been spotted so he drew a nice silver-plated .45.

He was a careful shooter; I'll give him that: headshot each time. But, then he was out.

A slider was coming after him. No working legs, just pulling itself along with its spindly little arms. It must have a busted spine or something. They had a grotesque little race, pulling themselves along the ground.

When the slider got close, Burke kicked him repeatedly in the head with his left leg. Clearly he was in pain, but he kept hammering the head with his boot until the slider lay still. If this was situation normal, he might have gotten away.

It wasn't. Two fastboys rounded the corner on him. They were late for the party, but they hadn't missed out completely. They pounced on him more or less simultaneously. Sid and I just watched. We watched his arms and legs flailing around. Then we watched a couple of slowboys moseying over for a chance at the leftovers.

I'm not sure where this leaves my sense of the sanctity of human life, but I do not regret what happened to him.

September 25
Our people in the top floors of Mary Berry evaced today. They were not sure what happened to Burke's people. They knew a few of them were dead, but the rest of them may have gotten out. They didn't hang about to look for clues.

September 27
We evacuated Dunn and moved to the chapel this afternoon. It was easier than I thought it would be. The other buildings knew we were going to make a dash. Sid and Lon supported me since I couldn't even hobble well. We got across without even seeing a Z. I'm a good shot, so I asked to be posted in the belltower. It has a 360 panorama and is a fairly small area, so it is ideal for me.

September 28
When the decision was made for most of our population to join the caravan, the tower had more people in it than usual. Some people were there on overwatch, but others just came up to gawk. It was like a parade. We hadn't seen that many people doing something together for a long time, and we honestly didn't know if we would ever see it again. It was a strange mix of magnificent and pathetic.

I'd volunteered to stay behind. I didn't do so out of heroism or anything. My busted knee just means that I need to be pretty much immobile. Taking up vehicle space didn't seem right when there are kids. Also, I feel pretty good about holding the belltower. We've got plenty of supplies – enough for weeks. I can't imagine Z getting up here. The only way would be if they climbed on top of one another's bodies and that would take thousands. Would it take tens of thousands? How many of them are coming again?

The rear elements of the caravan pulled out this morning. One guy on the back of a jeep snapped me a salute as his vehicle pulled out on to 65/69. I just watched him go. Sid sort of waved nonchalantly.

8.7 Photograph of Zac Bartels

Many of the "handmades" wielded by Simpson students in the early fall were fashioned in the theater department shops. Here a c-clamp mace is used to good effect.

8.8 Angela Bartonini, journal

Many college residents were enticed by the caravan and the promise of escape. By moving quickly, and looting college resources, the teachers from the campus elementary school were able to join the caravan with all of their charges. It is unclear from the entry if all of the children were orphaned, but by this point it was likely. After the chaos of the previous month, most families pulled their children out of the school for reasons of safety.

Since the perimeter breach, thirty kids, three teachers (including me), and two shooters have been holed up in the Art Building. There's not much room in here, but we're all doing alright. We have run short on food, however, just like everyone else. The kids cry and whine, they complain that their stomachs hurt from lack of food. I tell them they will be alright, but I know that we can't stay here much longer. They've been running food over to us from Mary Berry ever couple days, but they don't give us enough to begin with, so we have trouble rationing it out.

Food days are getting farther and farther apart since Pfeiffer fell. We don't know what food was contaminated and what wasn't, or if any food was contaminated at all. I don't think anyone's willing to find that out the hard way, though. I heard Wolf and his separatists have solved their supply problems with cannibalism. I know they've already eaten the dogs over there.

The other students in here were talking about their favorite professors last night. Delores saw what she swore was a zombified Mark Green yesterday. It shuffled around until a student took him out with a shotgun blast from the second story of Mary Berry.

It was food day. The kids were all anxious to get a good meal, which we allowed them on the day we got food delivered. We rationed every other meal, but we thought it best to keep them feeling positive and looking forward to the day they got to "pig out." Chase Miller's 16-year-old sister, Carrie, delivered us our food. He was a friend before all this started. Well, more than that I guess: a friend with benefits. He'd been bitten during fight to seal the breach. She'd ended up having to kill him. When I found out about Chase's death, I cried like a baby. I didn't think I had the tears in me anymore. I'd known plenty of others who had been killed, and a few people who had been killed the way Chase was. I don't know what it was this time, but the tears just started spilling out of me. Nikki Snyder drew a picture of a smiling sun to try to cheer me up.

A few days later she was back and she was excited. She told us about the approaching caravan. The teachers all immediately agreed that we should go, but then Carrie told us about the toll. We had to bring our own food. What about the kids? Them too. Gloom.

But Carrie had a plan. It was a desperate plan, but it was our only chance. The Governing Council had never really been reconstructed, and every building was kind of on its own. I wasn't sure what the situation was in Pfeiffer, but we needed to find out, and we needed to find out fast.

Delores grabbed her baseball bat and made her way up to the window Carrie had come in. They dropped the fire ladder and took off toward the grain stores while I started rounding up the kids. I was nervous, but I didn't want to show it, so I tried to channel it into excitement. I think I actually said, "We're going on a field trip!"

I was finishing up preparing the kids when Delores and Carrie returned with backpacks bulging full of dried soybeans. Both were tired, but satisfied and ready to get out. Carrie told us that we should get moving as soon as possible. She didn't know how much longer the caravan was going to be around before it headed south and she'd heard some rumors that more zombies were one the way. They made three more trips back and forth to Pfeiffer.

We needed to keep the kids together as a cluster and move as one unit. There would be people on all sides to protect the kids. The shooters were named Dustin and Wayne. Even though we'd been living in the same building it was kind of hard to tell them apart. They both had the same weary and dazed expressions and underneath their baseball caps. I thought they might try to exert their male authority or something, but they didn't. They never questioned the plan. Maybe they should have, but they didn't.

The children were scared, excited, nervous. Too many of them had seen their parents die. They had nightmares about the zombies eating their families. Now they had to face their fears in order to survive. Delores told them to take a deep breath and grab the hand of the person next to them. We were going to go in a daisy chain. She told them we needed to stick together, as close together as we possibly could. We could protect them better that way. Carrie looked to all of us. It was time to go. Delores smiled, looked at us and whispered, "Let's get the kids out of here. Let's get those motherfuckers!" We all smiled at her enthusiasm.

We slipped out of the building and the kids were totally silent. Somehow, we made it all the way across campus without incident. Carrie had found a place where someone had snipped the wire. We let ourselves out and made our way to the caravan's encampment.

They were already getting ready to leave. We weren't the only people from inside the perimeter who had decided to join up. The two armed men who screened us raised their eyebrows when they saw the Ziploc bags full of soya in each of the students' backpacks, but they didn't say anything about it. They just made checks on a manifest and led us over to a tent for physical examinations. I was so happy, I didn't actually mind the strip-search and delousing spray. The kids had to keep their clothes, but they gave us clean BDUs. Susie Parker thought it was funny, and started calling me "Sergeant Bartonini." We were assigned a cohort captain and a place in the column. They even found a place in a bus for the smallest kids. Everyone was exhausted but elated. Most of the kids were able to grab six or seven hours of sleep, but I was wide-awake the whole night through. Every rustle set me on edge.

It was a few hours before the caravan started moving. We all marveled at the sheer size of the group. We set out at first light of dawn. I hoped that the people inside the perimeter would get out while they still could. The last thing I remember about Indianola is the way it looked as we were driving away. We knew that in what was probably hours rather than days, the whole city would be flattened, and the only thing left would be our memories of the place that had kept us safe for so long.

You know the world has changed when taking thirty children on a walking tour of southern Iowa with nothing to eat but potentially poisoned soybeans fills your heart with joy.

Chapter 9: OCTOBER

9.1 Wesley Smyth, sermon

These notes were recovered from the basement of the Simpson College Chapel. Apparently Smythe was working on this sermon when the remaining survivors converged on the Chapel.

Chapel Reflection Notes
Chaplain Wesley Smyth
Preaching Text: John 20: 19 – 23

When it was evening on that day, the first day of the week (Sunday, Jesus died the previous Friday), and the doors of the house where the disciples had met were locked out of fear, Jesus came and stood among them and said: "Peace be with you." After he said this he showed them his hands and his side. Then his disciples rejoiced when they saw the Lord. Jesus said to them again, "Peace be with you. As the Father has sent me, so I send you." When he had said this, be breathed on them and said to them, "Receive the Holy Spirit. If you forgive the sins of any, they are forgiven them; if you retain the sins of any, they are retained."

My, what a rich text for us at this time! We need it now.

We are huddled in the face of this onslaught of foul viciousness.
Where did they come from – oh, I know about the biology of the disease by now. But my soul cries out in such anguish, my heart with such emptiness . . . .
We've lost so many and there doesn't look to be a sunrise on the horizon.
Did we deserve such a fate God?
This must be something like the feeling in that locked room where the disciples huddled.

They spent three years following, only to have it taken away in a week.

It was too quick, the time with Jesus too short. Like the time we have spent here on this earth with this zombie infestation, which has taken our families, our friends.

What's left? They must have been asking.
Where do we go from here?
Their question . . . our question.

Maybe I'll get the speakers cranked up and start with a couple of U2 songs.
There should still be enough juice in the batteries for that.

I'll start with *Walk On*.

The place we are "packin' for" is the place where the *Streets Have No Name*.
That's how I'll end the sermon.

We need some rock to fire us up,
Gets some energy going in this room, in this time of darkness and locked doors.

We are standing together in this darkness.
It is striking to me that the disciples only recognize Jesus after he shows them his scars.

What is the significance of having a scarred savior?
He continues to bear the marks of the cross, even in the resurrection.
Is everything supposed to be perfect in the resurrection time?
It is as though God's embrace has taken death in
And even God is scarred.
The God who rained down fire and brimstone at Sodom and Gomorrah
Has somehow shifted reality to take death in,
To be scarred by death itself.

Now this is interesting to me, possibly to all of us
In the face of the zombies and their living death
To have God so engaged.
Hope is restored

Next strong image: breath.
Do the zombies continue to breathe? Do they have breath?
Certainly not in the way we do.
THEIR BREATH SMELLS OF DEATH!

Jesus sends the Holy Spirit on his followers,
As breath, as Jesus himself has been sent. We continue to breathe and to
share this living breath.
Grants us the ability to talk and love one another. We breathing folk can
make choices about and for one another. It is this choice for life that the
resurrection holds out for us.

It is this breath which allows us to face what is coming.
That which was present at the time of creation
In Hebrew *ruah* – breath – that is what was present and hovering over the
chaos.

It is in that breath, that Spirit, that creation occurs.

How ironic, how wondrous
That Jesus breathes the Spirit upon us
This resurrection wind blows power and fullness
The resurrection wind blows us to the place
Where the streets have no name
Where all the colors bleed into one
You know, I believe it!!!
Hope in our future. Hope *is* our future.

9.2 Joseph Turner, note

Many of the inhabitants of the perimeter did not understand every dimension of Operation Hawkeye. The vast majority clearly understood that the caravan was moving south, but it appears that most did not know the caravan was towing a massive horde of zombies in its wake. Certainly, some volunteered to remain on campus to ensure the proper functioning of the ZED, but others were surprised when the deluge began. Most of them died, but a handful survived. It is easy to cast them as heroes, but the following account by Joseph Turner surely proves that they were not.

How can I continue without you? How can I pull myself through, day after day, alone? It's like a part of me has been missing since that day. I miss you Courtney. How am I supposed to live with myself after everything that has happened? I can't. No one knows the truth. No one knows what really happened that day. What we did. How we betrayed so that we could survive. How could we do that to them? Why didn't we just help them? They could have made it too Courtney.

We were fine. We only had to get to the chapel from Kresge. We met two other people on the first floor who decided to go with us. They were trying to decide whether to stay or run.

We left from the door closest to Pfieffer, but before we exited, we propped open the door on the western side of the building. If any Zs were lurking we wanted them to go in the building instead of after us. There were probably ten people still in Kresge. If they were staying, they were dead anyway. I justified it this way: if they died a little sooner and it helped us escape, their deaths would not be in vain.

We were cautious; there were groups of zombies already roaming the grounds inside the perimeter. We went around the north side of Dunn and almost made it to Wallace, but then they spotted us. A small group, maybe ten, but they were pretty fast. They were just rounding the corner of Barker. They say that the Zs don't have enough brain function to coordinate their actions, but I swear to God, this was a pack. They saw us and began sprinting toward us.

We both had the same thought. We couldn't outrun these monsters; we had to distract them long enough for us to get to Chapel. Our eyes met and I knew that we had the same terrible plan. . . Almost immediately we both did it. We swung our bats at the same instant, me breaking the girl's leg, Courtney breaking the guy's. They both fell to the ground in pain and surprise. Then we were ran.
How could did we do that, Courtney?

When we got to the Chapel I saw about thirty people on the steps, and it was set up for defense. It was a fortress, but when we looked out at the advancing sea of zombies, we knew that we had to get out. A pickup came crashing across the quad. It plowed through at least a half dozen of the infected. It was some west campus people. They were heading south. They wanted to catch up to the caravan. Suddenly, in the face of the horde, we were friends again. We leapt over the barricades and jumped on board. Three other people came with us. There wasn't much room on the truck, but we all held on while the diver accelerated and smashed through the fence. The impact threw one person out. I'm not sure if the driver noticed, but we didn't stop. The fallen man had the wind knocked out of him. He started to get up when he was swarmed by five or six fast ones.

We headed toward the square and the courthouse. The driver swerved to hit Zs along the way. One of the ones that slipped under the vehicle must have been dragged up into a wheel well or something. I'm not sure what did it, but the driver started to lose control. Then he overcorrected and we fell out of the bed, and dropped down into the street.

The truck righted itself and drove on. I was banged up, but nothing was broken. You jumped up too.

The street leading to the square was swarming with those moaning, flesh-eating, mindless monsters. We worked as a team. We had each other's back, just like we had since the beginning of all this. As we were fighting we saw a little single cab, two seat, truck parked along the street. We made a run for it. I made it to the driver's side door and jumped in. That's when I heard the pounding on the passenger's door. I looked over to see you beating on the door with a look of panic and fear on your face. I could see them coming for you, five of them sprinting from the alley. I lunged for the manual lock, trying to reach it before they reached you. As my hands, slippery with blood and entrails, fumbled with the button I watched and screamed. They overwhelmed you, tearing, ripping, and mauling you. If I hesitated I would have been lost; I opened the door and I ran.

They were shooting zombies from the courthouse steps. They saved me. They shot every Z that was focused on me instead of you. I'm not sure what happened next.

I never realized it, but I'd taken a heavy blow to the head when we tumbled out of the truck. Apparently, I lost consciousness, and two men dragged me to safety. One of them was killed. He gave his life for me. The bombing happened without me even realizing it. The first thing I remember is seeing dust dancing in a sunbeam. I was in a strange room. I wanted to be with you.

I went back to find your body, but there was nothing left: Just the charred shell of the truck. Everything had been destroyed.

I crippled an innocent girl and her boyfriend, and left them to the most agonizing death imaginable, so we could escape. They didn't deserve that. What gave us the right to swing the bat? What made them less valuable than us? Nothing. I convinced you to endanger a whole building full of people we once considered our closest friends. I don't deserve to be here, to be alive. I couldn't even protect you after we committed those murders. It's my fault you died. I should have died with you there that day. Instead I ran. I ran to safety and left you behind.

9.3 Adam Floyd, audio recording

When the zombie horde arrived on the north side of campus, many fled for the perceived safety of the chapel. Most of those in SAE apparently stayed in place. Others attempted to find shelter in various places throughout campus.

TESSA: -ot that thing!

ADAM: Too late, already on.

TESSA: Why do you bother carrying that around?

ADAM: Making a mark, you know? So people know our story.

TESSA: Know *our story*? It's the end of the world and we're trapped up in the theater light booth. I don't really imagine that is material for the epic poetry of the future.

ADAM: The *Zombiead?*

TESSA: Yes, very good. The *Zombiead.* Well done. Your liberal arts education is really showing.

ADAM: Well, I *did* read the Sparknotes.

TESSA: I was thinking more along the lines of Spencer's *Faerie Queen*, but that'll do pig.

ADAM: Hey, it was your idea to hide in the theater.

TESSA: Yeah...well I knew it would be safe.

ADAM: Failing to realize that once we're up here there's no way down. Thus making us totally trapped.

TESSA: I don't think clearly when things are trying to eat me!

ADAM: Did you grab the rolling papers?

TESSA: Hmm...?

ADAM: The Zig Zags. I really need to smoke a joint.

TESSA: [coldly] No. I did not grab the rolling papers. Nor did I grab *the bong* or *the stash*. I did not do these things because we ran out of pot in late May.

ADAM: Hm. Right, right. Late May. Right.

TESSA: I know I'm supposed to be terrified and everything, but I'm actually kind of bored. I wish there was something we could do.

ADAM: What would we do? There's no way out, there are zombies everywhere, and we've got no supplies. We'll just have to wait.

TESSA: Wait? Wait for what? The cavalry? Gandalf? It's still just so stupid...zombies. If it was vampires, at least we'd have a shot at eternal life.

ADAM: So...what do we do while we wait to starve to death?

TESSA: Well, I could show you my belly dancing routine...or play "I Never."

[Loud crash.]

ADAM: Shit! They've broken the windows in the lobby, they're coming in.

TESSA: Can they reach us up here?

ADAM: No chance.

[Distant moaning]

TESSA: Wanna throw stuff?

ADAM: ...What kind of question is that? Of *course* I do!

9.4 Photograph of Erin Larson and Ben Murga

By fall, most of Simpson's defenders relied on melee weapons.

9.5 Dietrich Motter, journal

Many of the people who remained on campus after the caravan moved south were not fully aware of the size of the approaching zombie horde. Some estimate it numbered close to 100,000. The defenders of the chapel were the exception. As the protectors of the ZED device, they had been fully briefed on the peculiarities of its operation.

The advance guard of the horde arrived on the highway about ten minutes after the caravan rearguard pulled out. They were all shamblers and they looked hungry. Even though it was at extended range, we followed the plan and took a couple of shots at the ones in the lead – enough for them to zero in on the source of the sound. Not all of them took the bait, so Sid started banging the bells with a mallet. That did not work very well either (although it did give me a headache and an unpleasant Disney flashback), so we spent a few more rounds trying to get their attention. We got some hits, but no killshots.

Everyone was ready below when they hit the campus. There was some gunfire on the north side, but most everyone on the chapel steps was a pro with handmades by now. Still, that was all too quiet to attract much attention. We needed Z to come to us. The buildings also blocked and reflected a lot of the sound, so we had to keep firing. We'd gotten additional ammo from some guys in the caravan when they got ready to pull out. They dropped it off a few minutes before they pulled out. From up in the belltower the sound echoed all over the north side of town.

Sid radioed the caravan on the two-way to let them know that the advance guard of the horde had arrived early. About fifteen minutes later, one of their SUVs came tearing back into town and went north. I'm not sure what they were trying to do – attract attention, I guess.

234

By this point there were hundreds of them. More than I've ever seen. The first ones had appeared on the highway, but then they started filtering down the streets and yards. I've seen a lot of Z in one place before – I was in the fight to retake the cafeteria and that was *a lot* of zombies – but this was truly awe-inspiring. Soon there were thousands of them. Maybe there were tens of thousands. The tower started feeling insufficiently high, but I hit the switch and the ZED hummed to life.

9.6 Paul Dule, journal

Irrepressible and cocksure, Paul Dule survived infection, medical testing, and the perimeter collapse. Somehow, he also survived the final stages of Operation Hawkeye.

I don't know how it happened. It really can't be possible. But fuck a duck, here I am! It's been a while since I've had a chance to jot anything down. First of all, I thought I was a walking corpse after my building superintendant caught me. Damn wound started bleeding and I didn't even catch it until Bryan's eyes lit up like a priest spotting a copy of *Hustler*. They treated me like some dumb animal! For all they knew I had tetanus.

During my delightful stay at motel hell, some power hungry rednecks decided that the wheels of the perimeter needed a fixin'. Well *git er done,* hicks! Their little coup de tat was appealing to me at first. The medical staff was so bamboozled they couldn't distinguish a cold sore from a decapitated moron. I figured I might have been able to escape, but things just became worse. The new doctrine announced by the "rebels" was a zero-tolerance policy. I would be killed immediately as a "tangible threat to the safety of the community." Fuck that!

This was starting to look really shitty, but one morning while I was having a bit of a tug, a ton of commotion came from somewhere outside. Everyone was running around and screaming. I used the opportunity to check out from the worst free clinic in the world. I exited the building to find people running in a single direction like an opening of *Mal*mart on Black Friday. I ran in the opposite direction only to find that the humans were being outnumbered by zombies. I figured that I may not turn into a zombie, but the last thing I need is to have my head ripped off by an infected jackass. I quickly ducked into Kresge, which happened to be the closest building.

I hung out there for the rest of my time at Simpson. Given that the perimeter was fucked and we had no power, life was pretty fun. The only issue was that my notebook was still in my room in Picken and those cowards in Kresge wouldn't even let me open the door. This was fun for a couple of days, until I started having trouble making the lies work. Refugees had run in when the perimeter went down and they'd popped up in the building. Everyone who wasn't a resident had to be screened. I didn't think "zombie bite ward veteran" was going to impress anyone, so I went into the bathroom on the second floor and jumped out the window.

I scurried to get away, thinking that I would never get to write my expose on this cluster fuck, but I survived. I got away with only a sore ankle which, by the way, still feels like shit today.
I decided to avoid the main part of campus because of the infected activity and took a walk through the park. I figured I would go to the part of town that had the least humans. I was taken aback by the school bus that decided to redecorate our perimeter. It looked nice. It looked so nice that I decided to spend the night in it, but the sounds of zombies wandering around is just not conducive to a good night's rest, so I made my way toward my old dorm.

When I finally made it, I freaked out. The bastards I had been living with for these long and hellish months had barricaded the doors and vestibules. Good news for me, one of the barricades fell. I guess that's karma. I snuck in and was able to get to my room without seeing any infected people. Actually, I didn't see *anyone,* but one thing's for sure: bodies and blood were not in short supply. I cleaned up my room and started looking in the other rooms for supplies. The place had been deserted in a hurry, and I ate pretty well off of everything that had been left behind. I had no idea Janice had a cache of Snickers bars. That bitch was holding out on me. *Me!* Number One on her fornication license.

I just bunkered down. Looking for help wouldn't do any good. They'd probably just put me down. Then, to my eternal delight, my wound started healing. Mom, Dad, I don't thank you for much, since you are crappy parents, but your genetic material – *it rocks!*

I woke up to the damn church bells ringing. I decided to see what was going on, so I peeked out the window and WTF? It was the whole zombie army -- thousands of them, slouching along, moaning and such as they usually do.

It was time to move my ass, and within ten seconds of leaving the building I should have been dead. I almost plowed straight into a big, fat Z. He barely even acknowledged my existence; he just kept keeping on.

That's when it hit me: I had been bitten, but I was immune, and now they must read me like a zombie. I must *smell* like a zombie or something. I didn't jump up and shout *Eureka!* or anything. Since singing and dancing were not a regular part of the zombie repertoire I didn't launch into the Hallelujah chorus. If they thought I was a zombie, I would act like a zombie.

This group was massive. There had to be millions of walking pusbags extending to my right and left as far as the eye could see. I noticed groups of people from the fraternities trying to make their way east. They were pretty gunned up and had a couple of vehicles.

I wondered if zombies were the only ones who thought I was living dead.

I ducked into the doorway of the Art Building. It was real chaos. The frat boys were cutting to the south, so I decided to go due east – toward old motel hell. I walked out the other side of the music building and followed the street south. I watched someone get torn limb from limb, crying out for help. One guy I walked up to was reaching for me as his intestines were being unraveled like an extension cord. You know, I never realized just how long that shit is.

There was gunfire, but it was sporadic. I guess the ammo was running out. Epic, you know. I kept out of the line of fire and kept moving south, towards the courthouse. Then, when there was a lull, I waved to one of the shooters on the roof.

I casually walked into the fortress of solitude, ignoring the dumbfounded look on their faces. They closed up the doors when it became clear that no one else would be coming. Then they gave me the most thorough fucking physical examination of my life. I didn't have time to spin a yarn about the bite marks. The important thing to them was that they weren't fresh.

Then we sealed ourselves in the bomb shelter. We only had to wait about five minutes before the bombing started. It went on for about ten minutes. The ground just kept shuddering. No one said anything; we just watched the dust jump in the beam of the crank flashlight.

9.7 Mitchell Kramer, interview

This interview with Mitchell "Dragon" Kramer was conducted in a sparsely furnished, partially padded room intended for both his, and others', protection. While not violent, his tenuous grasp of reality makes him a possible danger. He is friendly enough, but seems very distracted and restless.

Hello Mitch-
   Dragon, please. It's what everyone calls me now.

Certainly. How are you today?
   I could be better. I'm waiting for assignment to a new op. I'm hoping for long-distance recon.

So, after all that you've been through, you are ready to go back into combat?
Lady, I was *born* ready.

Let's pick up where we left off last time. What can you tell me about the day of the bombing? Where were you when the horde arrived?
   I was getting pent-up from lack of action. I just wanted something to happen. I considered going with the caravan, but ever since the perimeter fell, zombies regularly appeared on my doorstep. You just can't beat that kind of convenience.
   Anyway, after the caravan pulled out, a guy started running around the building screaming that we're all going to die. He kept going on and on about how a huge zombie horde was approaching and that we needed to get away because the military was going to bomb the Zs.
   Bomb the Zs? With what? Kites? I discounted the military part, but what he said about zombies caught my ear. "Huge zombie horde" was enticing. It could help me up my numbers. I wondered what the world record for kills was. I mean individual kills, of course, not cheating with grenades or bombs or anything. [Parenthetically] Blowing Hoover Dam

239

was pretty cool, I guess. Tens of thousands of Zs carried away by a wall of water and dumped in the ocean – I bet it was spectacular and everything, but how much of a rush did the guy who pushed the plunger actually get from doing that?

How did other people react?
At first they weren't too eager to go outside, but more and more people started saying that we needed to get out. I didn't care, really, but I guess some of them panicked and bolted, but they left a door open in the downstairs. This settled the decision. I was sniping out the window with my last few rounds for the Mosin-Nagant when Kyle Munson, who (for a journalist) was a really nice guy, got his ear bitten off by a zombie that just wandered in out of the hall.

I killed them both pretty quick and cleared the hallway. (If you are infected in a combat zone, you are a good, clean kill. The percentage chance for immunity is too low. If you're bit, you get hit). Anyway, people were yelling and such, but they still armed themselves with whatever was available. They got whatever armor or covering on they could.

I was good to go, of course. I don't make it a habit of *not* being ready to kill zombies. I had Baby, my trusty old katana, oiled and ready to slice at a moment's notice. My rifle was slung on my back along with my go-bag; my Glock was holstered, and I had another Beretta 9mm in the back of my belt; I found it on a dead guy a couple of weeks ago. I'd also gotten a sturdy twelve gauge off one of the dead guy's friends: good for close quarters. For protection I had the biker's jacket I'd picked up from *another* dead guy, complete with gloves that had superb grip. My sunglasses had polycarbonate lenses to keep them from shattering and fogging up; the wraparound plastic frame gave me complete eye protection. In a melee, blood had a nasty habit of getting in your eyes and turning you; the same goes for the mouth, which is why my double layered bandana was tied tightly around my face.

They would have to eat me alive; I wasn't going to end up as one of them. I was one of the first people ready, so I went to the window over the south entrance. I fired five carefully aimed shots at the closest zombies to the door. I took my time, ensuring a kill. By the time I was done most of the people who were going to leave were ready.

As I got ready to run down the stairs, I stared sadly at my Mosin-Nagant. It was a trustworthy weapon, but some sacrifices would have to be made. At this point, getting more ammo for it was a futile dream, so I gently laid it on the floor and wished it well.

What was your plan?

We came out the door in sort of a flying wedge. Almost all the ammunition was gone by this point, so we needed to use our hand-to-hand weapons. We opened the door and ran outside, trying to fan out as quickly as possible. I don't know how many of us were leaving, probably at least fifteen. They saw us and started heading our way.

Naturally, I took point. I used my shotgun to force a path through them, but we hadn't gotten more than twenty meters before I ran out of shells.

In order to get across campus to the fortifications in the chapel, I had a simple strategy in mind. It was all well and good to kill zombies, but when fighting a bajillion of them, it would take too long to finish them off. The others would take you down while you issued the *coup de grace*. This meant I had to settle for mostly crippling blows. I went for arms and legs especially. Baby was sharp enough to get through bone if I used enough strength and hit it at the right angle. I'd practiced extensively, of course.

I know what you're thinking: "But Dragon, that goes against your kill-them-all rule." I'd struggled with that myself, but came to the conclusion that a severed limb *is* a kill, eventually, okay? Even on zombies. No one can argue with that logic. Sure they bleed out slower, but they still *die*. Also, I was going for *lifetime* kills. If I went out in a blaze of glory there was probably some guy in Botswana who would eventually eclipse me by racking up a few every week.

So we charged them like that, with a big mass of people. I knew there were other groups trying to get to the chapel, or just trying to get *away*, but it was pointless to combine into a big group. All the zombies would go for us and there would be less chance for one of the groups to make it. So we hit them hard and fast.

The first one I hit with the katana was an old, rotting shambler. I'm not even sure he had functioning eyes left. Poor guy was homing in on me with his sniffer, so he didn't know what hit him. I took most of his left leg off and swept by him, already chopping at another zombie's shoulder. She moved right before the hit, so a lot of the impact force ran back up my arm and numbed it slightly, and she didn't get as hurt as I'd have liked. She was about to go straight for my face with her teeth, but one of the guys behind chose that moment to slam a golf club—God knows where he found it—right into her pretty face. Blood flew everywhere, it was awesome. She'd probably just turned S4.

For a while we were just cutting through them like that, one guy's trouble getting bailed out by someone else, sticking in a big group. Then we saw that the chapel was *not* where we wanted to go. Zombies were literally crawling over each other to get in there. I saw some people up in the bell tower, but I couldn't tell if the doors were holding.

I'll give credit where it is due – someone else came up with the idea of heading to the courthouse. I'd never been a fan of those guys, but the building was a real fortress. We kept going south.

The zombies were getting thicker by the second, and they didn't ignore us exactly, but for most of them, eating our brains seemed to be a lower priority than getting to the chapel.

Then three or four runners decided to hit us in the back. They must have been really well fed, because when I turned around, one of ours was trying to hold his throat together, while another was sprawled on the ground, but the runners were already lunging for others. This collapsed our wedge.

I saw our people just get swept up from all sides once our back lines broke. I used up most of my pistol ammunition, but the damage was done. Our forward momentum was stopped, and we'd lost almost a third of our group.

They faltered, but I kept yelling that we had to move through the ones ahead of us so fast that those behind couldn't follow in time. It was our only shot. The street was practically packed with them now, but I could see the courthouse over the top of them all. I could even see some figures moving around on top of it.

Then, a shambler hit me from the side. Its arms smacked into my left wrist so hard that I could hear the snap of breaking bone, even in all that chaos. The Glock flew out of my hand, and I swung desperately with the katana one-handed. I took the thing right in the skull with the flat of the blade; it busted its cheekbone, but that didn't slow it down much.

Someone busted the back of its head with a baseball bat. I don't know who it was because the impact blew about a gallon of black crap out of its mouth and nose on to my face. It was probably the girl – what was her name? Clementine? I pulled off the shades as I got to my feet. Four other people were left behind me, and we started fighting back to back. We were all scared, but both the girls had fierce looks on their faces. Just like Dana.

How did you survive?

Born lucky, I guess. Sometimes the odds just swing your way.

We were standing there resigned to die when all of a sudden we heard screeching tires and a truck came flying down one of the side streets, plowing straight through half the shamblers in our path. We suddenly had a pretty big corridor to run down.

I remember smiling, because the game was back on. The others followed close behind and covering my back. Our second chance had revitalized me. My wrist didn't hurt so much. My sword arm wasn't as tired as it had been. We practically flew through them; Baby was slick with dark zombie blood.

What happened to your companions?

The first one, Mike, was tripped up by a crawler. It had been smashed up by the truck, but it could still grab. It hooked his ankle and he went down. Clementine smashed a baseball bat into the thing's head, but it was too late. The zombies surged over the guy. More took her from the back. They piled up on them like some kind of blood-drenched NFL defensive line.

The other girl and I got to the nearest door. There was a barricade so we could not get in, but at least it covered our backs. She handed me a 9mm and took a two-handed stance with her steel pipe.

One zombie got close: BANG.

The next pushed past his corpse: BANG.

Two stumbled over the bodies: BANG BANG.

It was impossible to miss. Not that I would have anyway, you understand.

I fired like that, a steady BANG, BANG, BANG, until the gun clicked empty. I heard some movement behind us. They were trying to open the doors for us. I flailed around with Baby one-handed, but it didn't do much. My arm was just about to drop from such overuse.

The girl was keeping them off, and we were side-by-side when one of the shamblers she hit with the pipe grabbed at it and her arm. She had misjudged the angle, much like I had earlier. It grabbed her before she could swing back, and it clamped down on her wrist. It got some exposed skin between her gloves and her jacket.

She screamed with rage, and head-butted it – *head-butted it* – right on the top of its skull. It stumbled back. She looked at me with resignation in her eyes. I'd seen the look before.

She charged into the shamblers and started flailing wildly with her pipe. Hands grabbed my shoulders and pulled me inside. The door slammed shut, and few seconds later the whole world shook. The building seemed to be coming apart. Some rubble fell. I'm not sure if I got clocked in the head or if I passed out from lack of oxygen or something, but I passed out.

In seven months I'd tagged 1,108 infected. If it was time to die, I could die happy.

Thank you very much for sharing your experience.

Yeah, no problem. Just get the word out about my stats, huh? I feel like I deserve a little recognition, here. And don't let people forget about the girl who helped me, or the others who died. They would have been great fighters, with enough time and training. They deserve to be remembered for that.

Is there anything else you'd like to add?

No. I think that's about it.

Two weeks after this interview, Mitchell Kramer was inserted into the Dallas-Fort Worth area as part of a long-distance reconnaissance mission.

9.8 USAF, Operation Hawkeye Bombing Survey

Drawing upon some of its last reserves of aviation fuel, the Air Force used four F-16s from the Iowa Air Guard to execute the attack on the horde that had been gathered by the convergence of Task Forces Alpha, Bravo, and Charlie. Further concentrated by the ZED, which was housed in the bell tower of the chapel, the horde represented roughly 40% of the infected in the Upper Midwest between the Missouri and Mississippi Rivers.

Infrastructure damage: All wooden buildings within 1 km of ground zero have been destroyed. Stone, masonry, and concrete buildings sustained massive damage. Those that remain standing are no longer structurally sound. Rubble and debris are scattered throughout the area of the strike. Infected may be concealed throughout the killbox. US Highway 65/69 appears relatively undamaged. Much of the road surface is covered with debris, but there is no visible cratering.

Casualties: The estimated size of the horde varies significantly, from 100,000-150,000. A great deal of uncertainty remains about this figure. Satellite imagery is being processed to determine a more accurate count of horde strength, but tree cover prevents reliable visual estimates and various other factors make infrared sensing unreliable. An estimated 2000-4000 of the infected remained active immediately after the strike. The vast majority of these apparently sustained severe injuries. Within 48 hours, at least half apparently succumbed. Interviews suggest that as many as 100-150 were dispatched by survivors wielding improvised weapons.

Human survivors: Seven survivors were extracted from Indianola. They survived the bombing by sheltering in the lower level of the Warren County Courthouse. They varied in regards to health and mental stability. One was infected and was immediately euthanized by the reconnaissance team. The remaining five were transferred to Re-Hab Zone 16 for counseling and medical treatment. One of them subsequently committed suicide. A seventh possible survivor identified himself to US forces in Columbia, Missouri, 20 days after the bombing.

Overall Assessment: Considering the number of infected that this strike neutralized, collateral damage and the use of limited fuel and munitions resources remain within an acceptable margin.

9.9 Connor Ryan Williams, interview

Even after the departure of the caravan, many of the inhabitants of the perimeter were unaware of the specifics of Operation Hawkeye. Living on the west side of Simpson's campus, Connor Williams appears to have been particularly ignorant of the approaching danger.

Please state your name and age.
Connor Ryan Williams. I'm 23.

Where are you from, Connor?
Um, I used to live in Ames, Iowa.

Is that where you were born?
Yeah. My family's lived there most of my life.

Do you know anything about your family's whereabouts?
No. After we were evaced to the re-hab zone, I got on the Internet and had about a million e-mails from my mom. I had read through all of them, and it was like reliving the whole apocalypse for a second time. They started all normal, and then got crazy and frantic. The messages just got like she didn't expect me to respond—probably figuring I was dead. … But she sent them anyway. She sent the last one in June.

How did others respond to being cut off from their families?
How do you think?

Are you thinking of something in particular?
Yeah, I guess. There was this one chick, Tara, —I didn't really know her. Just had a Z-term class with her. Her family hadn't made it, and she knew it. They were in Chicago or something.

Things just started piling up on her. Family dead. Then her boyfriend died. Then she found out he'd given it to her. Pretty damn skippy.

Anyway, Tara just didn't show up to class one day. I wasn't really worried or anything. It's not like it's really mandatory to go to class during z-term, right? What would they do? Feed us to the zombies or something?

What is it Connor?

Well, that's what they did— in a way.

What do you mean?

Back in July, I heard about these guys who went on some recon mission, but nobody came back. And that's not what surprises me— plenty never came back. But, c'mon, from the looks of these guys you had to know they had no chance out there. It was a couple older guys, like late 50s, and this really scrawny chick I'd seen around.

I saw them all walking out of the perimeter together getting final instructions from some guy in cammies. I think it was that dick, Burke Wolf. They looked pretty confused. And I mean, the chick could barely hold the stick she was carrying. She had rickets or something. It's like they were just getting sent out for slaughter and everyone could see it but them. Well, maybe they saw it too.

Was this an isolated incident?

It was the only time I ever saw anything, but you heard rumors. I think it happened again. Luckily, I was pretty useful. I'm pretty good at chem, so I was always working on that kind of stuff. And I'm decent with weaponry. My dad always took me hunting and paintballing.

So what happened to the girl, to Tara?

She offed herself in quarantine. Not exactly sure how. But, I mean, stuff like that would happen every now and then. One guy shot himself in his room. There was a group of, like, three who all did it together... Lots of people just couldn't take it, you know? What could you really do?

What happened on the last day?

Good question. I don't know how I made it all the way out of there alive. I saw so many people dropping all around me. It was absolute *insanity.* Like nothing I'd ever imagined. When they're brushing up against you, pushing you every which way, when God only knows whose—or what's—blood is splattering all over you...

Could you start from the beginning? Try to describe what happened, what you saw.
Yeah. Well, I guess it started when I heard the bell—the chapel bell. A code had been developed back in the early days of the perimeter. One toll, perimeter threatened; two tolls, climbers on the fence – that kind of thing. The only other time it tolled five times was when the bus came through, and there it was again: five long chimes. It was a quiet day and I could hear them pretty clear where I was over by Picken. I was on my way to do a shift guarding the cistern. I stopped to make sure that was what I was hearing and like two seconds later there's all these gunshots and screaming.

Where was it coming from?
The north side. Then a bunch of people ran past me—through the parking lot, up the street, out from the IP houses. They were all running over and up E Street. That's where the northwest gate was. I had my bat with me—you take your weapon with you at all times—and I started up the street. When I got to the crest of the little hill I couldn't really see what it was all about because of all the people on the inside.

There hadn't been that much concentrated gunfire since the breach. Almost all the ammo was gone, but no one seemed to be holding back. I guess they figured that it there was a time to save up for – this was it. People were yelling and pushing. I kept going and was able to push myself through the crowd a little. The last time we'd had trouble with refugees our fence came down, and I wanted to make sure that didn't happen again. There was all that screaming like last time. But I got to the front and just *wished* that was our problem. Jesus... I've never *seen* so many zombies!

We were shooting them off the fence. And... I hadn't realized that all that screaming wasn't coming from our side of the wire. It was... It was the sub-E refugees on the other side. ... It's just... *God.* They were being just devoured over there. I mean, the most *literal* kind of devouring you can imagine. And so much screaming. That on top of the moaning and screeching from the zombies. Sorry.

That's all right. Take your time.

Then I noticed that…some of our gunners were actually shooting the refugees that were outside the fence. To save them, I guess. I imagine. We wouldn't let them in, but we'd kill them quick. Small mercies.

Hadn't most of the refugees joined the caravan?

Yes. I think almost everyone who was able went south; these were the rest: people with illnesses, people with malnutrition. Old people.

Seeing the approach of certain death animated some of them. They tried to climb with zombies grabbing at their legs, biting them while ripping them off the fence. I remember this one woman. She was clinging to the fence with both arms, she was horizontal in the air, like five feet off the ground. Four zombies had ahold of her legs, but couldn't really *get* to her around the people and zombies all around them—in between, behind, scrambling above, pushing on all sides.

She looked straight at me—super bright blue eyes. She was screaming, just… screaming. All of a sudden she wasn't making a sound – it was just this silent screaming that came out through these terrified blue eyes. I couldn't stop looking at her face, but I couldn't move to do anything either. One hand came loose. The fence was bowing back towards her. She was still looking into my eyes. Then they got one good tug and she was gone—yanked into that, that bloody, insane mess.

It was only a couple more minutes 'til the fence started to really waver. It just started, like, this exaggerated undulation—like flowing water. Then there was this unnatural second of silence as it fell—almost like in slow motion, you know? Or maybe that was just in my head. The whole front on our side had to back up pretty quickly—I practically fell over myself and the ones behind me. Then it was just this swarm of bodies coming at us—fast, slow, alive, dead—everyone was screaming.

I sprinted down the street with everyone else. And it was just this horde of zombies and refugees, everyone bleeding and yelling, and there's still all this gunfire. But where was I gonna go? There were dozens of people ahead of me all stumbling over everyone else, all going in the same direction but different directions at the same time trying to cut through to the front of the crowd.

My peripheral vision caught a Z coming at me. I wheeled and took her out with a quick swing to the face. I turned my face in time not to get any of her blood in my mouth—I was panting so hard I'm probably really lucky I didn't get infected from something so simple. I'd seen that happen to a couple people by then and they probably didn't even realize it.

And since I was so close to the fence, when the crowd turned I was in the back. I could feel those fingers snatching at me the whole way. Finally, one of them grabbed my jacket. He nearly whipped me down. I stumbled but regained my footing and could keep going. But he was just clinging to me with one hand and swatting at me with the other. I gripped my bat and did a quick spin and hit him in the side, but he didn't let go. I caught myself for an instant when I saw what was following me: it was a wall of death.

I dropped my bat so that I could shuck the jacket. I nearly tripped over one that had gotten ahead and taken down this smaller guy. He seemed to be holding his own with a couple of butcher knives, but it wouldn't be for long with hundreds of Z coming up. I knew I couldn't just leave him. I guess he could've been infected by that point – there was a lot of blood on him – but you never know.

In one long second I stutter stepped and gave the Z my best soccer kick to the head. It didn't get him off, but it got his attention enough for the little guy to drive one of his knives under his chin, up his throat, and into his brain. I grabbed his hand and yanked him up, having to drag him along with me 'til he found his feet.

By this time we were on the south side of the BSC. There'd been gunshots the whole time ringing out over the screaming and yelling, but here was a barrage just coming down. The third floor of Kresge was pumping out an impressive volume of fire. I didn't think the east side had that kind of ammo after the coup, but they really poured it on. I'm sure they were aiming for Zs but there were plenty of human casualties, too. I guess it's kind of inevitable when we were getting all mixed together. Some Zs had actually managed to get ahead of me.

In five minutes, I saw all the people – all my friends – people who had made it through over six months of this fucking shit get cut down. What kind of justice is it when after making it through all that you get cut down by a stray bullet or get your guts ripped out by some fuckall Z-girl who didn't even come up to your waist?

You know, right before the fence fell, I'd actually been feeling pretty optimistic – like, hey, we've got our act together. We've solved some problems. We're going to make it.

Can you tell me about it?

It was my roommate … my assigned roommate from Picken. Mark Arruguo. 17. He'd been let into the perimeter back in July, but his grandparents, they were processed out. They didn't have any special skills, and they didn't bring any supplies with them, so they got put on the C-list. They explained the situation to him and he took it. He accepted it. He accepted that they had to die so that he could live. It was fucking Auschwitz. Yes. No. In. Out.

What happened to him?

I saw him up ahead of me. He was running toward Kresge and he was covered in blood. I don't think he knew I was right in back of him. Then his head snapped back … back and to the right. Part of the top of it blew off. It was just, I guess, a stray round, or a ricochet or something.

Don't worry, take your time.

All that blood blasted in my face totally shocked me. I faltered back a step or two. And just in time—this big Z was coming across at me the same second but missed me when I staggered back. Hit this other guy that was next to me. Before I even realized it, they were lost in the screaming, senseless crowd. I had to keep going.

Then I'm between Kresge and Mary Berry, running toward central campus. We weren't so packed together because a bunch of people headed south on C Street or ran down a little to get a different way across campus. And, well, a lot of people were just gone.

I just headed straight toward Dunn Library and College Hall. I kept running and saw a Z on top of this motionless woman. Her… her face was half-eaten, but she was still alive, writhing around. Bubbling. Ordinarily this sort of thing would bring Zs like flies to honey, but this was different. It was like a feeding frenzy or something. It was like they didn't care about feeding – they just wanted to kill.

I rounded the corner of College Hall and this Z – early S4 – just popped up and jumped right in my face and knocked me down. I remember thinking, "I'm dead. I'm dead." I started saying an "Our Father," and instinctively put up my arms up to protect my face. Clawing and spitting, it knocked me right over. As we went down, it was trying to scratch at me and grab my arms and my head and trying to bite my arms. I'd never had one so close to me before. I probably became hysterical. I was just screaming and flailing at it. People were running all around us, and lucky for me, one of them was a good Samaritan. Without breaking stride he cocked back what must have been a ten-pound sledge and whipped it right in the Z's face. He arched up and his face basically imploded. The guy had to take an extra step to wrench his weapon out of the mush, and then he took off without a look back.

I'd already lost all my headway, but I got to my feet and made it all the way to the chapel. There were defenders on the front steps. It didn't look like many of the Zs had gotten here yet, but there were a few pulped up bodies on the group in front of them.

I took a few seconds to look back. Most of the Zs were preoccupied with people they'd taken down. Every body had two or three kneeling over it. Across the quad you could see a girl trying to get in a tree. Over by McNeil, a clutch of them were looking around frantically for any direction that looked clear, but the Zs were closing in. Then I saw a couple of people coming from the same direction I'd come from. Somehow, they made it too. Then some other people came through the same break. The Zs seemed to be confused now. I guess they were getting all distracted from the noise and movement so they wouldn't stay focused. They'd have a chance to get another person, and they'd just go.

Just when I thought I had gotten to somewhere safe, the chaplain said something like, "Time to get it fired up," or "let's light it up," or something like that. I asked someone what he was talking about, and that's the first time I knew what the ZED actually was. It wasn't some super-weapon; it was a zombie *attracting* device.

I guess this freaked me out a little bit. I started hyperventilating. One of the defenders took me inside and tried to help me calm down, but then, through a window, I saw a pickup hurtle through the south fence. Fine by me. Anywhere but here. I realized I had no idea where I was going—no plan, nothing. And I know this will sound incredibly, *incredibly* stupid, but... I just ran.

How did you end up at the Courthouse?

I think most of the Zs were within or around the perimeter, and then I guess they flipped on the ZED. I saw two Zs a block over, but they were loping back toward the chapel. It was like a magnet. They didn't even notice me.

I ran flat out all the way to the square. They'd deployed about ten fighters outside the garage door on the west side. It looked like they had some shooters on the roof. They saw me coming and waved me over. This kind of surprised me. I mean, I could've been infected. They didn't ask any questions. They let me though the line, and pulled me in.

Inside the building it was quiet. After complete chaos I'd ended up here. You could still hear yelling and gunshots but they were muffled. They seemed far away. Then Sara helped me down to the shelter.

Sara?

Sara Heikes. She was another Simpson student. I don't know how she ended up at the courthouse, but she seemed familiar with it. It was a pretty nice set up, but it smelled bad. Backed up sewage pipes or something. Anyway, she used a washcloth to get the blood off of me. I thought she was just being kind, but then I realized that she was making sure I didn't have lacerations.

She thought you were infected?

If they'd thought that, they would have just shot me down in the street. I think she was just making sure. It was nice for a minute, having a girl wash all that crap off of me with a damp sponge. Then the bombing started.

What happened afterwards?

Well, we weren't that keen to get out of our hole. The first bombing had caught us by surprise and we didn't know if we should expect another, so we stayed put until the air started getting stale. Then we discovered that we had to dig ourselves out because some of the courthouse collapsed. That took several hours. When we finally got through the rubble and looked out at the town it was pretty amazing. The courthouse was one of the only buildings left standing. The shops around the square were pretty much blown away. There were some walls still up, but nothing had a roof on it. Nothing had four walls. It was a mess. The trees were splintered; the wooden houses were blasted apart and burned. The whole town was basically blown wide open.

When did you begin exploring?

Right away. What else was there to do? It was late morning when we dug ourselves out. We spent the rest of the day walking around checking things out. We'd come across some Zs every once and a while. They were in rough shape. Legs gone. Arms gone. Sucking chest wounds. The works. But I'd still take them out. I used a bent piece of steel I'd reflexively picked up when we came out of the shelter. Bashed every bit of them I could—only stopped when my arms needed a break. We wandered around almost all day, looking for more survivors.

Did you ever see anyone?

No. No one. Just bodies and half-dead zeds.

What were you thinking at that point?

I don't know if I was thinking anything. Your brain can only handle so much. I think, apart from being able to remember things, that's the only kind of firing my brain could handle for days. I just couldn't process the shit that had happened. Everything I saw was hollowed out and destroyed. I felt kind of the same. Like, OK, we got through that one ... what next?

THE END

EPILOGUE

This book represents the beginning of an effort to encourage other survivors to share the stories of their communities. Every one of us is here because others perished for our benefit.

Let this history of Simpson College and its unwavering commitment to education, human decency, and the liberal arts stand as a beacon of light in our darkened and dangerous world.

We close with Simpson's *alma mater,* the "Red and Gold" by Lucian Waggoner.

Come we will sing together.
Once more the ringing song,
A strain that the coming classes,
Unceasingly shall prolong
The praises of our Alma Mater
Dear Simpson will e'er be told
Cherish thy recollections
And swear by the Red and Gold

Though in years before us,
Life's skies grow dull and gray
The friends of our youth are scattered
We journey our lonely way
Sweet memories oft will linger
Of those dear days of old
When beneath the whispering maples
We flaunted the Red and Gold

CONTRIBUTORS

David Albrecht- I am a senior History major and Philosophy minor. I enjoy long walks on the beach, breakfast in bed, and killing zombies. *Viva La Humanity!*

Adrian M. Aitken- I am a senior with a corporate communication major, biology minor and am a member of Lambda Chi Alpha. I know Paul Dule and continue my studies of zombie virus epidemiology. I plan to continue writing post-graduation.

Zak Bartels-I am currently a senior majoring in history, looking at going into teaching, and am very involved in the theatre department. I saw this class as a good way to challenge myself while still being able to remember the fallen. I also enjoy drumming, reading comic books, and challenging people on their knowledge of Simpsons trivia.

Erin Kay Broich- I was a member of the marketing team for this class, and also transcribed several entries including the Anne Howard diary entries. This experience has given me a new appreciation of zombies. Preparation is important!

Keith Bryan- I liked Simpson so much, I came back for a fifth year after graduating (as a Super Senior) and completed a history degree in one year. What a way to end the year by getting slammed by the apocalypse. Thank you to my great group of friends who made long nights working on this fun! You know who you are!

Jacob Christy- I am a freshman engineering major. I am destined for greatness. My favorite weapon is the axe.

Michael Comer- I'm a freshman Math major. I contributed to the writing, editing, and research needed to complete this book. My favorite zombie killing weapon: the 9 iron from my golf bag.

Marc Dwenger- I am a freshman biology major. I took this class because it sounded really awesome. Favorite anti-zombie weapon: combine harvester.

Crystal Fisher- I am a junior Instrumental Music Education major and am looking forward to teaching high school band in the future. I worked on the fundraising committee and transcribed entries for Karen Grzesiak. I have an unusual obsession with anything involving zombies, all inspired by my Dad who saved me on multiple occasions. My choice weapons are a hunting bow and a twelve gauge shotgun.

Rachel Gull- I'm the veteran How-to columnist for *The Simpsonian*, and I co-wrote and directed an opera based on Lewis Carroll's *Alice in Wonderland*. I like coloring books, Disney movies, corndogs, and swing dancing.

Ted Haag- I am in my first year at Simpson College. In my free time I enjoy working out and playing for the school varsity football team. If I could have anybody turned into a zombie I would have to choose, Dwayne "the Rock" Johnson..... he just might be invincible in zombie form.

Eliz Hewitt- I am a 20-year-old Theatre Major at Simpson. I love reading, poetry, technical theatre, and French. I like to have adventures and tempt fate. Usually fate wins.

Thomas Hlad- I am a junior. I was involved in the art development, and created some of the artwork for our book. Overall, this book stretched my capabilities and was fun doing so. My favorite weapon used to kill zombies is a machete.

Kari Kennedy- I am a Biology and Spanish major with a Chemistry minor. I learned a lot putting this book together -- including that I would prefer to have in my hand a machete above all else.

Jacob Kirby- I am a psychology major. This class was only three weeks long but it felt like months of work, but it was all enjoyable. I helped out by being the chapter nine editor and I transcribed the entries of Llewellyn Morse. This was an amazing experience that I will never forget. Maybe I'll do it again.

Erin Larson- I was so excited when I read what the course was about and couldn't wait to get started! This has been the highlight of my whole sophomore year!

Tessa Leone- I'm a sophomore art major with a photography concentration. I shot all of the photos in this book and make frequent use of the phrase "aim high." You neglect the head and they are sure to get back up.

Ben Lucas- I am a Journalism and Mass Communications major, so this class stuck right out as something that could give me experience and quite a bit of fun. Remember, the best armor in a zombie fight is confidence and calm. Panic never solves anything, just ask Wall Street.

Ben Murga- I worked on the cover concepts among other artistic areas of the book. I enjoyed working on this project as it was the last project I ever worked on for my four years at Simpson College. It was a great class to end on.

Tyler Pawletzki- I'm a freshman at Simpson College where I am on the baseball team. My favorite anti-zombie weapon would be a shotgun.

Corrina Pilat- I transcribed Susan Dodge's diary and other entries. I was also part of the fundraising committee and an assistant chapter editor. I discovered that a crowbar is a fantastic weapon. Julia D., Thank you!!!

Nicolas Proctor-I am a professor of American History, and I am currently attached to the Midwest division of the Historical Documentation Project managed by the Department of Recovery. In my experience the most dependable weapon is a pump-action shotgun, but in a pinch an aluminum baseball bat can be invaluable.

Antonio Reyes Jr.- I am a freshman, and I'm originally from Des Moines, Iowa. I dedicate my work on this book to the Reyes family, Lisa Klein, and Des Moines North High School.

Lucas Riesselman-I was part of the weapons availability team, as well as the editor of chapter seven. I did my research paper on the utility of animals like horses and dogs in the event of a zombie apocalypse. P.S. Jim Kirk is the MAN!

Lex Scott-I am a junior, and an equestrian world cup gold medalist. I was the only female presence on the weapons acquisition team. My kill playlist includes Drowning Pool, anything by Lady Gaga, and "Take on Me" by A-Ha.

Lynnette Snyder- Before heading off to be in the real world after four years of mathematics and computer science, helping edit this book has been the topping to a great four years. In my minimal spare time I enjoy all things Disney, music, sidewalk chalk and blowing bubbles.

Annie Spencer- I have really enjoyed this writing and learning experience. I was part of a group that investigated the development of an understanding of the zombie virus at Simpson and I was part of the marketing team. While the zombie aspect of this class terrified me, the old adage holds true: *Know thy enemy*.

David Ward- Potent and heartwarming; this book really opened my eyes to the potential of no holds barred, knock-down, drag out, hardcore zombie apocalypse carnage as a history book. A great gift for grandparents, recommend it to your favorite book club! Preferred anti-zombie weapon: frying pan. Hi mom!

John Warnke – I'm a freshman, majoring in Mathematics and Secondary Education. Member of the Publishing, and Continuity teams, also the editor for July. "Their flesh shall consume away while they stand upon their feet, and their eyes shall consume away in their holes, and their tongue shall consume away in their mouth." Zec 14:12

Fritz Wehrenberg- I am the new Chaplain at Simpson College, after serving 10 years at Iowa State University and the University of Minnesota – Twin Cities. Always on the lookout for nimble professors and creative students, this course looked chock full of both. When dealing with Zombies, I draw upon Martin Luther's observation about faithful people: Sin boldly and believe more boldly still!

Robin Whitford- I am an English major with a Journalism & Mass Communications minor. My Zombie Apocalypse advice: You know the people who die in zombie movies? Don't do what they did.

Avalon Woodard- I'm a sophomore Pre-Engineering/Physics and German double major. My great enjoyment in "binking" zombies (a.k.a. blowing their freaking heads off), led me to join this course.

CONTACT

For more information on the Zombie History Project and our ongoing work to document the Great Zombie War in North America, please contact us at: nick.proctor@simpson.edu

IN APPRECIATION

We could not have brought this project to fruition without the good people at Kickstarter.com. Since the Ford Foundation and the National Endowment for the Humanities were unable to extend funding (largely due to most of their staff being zombies), the Kickstarter community stepped in and provided generous support that reached 397% of our fundraising target.

PROJECT SUPPORTERS

Our supporters are wonderful people who deserve the undying gratitude of people everywhere. Without them, this project would not have been possible.

Angela Glover, Anne Christians, Willemijn Schmitz, Bobby Nalean, Mark Pritchard, Kara May, Heather Bardole, Karl Serbousek, Ben Vosatka, Tyson Wirtz, Taylor Norland, Kevin Ripp, Linda Luise Brown, Todd Little, Jamie Aitken, Chris Schacht, Ryanne Skalberg, Cate St. Clair, Kendra Halliwell, Ryan Robinson, John Kirby, Christopher Jorgensen, Catherine, Kate Tillotson, Curtis DeVetter, Erin Green, Dottie Marzian, Erin Whitford, Kevin McCullough, Sharon Ruelle Kirby, and Tom Woldt.

SPECIAL THANKS

All of our supporters are wonderful, but some went above and beyond. Their generosity is truly awe-inspiring.

Sara Beth Estes, Kraig Thomas, Jim Kirk, Selden Spencer, FC Rash, Kristine Hennings, Lynette Snyder, Ryan Hervey, Erin M. Gentz, Joyce Bartels, Mitchell Shepard Kramer, Eric Francis, esq., Anastacia Fotiadis, Tessa Murphy, Sara Heikes, Martin A. Reiche, Patrick Lynch, Nathan Liebold, Mark Dalrymple, Ron & Marilyn Lambert, Valerie Rash, Delores T. Montgomery, and Nick Veneris of xomba.com.

Made in the USA
Charleston, SC
16 December 2011